ON THE WING

THE PERSONAL HISTORY, ADVENTURES, EXPERIENCES & OBSERVATIONS OF PETER LEROY

BY ERIC KRAFT

(so far)

Little Follies

Herb 'n' Lorna

Reservations Recommended

Where Do You Stop?

What a Piece of Work I Am

At Home with the Glynns

Leaving Small's Hotel

Inflating a Dog

Passionate Spectator

Taking Off

On the Wing

ON THE WING

ERIC KRAFT

St. Martin's Press New York

ON THE WING. Copyright © 2007 by Eric Kraft. All rights reserved. Printed in the United States of America. No part of this book may be used or reproduced in any manner whatsoever without written permission except in the case of brief quotations embodied in critical articles or reviews. For information, address St. Martin's Press, 175 Fifth Avenue, New York, N.Y. 10010.

www.stmartins.com

www.erickraft.com/peterleroy

Author's notes: The part of the Electro-Flyer on the cover and on page 13 is played by the Starlite Electric Runabout, a prototype conceived by the Nu-Klea Automobile Corp. of Lansing, Michigan, in 1960, but never manufactured; the image is reproduced from an advertising postcard in the author's collection. The passage on aerodynamic lift on page 25, and the accompanying illustration, are from pages 104, 105, 112, and 113 of *Elements of Aeronatuics,* by Francis Pope and Arthur S. Otis, copyright 1941 by World Book Company, Yonkers-on-Hudson, New York.

ISBN-13: 978-0-312-36374-1
ISBN-10: 0-312-36374-5

First Edition: July 2007

10 9 8 7 6 5 4 3 2 1

For Mad

There is a great deal of enjoyment to be gained in learning to fly a plane . . . but a new thrill is had when the pilot sets out on a cross-country trip.

Francis Pope and Arthur S. Otis,
Elements of Aeronautics

The Bird of Time has but a little way
To fly—and Lo! the Bird is on the Wing!

Omar Khayyam, "Rubaiyat"
(translated by Edward FitzGerald)

ON THE WING

Preface
Albertine Gets the Urge for Going

   . . . we are here as on a darkling plain
Swept with confused alarms of struggle and flight . . .
      Matthew Arnold, "Dover Beach"

THE STORY SO FAR: I had thought, when I began writing about my aerocycle, my trip to the Land of Enchantment, my sojourn at the Faust-roll Institute for 'Pataphysics (known to some of its alumni as the Faust-roll Institute for Promising Lads), and my return to a hero's welcome in Babbington, my home town—Clam Capital of America, Birthplace of Teen Flight, Gateway to the Past—that I would write one book of medium size . . . however, the single book that I had intended to write about my exploit has become three books, the Flying trilogy.

   This book is the second volume in that trilogy, which will, when it is complete, set the record straight on the subject of the celebrated solo flight that I made in the summer of my fifteenth year from Babbington, New York, to Corosso, New Mexico. (I was fourteen at the time of the flight; I would turn fifteen at the end of October.) In the first volume, *Taking Off,* I built the aerocycle, *Spirit of Babbington,* a single-seat airplane based on drawings that I had found in an ancient issue of a magazine called *Impractical Craftsman,* made my travel plans, and departed. In this volume, *Spirit* and I meander from Babbington to New Mexico, and in the third volume, *Flying Home,* I will return to Babbington, somewhat older and, possibly, somewhat wiser.

While I was writing the first volume, Albertine (my darling, my lover, my muse and inspiration, my constant companion, my wife) suffered a crash while riding her bicycle in Manhattan. Emergency medical technicians took her to Carl Schurz Hospital, just down the street from the apartment building where we lived. X-rays revealed that the accident had fractured her pelvis along a nearly continuous line from the symphysis pubis to the crest of ilium, cracking the bone badly enough to keep her off her feet for weeks.

During the several days of her hospital stay, days that were only the very beginning of her convalescence, she experienced a Baudelairean return toward childhood, regaining in the highest degree the faculty of keenly interesting herself in things, be they apparently of the most trivial, seeing everything in a state of newness, with the sensory drunkenness of a child. One consequence was her becoming infatuated with the "flyguys," a swaggering bunch of medical technicians who ferried the sick and injured to Carl Schurz Hospital in helicopters.

When Albertine finally earned her release from the hospital by demonstrating that she could hobble about with the aid of a walker, the flyguys announced their intention to take her on a celebratory joyride around Manhattan in their chopper. Her eyes lit up. The flyguys hustled her to the hospital roof in the wheelchair that I'd rented to take her home, and then they trundled her aboard their helicopter. I stood and watched the machine rise and tilt and chatter out over the East River. Then I remained for a long while on the roof waiting for the flyguys to bring her back to me.

I waited. Time passed. Foolishly, I had thought that the flyguys would deliver less than they had promised, just take her for a short spin, and bring her right back to me. When that didn't happen, I began to panic. What if they had conspired to spirit her off, take her from me forever? What if she had become so enamored of them that she couldn't live without them? What if she thought of this as an escape? What if she had come to think of me as an encumbrance, something that she had to shed before she could fly? What if she had left me on the roof like a broken shackle and had made her getaway?

Writing in the calm of a morning several years later, I can allow myself to think that I was deluded, and I can even allow myself to think that, despite my moods and my boundless ineptitude, I am not nearly so difficult to live with as I feared she might think, but at the time the likelihood that she would want to escape from me suddenly seemed very high. I waited some more—and I waited some more. Every time I heard the clatter of a helicopter, my heart leapt and raced like an excited pet eager for Albertine's tickling caress behind its ears. Every time the clatter passed or turned and trundled away, my heart sighed and slunk into a corner. As time passed, I began to sweat. I began to feel powerless, hopeless, impotent. There was nothing I could do to bring her back. I was standing on a rooftop, with no way to confront the flyguys, reclaim her, sieze her, carry her off, take her home to my cave. When another helicopter began to rattle into range, I decided—or some part of me below consciousness decided—that I wasn't going to let this one get away. I dashed to the elevator penthouse, punched the button, and banged the door with my fist until the elevator arrived. I rushed in and rode down to the ground floor. I hastened through the emergency room with an affectation of calm, as if I weren't insane, but as soon as I was outside I began running in the direction of the sound of the helicopter. I ran like a boy, a lovesick boy. After a couple of blocks, I stopped to catch my breath and to listen for the sound of the helicopter. It was south of me now. I began running down 2nd Avenue. I paused again at 86th Street. The helicopter had turned west. I began running along 86th Street. If you've tried running along the sidewalks of New York in midafternoon, you know that you step on a lot of toes. I stepped on a lot of toes. People shouted at me. People lashed out at me. One or two people tried to trip me up. I ran until I was out of breath, and even then I walked as quickly as I could, until I heard one helicopter approaching as another receded and realized that I was a man on foot chasing helicopters. I stopped, and I told myself that I was acting like a fool, then corrected myself and told myself that I *was* a fool.

Then, when I had caught my breath, I began running again, in the direction of the most recent helicopter, because, after all, it might be the one that she was in.

Did I think about calling the police, dialing 911? Oh, yes. I did. But then I thought about what I would say:

"My wife has been abducted by flying EMTs."

They must get a lot of calls like that on any given day. There must be a category for them.

Eventually, I gave up. I would tell you that sanity returned, if I thought you would believe it. The truth is that I surrendered to exhaustion and resignation. I walked back to Carl Schurz hospital. I decided that I would wait on the roof. I would wait all afternoon, all evening, all night if I had to. If she never returned, I would be able to say, "I waited all night." I found that consoling, somehow. I have no idea, now, why I found it consoling then, but I did. I also told myself that I would never tell her about my running through the city in panic, chasing helicopters, and I never have—until now, here, in the pages you've just read.

THE HELICOPTER eventually reappeared from the north. It swung over Carl Schurz Park and settled gently onto the hospital roof. The flyguys off-loaded Albertine, hugged and fondled her, and finally settled her into the rented wheelchair. We all descended in the elevator, and there was another leave-taking at the hospital door. Then I pushed her home to our apartment, and on the way I confessed to her, with some fervor, my hope that neither she nor I would ever see the flyguys again.

ALBERTINE WORKED HARD at her recovery. As soon as she was permitted to exercise, she began riding a recumbent bicycle in the vast, multistory gymnasium up the street from our apartment building, and she swam lap after lap in their 25-meter pool. She never missed a physical therapy session and did all the exercises that her therapists prescribed. One therapist was amazed by what he took to be her tolerance for pain.

"It's not that," she said. "In truth, I have a very low tolerance for pain, and I'm feeling terrible pain right now, while I'm trying to do what you tell me I should do, but I want to be back on my feet as soon as possible, and if you tell me that this exercise is going to be good for me, then I will do it."

She wasn't foolish; she didn't allow her urge to be up and about to drive her to excess. She began slowly, and she avoided any position or effort that was not prescribed, but as she felt her strength return and as the pain began slowly to diminish, she increased the work she did, going far beyond what the therapists had expected her to do. It hurt. I could see that it hurt, when she let it show. There were times in bed when she made the mistake, in sleep or half-sleep, of turning onto her side—or merely beginning to turn onto her side—and the pain made her scream.

I PUSHED HER EVERYWHERE in the wheelchair I'd rented, but she hated being in it. She yearned to graduate to the walker—a frame of aluminum tubing that would allow her to take some of her weight off her legs as she moved ahead one slow step at a time. Although she'd passed a "walker test" before leaving the hospital, she wasn't permitted to leave the chair and walk with the aid of the walker until the line of bone repair along the fracture was strong enough. When that day came, she began a determined assault on distance, beginning with a walk of just a few feet eastward from the front door of the building, along East 89th Street, and back. From that beginning, she extended her range until she could circle the block, working at it with determination and perseverance, as if she were in training for the walker Olympics.

ANOTHER CONSEQUENCE of Albertine's convalescent return toward childhood, and her thereby regaining in the highest degree the faculty of keenly interesting herself in things, be they apparently of the most trivial, seeing everything in a state of newness, with the sensory drunkenness of a child, was her surprising interest in the literature of home-built and kit-built aircraft. In particular, she became an avid reader of builders' logs.

If you do not belong to the relatively small group of builders of small aircraft or to the slightly smaller group of their fans, you may not be aware of the custom prevalent among the builders of keeping logs of their progress as they work. For accuracy's sake, make that "efforts" rather than "progress." These logs, known among the fraternity of plane-builders as "construction logs" or, for short, "clogs," are often posted on the World Wide Web. Reading them became Albertine's pastime, then her passion.

I get up earlier in the morning than Albertine does. We both wake at the same time, but I get up, get out of bed, make myself some coffee, and work on my personal history for a while. While I write, Albertine reads. Often, during her recuperation, when I returned to the bedroom after an hour or two of work to wish her good morning, I would find our bed covered with pages of online clogs that she'd printed out for ease of reading in bed.

"This isn't becoming an obsession, is it?" I asked her one morning when the bed was heavily clogged.

"A passion," she admitted, "but not an obsession," she claimed. "These are really amazing, Peter. There's such a wealth of human drama in these accounts of failed attempts to realize a dream."

"I have to admit that I haven't spent any time reading them," I said.

"I can understand that you'd be reluctant to expose yourself to them."

"Why?"

"Because I understand you."

"I mean why, in your estimation, wouldn't I want to expose myself to them?"

"Because they are so discouraging. They dash hopes. They shatter illusions. And you are a person who lives on hope and nurses illusions."

"That's true," I said. It is. She understands me well. I'm a muddle-headed dreamer. I once belonged to a muddleheaded dreamers' club, as you will see in the pages to come.

"The typical clog begins full of optimism," she said. "Here—listen to this: 'The U-Build-It-U-Fly-It kit arrived this morning, and when Delia called me at work to say that it had been delivered I immediately feigned illness and left. I can't describe the feeling of buoyancy that I felt in the car on the way home, knowing that the kit would be waiting for me there. But I'll try. It was as if the car and I were not quite touching the road. In a sense, I was already flying, and the car had become the UBI-UFI. Although I hadn't even opened the kit yet, I felt as if my work was already done, and done well. I felt capable. I felt—how can I put it?—wise. It was as if the lightness I felt were sufficient justification for buying the kit, for the sacrifices I'd inflicted on Delia and the kids. I could fly. That was worth it.'"

"That sounds delightful," I said, naïvely. "It sounds as if the guy is really off to a great start—"

"Then, typically, the tedium sets in. Listen: 'Eighty-three days so far, and I don't know how much more of this I can take. Night after night, alone in the garage, struggling to decipher the instructions, too bewildered to make any real progress, too proud to ask that wiseass Stan next door for help. Why, why, why did I ever begin this? I feel like a condemned man, condemned to isolation, laboring alone. It's like trying to cross a desert on foot, or sailing alone around the world, or trying to survey the vast frozen wastes of the Siberian wilderness, struggling to build a shelter out of reeds in the teeth of the cutting wind. Nobody understands what I'm going through, nobody could, nobody cares.'"

"Grim," I said.

"Often, there is a laudable effort to soldier on: 'Today I've discovered a new determination, and I'm proud of myself for that. I've found a strength of will in myself that I hadn't known was there, and I think I'm justified in praising myself for that. I've learned that I've got something I might have to call grit. Or maybe pluck. Or maybe it's good old American stick-to-itiveness. Whatever you want to call it, I've got it. It's me against this damned plane, and in the name of all that's holy, I'm going to come out on top!'"

"Impressive."

"And then, finally, defeat: 'This is the end. I just can't go on. Every day is torture. After hours wasted in the garage, I lie awake in bed trying to find a way out of this folly. For a while, I thought I might be able to persuade the kid next door—the eldest son of that wiseassed bastard, Stan—to take the damned plane off my hands. He spent a couple of evenings watching me work, and I thought I had him hooked, but then he just stopped showing up. Kids today. They've got no sense of purpose. They can't stick with a thing. My only hope, I've decided, is to get Delia pregnant. Then I'd have to convert the garage into a room for the baby. The plane would have to go. I recognize that this is a desperate plan. But I'm a desperate man.'"

"Chilling," I said.

For a while, Albertine said nothing. She was overwhelmed, I think, by the emotions occasioned by the builder's defeat. When, at last, she felt like herself again, she said, "I want to go on the road."

"Touring with your band?"

"Be serious, please," she said. "Maybe it's my long period of immobility that is making me feel this way," she said, "but I've got the urge to travel."

"Where do you want to go, my darling? I'll push you anywhere."

"Oh, please. I don't want to be pushed. You have been a darling to push me everywhere, and you have been a darling to help me into the pool and into the hot tub, to help me into bed, to help me out of bed. I've even enjoyed it. I've felt pampered. I've felt loved. And I love you for it, for all of it. But I've had enough. I don't want to be helped. I'd like to range beyond this block, beyond this island, and I don't want to be pushed. I'd like to do what you said not so long ago. How did you put it? 'Walk out our door one day and just *go*.'"

"That's it," I said. "I met a guy named Johnny on my trip to New Mexico who put the urge that way: 'Just *go*.'"

"'Just *go*,'" she said. "That's right. That's what I'd like to do."

"And stop somewhere at the end of each day for a hot shower, a delicious meal, and a comfy bed?"

"Exactly."

"By what conveyance?" I asked warily. "Plane, train, aerocycle?"

"By car, I think."

"We don't have a car."

"Let's buy one."

"Are you serious?"

"I think I am. Our little world is not enough for me just now. I want to get up and go. I want to be out in the big, wide world, wandering with you."

"And do you have a specific car in mind?"

"I'm afraid I do."

"Afraid?"

"Yes. Afraid that the car I have in mind is a foolish choice. But I think it's a choice that you'd make in my place."

"Now *I'm* afraid," I said.

I should explain the reasons for our fear. I should tell you about our cars—well, not all of them—that would tax your tolerance too much. I will tell you about two of them and you can extrapolate from those. Let's see. Which two? The Twinkle, I think, since it was our first car, and, of course, the powerful Kramler, since it was our most magnificent.

There was a time—a time that today seems very long ago—when Albertine and I were enthusiastic motorists. We took Sunday drives, we made rambling excursions, we were adept at double-clutching. In those years, we owned a number of cars that were great fun to drive, but were very little fun to maintain in driving condition. The first of them was a red Twinkle. This was a British car with right-hand drive. We bought it from an English architect. The Twinkle was all of ten feet long and had ten-inch wheels. It really was great fun to drive. It had two transversely mounted rotary engines. One, in front, beneath its diminutive hood (or bonnet), drove the front wheels; the other, in back, in its trunk (or boot), drove the rear wheels. Both engines were small, but their combined output gave the Twinkle considerable oomph. It went like a bat out of hell—a little red bat out of hell.

When I was the Twinkle's co-owner, I would have bristled if you had told me, Reader, that it looked like a toy, but when I see one on the street today I recognize that it must have looked like a dangerous toy to Albertine's parents. They had been worried enough about consigning their daughter to the care of the Birdboy of Babbington when we announced that we were going to get married. I must have looked like a dangerous toy myself.

Her mother asked Albertine, pointedly, "Wouldn't you rather go to Europe?"

Albertine chose me over the European tour, and not long after making the choice she found herself driving a Twinkle and discovering a love of speed. Alas, as the Twinkle aged, it developed a problem that apparently could not be solved. The engines began twisting on their mounts under acceleration or deceleration. Apparently, the art of mounting engines had not then attained its present degree of perfection. When we made an upshift and accelerated, the engines would twist rearward. This meant that the front engine twisted toward the cockpit until the top struck the fire wall. On deceleration, the reverse phenomenon occurred, with both engines twisting forward, the rear engine striking the back of the diminutive back seat. The only mechanic who even suggested a solution told us that the "constant velocity joints" had to be replaced at a price greater than what we had paid for the car. Putting to work the mechanical skills I'd acquired in building—or attempting to build—a boyhood's worth of *Impractical Craftsman* projects, I designed a set of braces for the engines, had a machine shop fabricate them to my specifications, and bolted the braces between the engine block and the fire wall, in front, and between the engine block and the back of the back seat, in the rear. The engines no longer twisted. Success? Not quite. The cabin roared with the sound of every moving part in both engines, since every vibration and detonation was transmitted via the braces to the steel shell of the car itself. It was like driving inside a hi-fi speaker during a fuzz-bass solo. Clearly the time had come to trade the little baby in on another car or find some sucker to buy the Twinkle from us. My parents had taught me that one never gets a car's true worth when trading it in, so I advertised it for private sale. When I was demonstrating the Twinkle for potential buyers, I kept the radio volume high and sought out extended fuzz-bass solos. Some sap bought the car. I like to think that he is driving it still, and that it pleases him, noise and all.

After the Twinkle, we owned a succession of British sports cars. (I wish that I could say "other British sports cars," but the Twinkle, a four-passenger car, was never regarded as a sports car by the drivers of two-seaters, who scorned to wave at Albertine and me in the clannish way they greeted the drivers of other two-seaters. The Twinkle was faster than all but the most expensive and exotic of them, but that didn't matter; in fact, one roadster driver dismissed it as a "hot rod.")

With each of our sports cars, we experienced a brief honeymoon, a euphoric period during which we took several pleasant drives. Then the car would begin breaking down. The drives would become less pleasant, and many of them ended at repair shops. We got to know a number of interesting mechanics. We learned how to whack a fuel pump in just the right way to get it pumping again after it had quit in the fast lane of a highway. We would invest some money—sometimes quite a lot—repairing the sporty little thing, and we would try to convince ourselves that it was now as good as new, but it would keep breaking down, and in time we would sell it and buy another. We had in those days the naïve belief that somewhere there was a reliable British sports car that we could purchase, used, for a reasonable price. Perhaps that belief seems ludicrous to you. Perhaps you cannot imagine that two intelligent young people—which we then were—could labor under such an absurd delusion. If you feel that way, I just want to inform you—or remind you—that a large segment of the population of the United States believes that the sun revolves around the earth, and so I say, in the manner of Bosse-de-Nage in Alfred Jarry's *Gestes et Opinions du Docteur Faustroll*, "Ha-ha."

As we traded in, we traded up. We would rid ourselves of one limping sports car and promptly buy another that was more powerful, more expensive, and more difficult to keep running. We always had an automobile loan, and the balance kept increasing. Little by little, we progressed from one of the most basic sports cars, a Benson-Greeley Gnome, to one of the most sophisticated, the powerful Kramler.

Our Kramler was powered by a V-12 engine with four camshafts and nickel-plated cam covers, a thing of great beauty. The entire front of the car's body tilted up to reveal this engine, in a far more dramatic and aesthetically effective manner than the ordinary hood would have done. Tilting the front end forward did not, however, allow easy access to the engine for the servicing and repair that it required at frequent intervals. That access might have been better provided by the conventional hood arrangement. Instead, the Kramler people required the mechanic to remove the engine and work on it outside the car. A disconcertingly large number of repair and maintenance procedures in the shop manual, which we owned and which I sometimes used as bedtime reading, began with the words, "First remove the engine; see page 19." One of these procedures was changing the oil filter.

We haven't owned a car for years. Living in Manhattan makes a car unnecessary, and the cost of garaging a car in Manhattan makes a car insupportable.

Sometimes I miss driving. I can't manage to get as excited by a car as I used to, but there are several available now that I would like to drive. I don't want to own any of them, but I still have the urge to get into something sleek and powerful and just take off, heading west.

"What is this fearsome machine you have in mind?" I asked.

"It's a Prysock Electro-Flyer."

"I don't think I've ever seen—"

"It's the only one of its kind. And there will never be another."

"Is it a dream car? A concept car? A show car?"

"It was built as a prototype. The designer-builder hoped to put it into production, but he has since abandoned the plan and moved on to other things."

"Mm."

"It's a sleek little thing with a top speed of 140 miles per hour."

"Impressive," I said.

"Especially for an electric car."

"An electric car? Wow."

"And the Electro-Flyer is, as I'm sure you'll agree in a moment, when I show you some pictures, a thing of beauty."

"Can't wait. Somehow 'Prysock' does sound vaguely familiar—"

"In the spirit of full and frank disclosure, I have to point out that the Prysock Electro-Flyer is—how shall I put this—derivative."

"Oh?" I said, puzzled.

"The design was heavily influenced by the 1960 Nu-Klea Disco Volante Runabout."

"Disco Volante? As in—"

"As in 'Flying Saucer.'"

"Oh," I said, disappointed. "We'd be buying a replica."

"Not exactly. The mechanicals are original with the designer-builder."

"But still—"

"I know how you feel about replicas," she said quickly, "but this is different. It's the work of a madman obsessed with detail and accuracy."

"Oh!" I said, brightening.

"Here's his ad."

I looked at the picture. I read the copy.

"You mean Norton Prysock built this thing?" I asked.

"Built this beautiful car. Yes."

"I seem to recall that you had a low opinion of Nort and his skills when you examined the photographs of the Pinch-a-Penny on his Web site."

"I still think that as an aeronautical engineer he's not much use."

"But you think he could build a good car?"

"I'll want to examine it carefully, of course, take it for a spin, and have a mechanic go over it thoroughly, but I suspect that this car is the one good thing Norton Prysock ever made—and remember, too, that in the case of the Pinch-a-Penny he was asking me to believe that he could get me into the air and keep me there, while in the case of the Electro-Flyer he is making no such claim."

"I don't know," I said. "I see a dangerous parallel between Nort's situation and my own when I began building the aerocycle: I had drawings of a finished plane, but no plans for building it, so I had to improvise. Nort had nothing but pictures of the Disco Volante, which were the equivalent of the drawings I had, invaluable as inspiration but useless in terms of

engineering—so he must have had to do a lot of improvising—and the result—"

"Oh, Peter."

"I'm trying to be realistic."

"Don't."

I looked at her, looked into her eyes, saw the longing there, and said, "Okay."

DESPITE WHAT HIS AD CLAIMED, Norton Prysock was not willing to let the world's only Electro-Flyer go for what we considered a reasonable offer. Even after a long negotiation he wanted much, much more than I thought Albertine would be willing to pay.

"He is asking us to pay for a car more than twney-six point three percent of the cost of the average studio apartment in Manhattan," I said as Albertine and I huddled at the end of Nort's driveway, conferring.

"Where did you get that bit of information?"

"I'm basing it on a survey reported in this morning's *Times*," I said, unfolding the paper to the story.

Albertine skimmed it quickly and announced, "But he's asking less than one percent of the average price of a Manhattan property with four bedrooms or more."

"Are you kidding?" I asked her.

"No," she said, pointing to the relevant figure. "Peter—"

"Yes?"

"If we sold our apartment—a two-bedroom apartment, I remind you— we could buy this car—and have lots and lots of change left over."

"Shouldn't we save that for our golden years?"

"Yes, we should. That would be wise. It would be prudent. We try to be wise. We try to be prudent. Well, I try to be prudent. However, after my fall I find that I am feeling the cold breath of mortality on the back of my neck, and it's making me impulsive and foolish."

"Are you sure it's not the hot breath of the great god Urge that you feel?"

"Could be," she said coquettishly.

"Urge couldn't be appeased with some shoes, could he?"

"Not this time," she said.

I was about to speak again, but she put a finger over my mouth, shushed me, and said, "Listen." I listened. I expected her to speak; I thought she wanted me to listen to her, but after a minute, she said, "Sometimes, more and more often, especially at night, I can hear them, out beyond us, ranged in rings and rings around rings, the angry, murderous, rapacious numbers of our species, growling and cursing and gnashing their teeth, brandishing their weapons, blowing one another to smithereens, feeding their hatred with hatred, stoking their anger with anger, fueling their selfishness with arrogance. There's no getting away from them, but we could do as your pal B. W. Beath advised and, for a while at least, just pass through the squabbling world without being a part of it, like a breeze."

"In an Electro-Flyer?" I asked.

"In *the* Electro-Flyer," she said.

We paid Nort's price.

Peter Leroy
New York City
February 15, 2007

Chapter 1
Without a Map

Traveling ought [. . .] to teach [the traveler] distrust; but at the same time he will discover how many truly kind-hearted people there are, with whom he never before had, or ever again will have any further communication, who yet are ready to offer him the most disinterested assistance.
Charles Darwin, *The Voyage of H. M. S. Beagle*

LO! THE BIRDBOY WAS ON THE WING, figuratively speaking. I was on my way, taxiing westward, urging *Spirit of Babbington* up, up, and away, but not managing to get the thing off the ground. Had I been my present age, I might have blamed the flightlessness of *Spirit* on its weighty freight of metaphorical implications, its heavy burden—in the old sense of "meaning." It stood for the contrast of lofty goals with leaden deeds, of grand urges with petty talents, of soaring ambitions with earthbound achievements, but at the time I wasn't thinking of the weight of *Spirit*'s significance, or even of the reason that it wouldn't fly; I was simply frustrated and annoyed and embarrassed. I believed that the well-wishers along the roadside were beginning to consider me a hoax or, what seemed worse, a failure. Actually—as I learned from their testimony years later—they thought that I was being generous to them, staying on the ground as I passed to allow them a good look at me and my machine, to allow them to hoist their babies onto their shoulders and afford them the inspiration of a good view of the bold Birdboy. In a letter to the *Bab-*

bington Reporter on the twenty-fifth anniversary of my flight, one of them recalled the experience:

> I'll never forget that day. I watched him as he passed by, and you could just see the determination in his face, the keen gaze in his eyes, the way he looked straight ahead, toward the west, and you said to yourself, "This is a boy who knows where he's going." It was inspiring, I tell you. It was inspiring, and it was a little daunting, too. Seeing him go by, on his way, made you ask yourself, "Do *I* know where *I'm* going?" It is no exaggeration, no exaggeration at all, to say that his example, and the introspection it inspired, made me what I am today.
>   Anonymous Witness

I HAD PLANNED MY TRIP to New Mexico as a series of short hops, because when I was in the fourth grade my teacher used to begin every school day by writing on the chalkboard a few of what she called Pearls of Wisdom, requiring us to copy them into notebooks with black-and-white mottled covers, and among her pearls was Lao-Tzu's famous statement of the obvious, that a journey of a thousand miles begins with a single step, and also because I had been required, in fourth-grade arithmetic, to calculate how many steps my fourth-grade self would have to take to complete that journey of a thousand miles. (I've forgotten the answer; but my adult self has just measured his ambling stride and calculated that it would take him 1,649,831 steps.) In advance of the journey to New Mexico, I tried to calculate the number of hops that would be required. At first, I imagined that I might cover 300 miles per hop, 300 miles per day. At that rate, the trip out, which I estimated at 1,800 miles, would require just six hops, six days. However, when I daydreamed that trip, it felt rushed. I didn't seem to have enough time to look around, explore the exotic sights, sample the local cuisine, meet the people, talk to them, fall in love with their daughters, get gas, or check the oil. So I decided to cover only 100 miles per daily hop. At that rate, the trip would require eighteen hops, eighteen days. (That was my calculation. It would have worked for a crow; it didn't work for me, as you will see.) My friend Matthew Barber would be making the trip to New Mexico by commercial airliner, in a single hop, which seemed to me pathetically hasty.

When I had decided on eighteen hops, I phoned my French teacher, Angus MacPherson, who was one of the sponsors of my trip, and said, as casually as I could. "I figure I can do it in eighteen hops."

"Do what?"

"Get to New Mexico."

"'Eighteen hops'? Why do you say 'hops'?"

"That's the way I see it," I said. "I take off, fly a hundred miles, and land. It's just a short hop."

"I wouldn't call it a hop."

"Why?"

"'Hop' makes it sound too easy, Peter. It makes it sound as if any boy could do it, as if not even a boy were required. A rabbit, for example, might make the journey in a certain number of hops, given enough time and carrots."

"Oh."

"Say 'stages,'" he said, suddenly inspired, "like pieces of the incremental journey of a stagecoach. That has some dignity, given the weight of its historical association with western movies, settler sagas, and the lonely yodeling of cowpokes on the vast prairies. As a traveler by stages, you will be putting yourself in the long line of westward voyagers, making yourself a part of America's restless yearning for what I think we might call westness. And *stage* has a nice ring to it. *Hop* does not ring at all. It sounds like a dull thud on a wet drum. Take it from me: go by stages, not by hops."

So I went by stages, though I had planned to go by hops. I think that I would have reported here that I had gone by hops, despite Mr. MacPherson's counsel, if it were not for the fact that *hops* suggests too much time spent in the air. Because being in the air is what makes a hop a hop, *hop* suggests, it seems to me, that the hopper is in the air for the entire length of each hop. "The entire length of each hop" would be more time in the air than I actually did spend in the air, and I am firmly committed to total honesty in this account. I went by stages, on the ground, along roads, with a great deal of divagation and an occasional hop when I was for a moment a few inches, sometimes a foot, in the air.

Making the trip in stages confirmed in me a tendency that had been growing for some time: the preference for working in small steps, for making life's journey little by little. I think that this tendency may have

been born on the earliest clamming trips I made with my grandfather,
when I watched him clamming, treading for clams by feeling for them
with his toes, and I learned, without giving it any thought, that a clammer
acquires a peck of clams one clam at a time, that the filling of a peck basket is a kind of journey. Whether Lao-Tzu had anything to say about the
connection between clamming and life's journey, I do not know, but I do
know that there came a time, sometime after my youth, when I turned my
step-by-small-step tendency into a guiding principle, and I began deliberately to live one small step at a time. Living according to this principle
has meant that many of life's jobs have taken me longer than they might
have been expected to take. Many of them are still in the process of com-
pletion, and I know people who would count "growing up" among those,
but I swear to you that I do work at them all, a little bit at a time. So, for
example, I write my memoirs as I've lived my life, a little bit each day,
hop by hop.

I TRAVELED WITHOUT A MAP, though that was not my original intention. I had intended to travel with a map, because I had thought that I
needed a map, and I was convinced that I needed a special map, a superior
map, that "just any map" would never do. I already had maps of the United States, of course—several in an atlas, more in an encyclopedia, and
others in a gazetteer that showed the typical products of various regions—
but I felt that none of those would do. They were maps, but they weren't
aviators' maps. I supposed that I needed maps like—but superior to—
those that automobile navigators used, the sort of map that my grandmother wrestled with every summer when my parents and I traveled with
my grandparents to West Burke, Vermont—and, later, West Burke, New
Hampshire—my grandfather at the wheel of their Studebaker, as pilot,
and my grandmother beside him, as navigator.

   I should explain the two West Burkes. In 1854, fugitive transcenden-
talists from Burke, Vermont, established West Burke, Vermont, as a uto-
pian community. When, in time, some of West Burke's residents came to
feel that the town had, like Burke before it, fallen toward an earthbound
state, that commerce and government had become the preoccupations of
the majority of their fellow citizens, that the community's increasing ma-
terialism was no longer hospitable to their pursuit of spiritual truth, no

longer conducive to their everyday effort to see the world globed in a drop of dew, they left the town, headed in an easterly direction (rejecting, resisting, or reversing that restless American yearning for westness), passed through the town of Burke, and moved to New Hampshire, just a short eastward hike away. There they established a new settlement of their own. Logically, this new town might have been named East Burke; defiantly, however, the erstwhile residents of West Burke, Vermont, named this new town West Burke, as an assertion that it was the true West Burke, and that the Vermont version had become a travesty of everything that it ought to have been. (Later still, New Hampshirites disturbed by the presence of a West Burke in their state where one did not logically belong, incorporated their own town of Burke, just east of West Burke, thereby legitimizing the name geographically.)

On our trips to West Burke, whether we were on our way to Vermont or New Hampshire, my grandmother did the navigating, and I remember well how she struggled to control a huge, ungainly map, on which the routes were laid out in a code of width and weight and color that indicated their place in the hierarchy of roadways. That, I thought, was the kind of map I needed.

In those days, one could have maps for free from local gas stations (which were not yet billed as service stations, though that appellation and the diminishing level of service that it was meant to mask were just around the corner). Since my father worked at a gas station, I could get maps there, of course, but the station stocked only maps of New York and contiguous states. Those would not be enough. I wrote to the company that owned my father's station and supplied him with gas, and I received maps of Pennsylvania, Ohio, Indiana, Illinois, Missouri, Kansas, Oklahoma, Texas, and New Mexico. I stapled them to the walls of my room, along with my maps of New York and New Jersey.

While I was studying them, the thought occurred to me that wind and weather might drive me off course, make me drift. I would need maps of the states north and south of my route. I wrote for those, and when they came I added them to the walls of my room, and when I had filled the walls I tried taping some to the ceiling. The ones on the ceiling sagged and billowed, and their corners came unstuck and curled downward. After struggling to keep them flat and fixed, I persuaded myself that I liked the billowing and curling, and I allowed them to billow and curl as they would.

Studying these maps as I did, whether standing at the wall and leaning in at them or regarding them from my bed with my hands clasped behind my head, I made my trip to New Mexico many times before I ever left the family driveway. I felt in imagination the surge and lift of my winged mount beneath me. I saw my flightless coevals, the nation's little ground-lings, below me, watching and waving, wishing that they could be me. I saw America's yards and farms laid out like patches in a quilt. I saw it all as others said they had seen it. I was seeing it at second hand, but still something of it came from me—all the pretty girls, to name just one ex-ample, sunbathing in their yards, waving at me, beckoning to me, blowing kisses. After a while, I began to fear, as I suppose all armchair travelers do, that the actual journey would be a disappointment, and, little by little, the thought occurred to me that the maps might not be accurate.

"I got these maps from the company that owns my father's gas sta-tion," I said to my friend Spike, "but I'm worried about them."

"You're afraid that they'll fall on you while you're asleep and smother you?" she suggested.

"No," I said. "It's not that. It's—look at the way the mapmakers vary the thickness of the lines that represent roads and highways, and the way they use different colors."

"Very nice," she said.

"But—suppose they make these maps in such a way that they tend to lead the traveler astray?"

"Astray?"

"I mean, what if they lead people to their gas stations?"

"What?" she asked.

"All the gas companies make maps like these and give them out at their stations, right?"

"Right."

"Suppose they make the roads going past their stations look more at-tractive or more interesting, so that people will choose those routes and won't choose other routes, where the gas stations that sell other kinds of gas are located."

"You're nuts," she told me.

"Maybe," I admitted.

To test my theory—and Spike's, I suppose—I wrote to other gas companies. I compared their maps' depictions of the roads along the route that I intended to follow with the version offered by the company that owned the station where my father worked. I imagined traveling the routes that the maps depicted, and tried to decide whether I was being steered toward each company's gas stations. After many long hours of thought experimentation, I came to the conclusion that the maps could not be trusted—and, simultaneously, I discovered that the trip so often taken in my imagination had grown stale.

So I refreshed the trip that had grown stale by deciding to travel without a map. Why travel with a map that you've decided you can't trust anyway? I took all the maps down from my walls and ceiling, folded them up, and put them away in my closet.

Having no map forced me to ask directions of strangers, and along the way I learned that doing so leads to fascinating exchanges, exchanges that are, more often than not, useless, but fascinating nonetheless. If I had it to do over again (in actuality, not in memory, as I am doing it now), I think I might travel with a map. I've decided that they're more trustworthy than I thought—and they are much more trustworthy than the advice of strangers.

Chapter 2
Our Little Secret

I AM SOMETIMES asked to explain the secret of the happiness that Albertine and I have found in each other's company over all the years that we have been together, through thick and thin and through thin and thinner, and when asked I admit quite frankly that the secret is our nearly perfect balance of induced and dynamic lift.

Lift, on a wing, on an airplane, is a matter of relative pressure: less pressure above, pressing down; more pressure below, pushing up. When the pressure's off above and on below, we rise. I am a great believer in lift, unlike Wolfgang Langewiesche, who, in his *Stick and Rudder: An Explanation of the Art of Flying,* disparaged lift. It might be fair to say that Langewiesche pooh-poohed the whole idea of lift, coming very close to calling it an illusion, as close as Kurt Gödel came to calling time an illusion in "A Remark About the Relationship Between Relativity Theory and Idealistic Philosophy," his contribution to the 1949 Festschrift volume, *Albert Einstein: Philosopher-Scientist.* For Langewiesche, the upward mobility of a forward-moving airplane is the result of the reaction of the undersurface of the wing to the force of the air below the wing when the airplane's engine pushes the wing against the air below it at a sufficient angle of attack—that is, with a sufficient upward slant. The air pushes the wing up, in Langewiesche's view, and the wing needn't be an airfoil; it might as well be a sheet of plywood; it could be any plane surface at all. Hence, Langewiesche points out, the name of the vehicle itself, an air(borne) plane. So, which is it: the lowered pressure on the upside of an airfoil or the greater pressure on the underside of a plane at the proper angle of attack? (In certain circles, this is still the subject of lively debate.) For the answer, I turn to Pope and Otis, my quondam mentors Frank and Art:

> When an airfoil is presented to the wind at a positive angle of attack, the impact of the air on the under surface of the airfoil produces lift. This kind of lift is called *dynamic lift*. [The] lift which comes from the reduced pressure of the air above an airfoil is called *induced lift*. The total lift is the sum of these values, which is merely the difference between the increased pressure below and the diminished pressure above the airfoil.

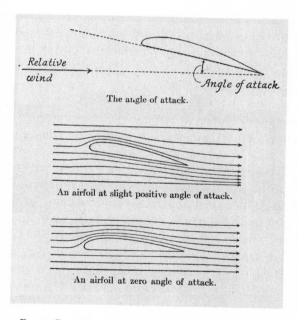

The angle of attack.

An airfoil at slight positive angle of attack.

An airfoil at zero angle of attack.

FRANCIS POPE AND ARTHUR S. OTIS, *ELEMENTS OF AERONAUTICS*

For Frank and Art, it's not a case of either-or. Both the dynamic and induced forms of lift play their parts.

As it is in flight, so it is in life—my life with Albertine, at any rate.

When Albertine commences an undertaking, she assumes a positive angle of attack and thrusts herself forward, attacking that undertaking head-on, with power and purpose and a plan. The undertaking could be something as simple as a cross-country drive or as complex as "taking Peter out for an airing so that his outlook on life will be refreshed." The result is the same: the woman produces lift. Her kind of lift is called *dynamic lift*.

When I commence an undertaking, I begin conducting thought experiments at once, and in a remarkably short time my head is in the clouds. My kind of lift is called *induced lift*.

Through the combined effects of dynamic and induced lift, Albertine and I manage to transport each other over many of life's little obstacles. Ordinarily, she provides the dynamic lift, and I'm the simple airfoil, providing the induced lift. Together, we are a complex airfoil like the one described by Frank and Art.

So it has been for many years, but something happened to Albertine during her recovery from her crash and fracture. She underwent a Baudelairean turn toward childhood, and to my great surprise began to exhibit an inclination and talent for producing induced lift, culminating in her selection of the Electro-Flyer as a vehicle suitable for a cross-country trip. I found this a little alarming. What would such a trip be like with two agents of induced lift and none of dynamic lift? I was relieved to find, while we were packing the Electro-Flyer, that she had reverted to form.

"You know," I said, squeezing a small bag into a small nook in a corner of the trunk, "in recent years, my favorite journeys, my best journeys, have been the ones I've made in my mind. They have required no shopping, no tickets, no luggage, no packing, and no maps."

"Mmm," she said, thereby displaying her practical dynamic-lift side by disparaging my impractical induced-lift side.

"Armchair travel is surely one of the greatest benefits of the human imagination," I asserted.

"One of its virtues," she admitted, "is that you get to sleep in your own bed." She frowned at the pile of things we hadn't been able to find nooks for. "I'm beginning to think that we should have bought a car with a bigger trunk."

"The tiny trunk makes it more like my aerocycle—which hardly had room for a change of socks."

"Oh, I do hope we're not going to find it difficult to get our laundry done," she fretted. "We have only a week's worth of underwear each."

"We could stuff some more into the pockets in the doors if we got rid of all those maps and turn-by-turn directions and just trusted to hunch, whim, and serendipity."

"If you're going to travel with me, Peter, you're going to be in a car driven by a woman who knows where she's going."

"Yeah. I know. I just thought I'd give it one last try."

"I'm sorry. That's just the way I am."

"But did we really have to make all our hotel and motel reservations in advance?" I asked. "Couldn't we maybe just wing it, trusting to chance that we'll find a cozy place for the night when night comes on?"

"I used to run a place like the ones we'd be likely to find if we trusted to chance," she reminded me. "That's why I made reservations at places where I think we can remain dry on rainy nights."

We took our places in the car. Albertine switched it on, put it into gear, pulled out of the spot in front of our building where we'd parked it for packing, and headed for the corner.

"Well," I said hopefully, "there's always the chance that we'll get lost."

Chapter 3
West Bayborough

It is often necessary while flying to determine where one is, or was, or will be, at a given time.

Francis Pope and Arthur S. Otis, *Elements of Aeronautics*

I HAD BEEN ON THE ROAD for a couple of hours, enjoying myself quite a bit despite the fact that I couldn't get *Spirit* off the ground, when I began talking to my mount. At first I was just urging her to get up and go, but then, little by little, I began conversing with her as I would have with a traveling companion.

"Do you think that means something?" I asked her as we came to a stop at a red light. "The way talking to yourself means money in the bank?"

"Doesn't that mean company's coming?" she asked.

"Money in the bank, company's coming, something like that."

"I think it's just an inevitable consequence of traveling solo," she said thoughtfully. "Sooner or later, a solo traveler will talk to himself—or to his beautiful aerocycle if he's fortunate enough to have one. That's just the way it is."

"What?" asked the driver of the car beside me.

"Oh—ah—nothing," I said. "I was just talking to my—ah—myself."

"Means you're nuts," he claimed cheerily. "You want to try to keep that under control."

"Yes, sir," I said.

Embarrassed, I chugged along for a while without saying a word to anyone.

"So!" she said after a couple of blocks. "I embarrass you!"

"Oh, no. No. Of course not."

"Then why wouldn't you admit to that fool that you were talking to me?"

"I—"

"That was a person of absolutely no consequence to you, someone you are not likely ever to see again, and yet you wouldn't acknowledge me."

"Please, I—"

"Don't talk to me."

"Okay."

We rode on in silence until the silence grew awkward, whereupon I broke it by remarking, as if there were no ill feeling between us, "So this is traveling without a map, free as the wind!"

"I like it!" said *Spirit,* apparently as eager as I to put the past behind us.

"It's easier than I thought it would be," I said.

"I agree!"

For a moment I thought of using that remark as an opening to point out that she wasn't putting as much effort into transporting me as I had expected her to, but I think that—tyro traveler though I was—I realized that it's not wise to antagonize one's traveling companion or one's conveyance or both so early in the trip.

"Now that I think about it, I realize that I had begun to worry that it was going to be boring," I said instead, "just one straight road to New Mexico without any diversions."

"It was studying all those maps that did that."

"But now I'm finding that although I have a general direction in mind as a goal—"

"A kind of Emersonian tendency."

"Um, yeah. You could say that. A tendency. Right. A kind of westness. But I can choose the roads that seem most appealing, the ones that seem to offer the most pleasant route to—or at least toward—the goal."

"I see what you mean. You don't have to go right at it."

"Right," I said, inspired. "I can tack."

"Well put."

"A sailor soon learns that he almost never takes a direct route," I declaimed under the influence of her praise, or flattery. "He learns that wind and tide and currents will alter his course, and he learns to live with that, even to enjoy it."

"'A tar rolls with the swells,' as Mr. Summers said—"

"Well, yeah," I said, surprised that she should know about Mr. Summers, leader of the Young Tars, and the mottoes he tried to persuade his followers to adopt, surprised that she should have access to my memory.

"—enjoying the diversion of wind and tide and currents and swells the way that you're enjoying the wandering course of this journey."

"Yes."

"You seem to have learned a lot from the days you spent as a boy, sailing with your grandfather on Bolotomy Bay," she said, mining my memory again.

"Those were wonderful days," I said with a sigh.

I went on for a while, reminiscing happily about those carefree days on Bolotomy Bay, until, suddenly, to my surprise, there was Bolotomy Bay right in front of me. I throttled down and rolled slowly to the water's edge, where a bulkhead formed the margin of the bay. Somewhere, I realized, somewhere in my recent past, I had made a wrong turn.

Long Island is long and narrow, running east-and-west. When I set out from Babbington I had been headed west, in the general direction of New Mexico. My intention had been to continue heading west, and if I had succeeded in doing so, the bay, which stretches along Long Island's southern shore, should have been to the south of my route. I should have been traveling westward, paralleling the bay, not heading directly into it. I should have arrived in New York City, not at the West Bayborough Municipal Dock, which was where I found myself, or where I found myself lost.

I turned away from the water and in the manner of all lost people began trying to retrace my steps, hoping to find the place at which I had gone wrong, and there to go right, to regain the westward tendency that I had hoped to maintain throughout my journey.

After spending some time in that effort, I began to understand that I must have made many wrong turns. The first one must have been made quite some time ago, not very far from Babbington, and then I must have spent most of the afternoon and early evening making one wrong turn after another. The pleasure I had found in traveling had been a false pleasure, founded on ignorance, a bliss that I felt only while my ignorance lasted, a bliss that vanished when my eyes were opened.

"I blame it on the weather," I explained to *Spirit*. "When the day clouded over, I had no sunlight or shadows to help me tell west from south or north or even east. I was flying blind."

"In more ways than one," she muttered.

"Okay. You're right. It's my own fault. I should have brought a map."

I thought she might offer me some consolation, perhaps even tell me that I shouldn't blame myself, but she didn't. We rolled on in silence, retracing my steps, but I retraced my steps so badly that I found myself back at the West Bayborough Municipal Dock again.

I stopped. I sighed. Beside me, a grizzled fisherman sitting on the bulkhead heard me sigh and guessed the reason for it.

"Lost?" he asked.

"Yes," I admitted.

"That's nothing to be ashamed of," said a lovely dark-haired girl beside him. "Everyone gets lost now and then."

"In my case, there is something to be ashamed of," I confessed. "This is trouble of my own making, and the making of it began when I chose to travel without a map."

"That's quite eloquently put," the fisherman said.

"I've been practicing," I said. "I've been rehearsing that for the last hour or so, while I was trying to retrace my steps."

"In the manner of all lost people."

"I suppose so."

"It's a pity we didn't speak earlier, the first time you arrived here at the dock."

"I didn't notice you."

"Perhaps."

"Really. I didn't."

"Perhaps you were reluctant to ask directions. It's a common failing."

"No. Really. I just didn't notice you."

"And yet I have rather an unusual aspect, wouldn't you say?"

"Well, no, not really, to tell the truth. Back home, in Babbington, there are quite a few grizzled—"

"Old salts?" offered the girl.

"Yes."

"Here I'm considered quite a character," the fisherman asserted.

"That's true," said the girl.

"Well—"

"I make a considerable contribution to local color."

"I'm sure."

"And I'm considered an important source of folk wisdom."

"That's the way it is back at home. There are many—"

"If you had asked my advice," he said, with an unmistakable note of irritation in his voice, "I would have offered you a bit of that wisdom: I would have told you not to try retracing your steps."

"Why?"

"Retracing one's steps is repeating old errors. It's a miserable way to live one's life."

"I only spent a couple of hours—"

"Now you take me," he went on. "I've made mistakes in my life—who hasn't—but do I dwell on them, do I keep returning to them and regretting them? No. Certainly not. What's done is done. You can't change the past. You can't go back to the place where things went wrong and make them go right."

"But what should he do, Grandfather?" asked the girl.

"Yeah," I said. "What should I do?"

"You should go on from where you are."

"But it's getting dark. It feels late. And I've been on the road so long."

"How long have you been away from home?" asked the girl, placing a gentle hand on my arm.

"Hours," I said importantly.

"Grandpa," the girl said to the grizzled fisherman, "this boy must be tired and hungry. I'm going to take him home, give him a hot bath, cook him some supper, and tuck him into bed," and then she simply faded away, vanished, returning to the land of wishful thinking, from which she had materialized for the few moments that she'd been standing there.

"Did you?" asked the fisherman.

"What?" I asked, bewildered by the way the girl had disappeared.

"I said, 'You must have had many adventures,'" the fisherman repeated. "Did you?"

"Huh?" I said, still befuddled.

"Never mind," he said. "Time for me to pack up and head for home—a hot bath—a hearty meal—and a good night's sleep."

I needed a place to stay. I'd been away from Babbington for only a few hours, but I had already begun to feel the chill of separation. I missed the place—my home town—and the people in it. I felt very much alone and in need of someplace that would make me feel, if not at home, at least in a place like home. I had intended from the start to rely on the kindness of strangers, to ask the people I met along the way to give me shelter, and to exploit the good impression that I, a daring young flyboy, was likely to make on the easily awed populace of the towns I would be passing through. The grizzled fisherman didn't seem easily awed, but he was the only current candidate for the role of kindly stranger.

"Please, sir," I said, "I've been traveling for some time—I'm tired and hungry—and I need a place to stay for the night."

"Mm," he said as he began to pack his gear.

"Could you—?"

"Mm?"

"Could you—um—put me up?"

"For the night?"

"If it wouldn't be too much trouble."

"I suppose you'll want supper, and a bath, and clean sheets."

"Well—"

"You'll have to eat fish," he said, indicating the fish in his bucket.

"I like fish."

"You'll have to bathe in cold water."

"I've done that at camp."

"You'll have to sleep with my granddaughter."

"That would be—I—really?"

"In your dreams," he said, cuffing me behind the ear.

His humble home was not far. It was a little cottage, not much larger than the cabin of a boat and outfitted just as efficiently. The fisherman's wife greeted me as if a wayfarer in need of a place to spend the night were not at all an uncommon sight. She had bread in the oven, and as soon as the fisherman had cleaned the fish he'd caught she began making a plain but hearty chowder. Dinner was wonderfully satisfying, and I paid for it

by regaling them with tales of my adventures on the road until their eyes
began to droop and they began to list the many tasks that awaited them on
the morrow. The fisherman showed me to a tiny loft above the kitchen,
and there, in a narrow bed with a thin mattress, I slept soundly, with visions of the dark-haired girl dancing in my head.

THE NEXT MORNING, after breakfast, I was surprised to find that I was
reluctant to leave the cozy cabin. The grizzled fisherman must have noticed my reluctance, because he took me aside—actually, he grabbed my
arm above the elbow and dragged me from the house—and said, "You'll
be on your way." I decided to interpret it as a question.

"Yes," I said with a sigh, "you're right. You and your wife have been
wonderful hosts, and I've enjoyed my stay, but if I'm going to get to New
Mexico I'll have to be on my way."

"It isn't wise to sail without a chart," he said.

"I realize that now."

"It's folly, really."

"I suppose you're right."

"But," he added with a twinkle, "as the poet says, 'If the fool would
persist in his folly he would become wise.'"

"You mean you think that I—should continue to sail without a chart?"

"Yes."

"That's your advice?"

"That's my advice."

"And you think I'll become wise by persisting in my folly?"

"You might."

"All right," I said, extending my hand, "I'll take your advice."

We shook hands. I mounted *Spirit* and started her up. I looked around.

"Which—um—which way—"

He pointed in a direction that I hoped was westerly.

Chapter 4
Riding Shotgun

> Kurt [Gödel] liked to drive fast. This, combined with his penchant
> for indulging in abstract reverie while behind the wheel, led his
> [. . .] wife, Adele, to put an end to his driving career.
>   Palle Yourgrau, *A World Without Time: The Forgotten Legacy*
>   *of Gödel and Einstein*

ALBERTINE WAS BEHIND THE WHEEL of the Electro-Flyer, driving, and I was beside her in the passenger's seat, asking myself what, exactly, my role was in this adventure. Co-pilot? Navigator? Faithful
companion? Sancho Panza? Dr. Watson, Jim, Tonto?

"You're talking to yourself," said Albertine.

"Not audibly," I said.

"No, but I can see your lips moving."

"Keep your eyes on the road."

"Why do you talk to yourself?"

"I know not why others may do so, but as for me it has always been a
way to clarify my thinking—"

"Clarify somewhat."

"It has always been a way to clarify my thinking somewhat, and in the
years that you and I have been together, it has been a way for me to prepare the witty aphorisms, entertaining anecdotes, and penetrating com-
mentary that I use to impress, entertain, and seduce you."

"Do you have anything ready?"

"More or less."

"Speak."

"I've been reflecting on my role in this adventure."

"Are we having an adventure?"

"Life is an adventure."

"Not when I'm waiting on line at the pharmacy."

"Okay, but this part of our life together is an adventure, and I've been reflecting on my role in it. After all, there you are, at the wheel, clearly the driver, or pilot, and here I am, beside you, with a folder of maps at the ready—"

"A handsome leather folder of maps."

"Yes. Very manly. I appreciate that. But even with my maps I can't be considered the navigator, since you have chosen the route in advance and printed turn-by-turn directions from three map sites on the World Wide Web."

"Oh. I see. I'm sorry—"

"No need. No need. I've defined my role, and I'm happy in it."

"Stud muffin?"

"Not while you're driving."

"Ye gods, what good are you, then?"

"Exactly the question, I think, that teenage boys used to ask themselves when they cadged rides from friends who had driver's licenses and the use of the family car when they had neither themselves."

"What good am I?" she cried to the open sky above the crystalline plastic top of the Electro-Flyer in excellent imitation of the wail of a boy whose voice is still changing.

"And the answer, I've decided, is that I am fulfilling the role that in my teenage years was called 'riding shotgun.'"

"Now why did you call it that?" she asked, speaking this time in the manner of Mr. MacPherson, my high school French teacher, an enthusiastic student of idiom.

"I'm glad you asked," I said. "I can answer with confidence because as a boy I spent many Saturday mornings at the Babbington Theater, watching westerns." In the voice of one who knows, I said, "My dear Albertine, we teenage boys used the term because when we were even younger boys we had heard it used so often in westerns that involved stagecoach travel. In those movies, there were always bands of marauding bandits. I should point out that many of those bandits were actually good guys who, through no fault of their own, often just because of a case of mistaken identity, had been driven out of polite society and found themselves forced to turn to banditry to make a living. I don't mean to suggest that all the bad guys were good guys forced to be bad—many were actually bad—most of them, in fact. Sometimes they were greedy, and sometimes they were just mean. They had been brought up that way, I guess, or perhaps they had been starved for affection during childhood. Something like that. Anyway, the point that was brought home again and again to an impressionable boy in the Babbington Theater was that driving a stagecoach through the Old West was a dangerous undertaking, especially if the stage was carrying something valuable that bad guys would want, like gold or the new school marm or somebody's bride from Back East. The hills out there were crawling with bad guys. So, a stagecoach required, in addition to a driver, a second man sitting beside the driver, his right-hand man, right up there on the seat where the driver sat, a man who could fight off the bad guys if they attacked. This second—but equally important—man held, across his lap, at the ready, a shotgun. He wasn't driving. He was 'riding shotgun.' And here am I riding shotgun for you, so that you can concentrate on your driving, secure in the knowledge that if any bad guys come galloping up beside us with evil intent—I will scare them away with the handsome leather folder of maps that I have lying across my lap, at the ready."

"That's my guy," she said.

What I hadn't told her, what I am telling her only now, in this sentence, on this page, is that the guy riding shotgun for her was on the alert for signs of flyguys in the sky, and if he saw them in the rearview mirror or heard the ominous sound of their blades chopping the air, he meant to use his handsome leather book of maps to suggest evasive action—a sudden side trip to someplace hard to spot from the air. He would insist. If necessary, he would plead. If it came to that, he would take the wheel.

Chapter 5
Once Bitten

Ladies and gentlemen, . . . I . . . hardly know where to begin, to
paint for you a word picture of the strange scene before my eyes . . .
   Carl Phillips, radio commentator, in Howard Koch's adaptation
   of H. G. Wells's *The War of the Worlds*

THE DAY WAS NEARLY PERFECT for traveling: clear and cool and
still. As I pulled onto the road, my heart was full of the mad hope that
Spirit might on this promising day take to the air and fly me to my next
stop.

"Let's go, *Spirit*," I coaxed her. "Let's rise up, leave the hard pavement below us, and soar into the clear, cool air. Come on, let's go!"

"Oh, please," she said with a yawn.

"What's the matter?"

"It's so early."

"But it's such a wonderful morning. Don't you feel the urge to get up
and go?"

"Not at all. I'm still tired from yesterday. All that traveling! I've never
done anything like that in my life."

"No," I said, reluctantly admitting the truth of it, "I guess you
haven't."

"Couldn't we just take it easy today and kind of glide along at a nice
easy pace? On the ground?"

"Okay," I said, but I didn't try to hide my disappointment.

"If I have an easy day today, I might be able to get up into the air to-morrow."

"If you're making a bargain, I'm going to hold you to it," I said.

"Of course. I'm an aerocycle of my word."

So, off we went, at an easy pace. I realize now, in retrospect, that, for the sake of my account, I should have stopped one night in Manhattan. If I had, this chapter might have included some Manhattan adventures. At the time, though, the city seemed an obstacle that stood in the way of my real journey and my real adventure, which lay beyond New York, in the West, so I pushed on through without stopping at all, and we traveled without adventures for the entire day, pleasantly and uneventfully, if slowly, stopping once for gas, and once for lunch, and briefly now and then so that I could stretch my legs and she could rest, until we found ourselves deep in New Jersey, late in the afternoon.

As the shadows began to lengthen and I began to turn my thoughts to dinner, I began to feel that something was odd, though I wasn't quite sure what made me feel that way.

"*Spirit,*" I whispered, "there's something strange going on."

"What?"

"I don't know—it's hard to put into words—I've just got a strange feeling."

"You're not giving me much to go on."

"Well, it feels as if people are watching me—watching us."

"I suppose it isn't every day that a kid comes flying through these parts on a graceful and gorgeous aerocycle. Of course people are watching."

"Yeah, but this is more like—surveillance."

"You've seen too many—" she began, but she broke off, and in a moment said, *sotto voce,* "You're right. We seem to be attracting notice."

"That's it," I said, "attracting notice. Am I right that there are some people—keeping an eye on us?"

"You are," she said. "They're acting as if they're going about their business, but there's something phony about them."

"They're evenly spaced," I pointed out, "as if they've been stationed there."

"Like sentries," she said with a chill in her voice.

"Uh-oh."

"What?"

"In the road—ahead—a roadblock."

"Wow," she said, and from her tone I could tell that, like me, she found two emotions vying for dominance within her: (1) a fear of the authorities, and (2) pride in our seeming important enough or threatening enough for the authorities to put up a roadblock against us.

I began slowing long before we reached the roadblock, lest the small mob assembled there get the idea that I intended to run it.

"This is my first roadblock," I confessed to *Spirit.*

"Mine, too," she said, as if I didn't know.

"I'm a little nervous."

"Me, too."

There were four police officers manning the roadblock. They wore enormous pistols on their hips. The people in the growing crowd around them were also armed. Shotguns, cradled like babies, were the weapon of choice, and pitchforks, held like lances, the tines directed at *Spirit* and me, were a close second.

I came to a stop, wiped my sweaty palms on my pants legs, swallowed hard, and said, "Hello," as innocently as I could.

"Don't come no closer," said the largest of the cops.

"Sorry," I said, pushing with my heels to back *Spirit* up a bit. "Was I too close? This is my first roadblock—"

"Don't try no funny stuff."

"No, sir," I said, shaking my head. "You won't get any funny stuff from me. Not at all. You can ask anybody—"

"Where have you come from?" asked the closest of the pitchforkers.

Tentatively, apologetically, fearing, for the first time in my life, that it might be the wrong answer, I said, "Babbington."

"Is that on our planet?" he asked, narrowing his eyes.

"Sure," I said. "It's just back that way—" I raised my arm to point, and the crowd stiffened, brandishing their weapons. The cops put their hands on their pistol butts. I held my own hands up to show that I was neither armed nor up to any funny stuff, and said, "It's on Long Island—in New York."

"Oh, yeah? New York?"

"Right."

"Quick: who plays center field for the Yankees?"

"Mickey Mantle."

"What does the Statue of Liberty hold in her right hand?"

"In her right hand? I—ah—" I struck Liberty's pose to ensure that I didn't confuse her hands. "A torch," I announced authoritatively.

"Who is Popeye's nemesis?"

"I—ah—his nemesis—um—Pluto? No—Bluto!"

At once the crowd that had seemed so hostile became warm and welcoming. My interrogator shifted his pitchfork so that the end of its handle rested on the ground with its tines pointing upward. He seemed as relieved as I that the interrogation had gone so well.

"You've got to excuse us," he said with an apologetic shrug. "Once bitten, twice shy, you know."

"Who bit you?" I asked.

"Martians."

"Martians?"

"You don't believe me?"

I sensed that stiffening again, so I was quick to answer, "Of course I believe you. I just didn't know that Martians—um—bit. I thought they used—well—ray guns."

"You trying to be funny?"

"No, sir! It's just that—I don't know—Martians that bite—"

"It's just an expression," one of the cops offered helpfully. "Probably derived from experience with dogs, but extended to a wide range of experiences, essentially suggesting that after a bad experience a person tends to be cautious when presented with a similar situation."

"Is your name MacPherson?" I asked. I couldn't help myself.

"MacPherson? No. Why do you ask?"

"Because my French teacher, back in Babbington, is named MacPherson, and he's very interested in words and phrases that don't mean quite what they seem to mean, like saying 'once bitten, twice shy' when you mean being cautious after a bad experience."

"In our case it was a bad experience with Martians," the interrogator said, evidently not particularly interested in Mr. MacPherson.

"That's incredible!" I said enthusiastically.

"I'm going to assume that you mean 'amazing' or 'astonishing' or something like that and not 'unbelievable.' Am I right?"

"Yes, sir. Definitely. Amazing. Astonishing. Um—tell me about it."

"That would best be done by Lem here," he said, beckoning to a venerable member of the armed mob. "He's kind of our local historian."

"Ahhh," objected Lem, with a dismissive flap of the hand. "He ain't goin' to believe me no more'n any o' the other outsiders."

"Now take it easy, Lemuel," said the largest of the cops, gently. "Don't go getting yourself into a lather. Why don't you tell the boy what happened? Then he'll be able to pass the truth along, and then someday everybody'll know what really happened here."

Lem shook his head petulantly and looked at his shoes.

"Once bitten, twice shy?" I offered.

"How's that?" asked Lem.

"I guess you've had a bad experience with people you've told the story to," I said. "Outsiders, I mean."

"Oh. Yeah. That's so. Say, you catch on right quick."

"I sure would like to hear about the Martians," I said.

Lem came forward, took a position beside *Spirit,* turned to me, incidentally, and to the crowd at large, primarily, and began, "Pretty near a score of years ago, Martians landed here, in Hopper's Knoll, at Gurney's farm."

One of the assembled multitude raised a hand, evidently acknowledging his status as Gurney.

"They came in a spaceship that they had disguised so's it would look like a meteor, but when you got close to it you could see it was more of a kind of yellowish-white cylinder."

Gurney took a step forward and volunteered, "When it come in out of the sky, I was listening to the radio, kind of halfway listening and halfway dozing, when I heard a hissing sound, kind of like a Fourth of July rocket, and then—bingo!—something smacked the ground. Knocked me out of my chair."

Lemuel resumed the narrative, and as it continued, with occasional eye-witness interruptions from Gurney and others, a thrill of recognition began to run through me. I knew the story they were telling. I knew it

well. It was *The War of the Worlds,* and the version that Lem was telling
resembled the version broadcast by the Mercury Theatre under the direction of Orson Welles, on October 30, 1938, six years—almost to the
day—before I was born. I had become interested in the story after seeing
a movie version of it at the Babbington Theater when I was nine. Inspired
by that experience, "once bitten" and infected in a positive rather than a
negative way, I had read the original version, by H. G. Wells, and I had
also read the radio play by Howard Koch that had been the basis for the
Mercury Theatre broadcast. It was a case of once bitten, twice eager. Not
only had I read Koch's radio play, but when I was approaching my elev-
enth birthday a friend and I had made our own version of the radio broadcast, using a tape recorder. Together we had created some sound effects
that we considered pretty realistic. For instance, for the scene in which
the top of the Martians' spaceship begins unscrewing, we put the microphone right up next to an empty mayonnaise jar while one of us slowly
unscrewed the lid. The effect was so realistic that when the kids in our
class at school heard it—

"You got something you want to say, son?" the interrogator asked.

I did! I did! I wanted to tell them everything about my experiences
with *The War of the Worlds.* I wanted to begin at the beginning, with
some background about the Babbington Theater and brief plot summaries
of the most memorable movies that I had seen there before I saw *The War
of the Worlds,* but in the moment of hesitation when I was deciding just
where I ought to begin, I noticed that Lem had grown perplexed and irritated, and from the way he was scowling at me I surmised that I was the
cause.

"Um—no," I said. "What makes you think—"

"You're moving your lips and twitchin' and bouncin' up and down on
the balls of your feet like somebody's got to go to the bathroom."

"That's it!" I said. "I didn't want to interrupt the story, but, you know,
I've been on the road for a long time, and I—I've really got to go."

"Well, heck, son, why didn't you say so? Gurney, your place is about
the closest. What say we all head on over there where the boy can relieve
himself and Lem can go on with the story?"

"It would be an honor," Gurney claimed.

ON THE WAY TO GURNEY'S FARM, *Spirit* had time to give me some stern, unwelcome, but necessary advice.

"That was close," she began, realizing, I suppose, that it's best not to launch right into stern, unwelcome, but necessary advice without some preamble.

"I know," I whispered.

"You just barely managed to keep your foot out of your mouth."

"I wonder why we say that?" I asked, because it was an expression that had puzzled me for some time, and because I didn't welcome the stern but necessary advice that I knew was coming.

"Never mind," she said in the manner of people who find that fate has given them an opportunity to deliver the kind of advice that is more pleasant to give than to receive.

"It just seems to me that it's backwards," I said. "Wouldn't it make more sense to say, 'You should have put your foot in your mouth'?"

"Listen to me."

"Okay."

"These people think they've got something that's uniquely theirs, a place in the history of these parts, of the United States, of the world, that is theirs alone. They've got a story to tell—and you almost took that away from them because you always want to tell your story."

"I know, I know. You don't have to tell me."

"But I think I do have to tell you to keep your mouth shut while you're here."

"Yeah, yeah. I know."

I really did know. What I knew, what I understood then but hadn't understood a few moments earlier, was that through many outward and visible signs I had betrayed my impatience with Lem and his story, my eagerness to tell everything I knew about *The War of the Worlds,* and my burning desire to make Lem's audience mine. Fortunately, those signs could also be interpreted as signs of a need to relieve myself, which, of course, they were. But I also knew that *Spirit* was right: from now on I was going to have to let Lem tell his story and let him have his audience and include myself in it. I'd have to keep my mouth shut—put my foot in it if necessary.

I HEARD LEM'S WHOLE STORY that night, and some parts of it I heard many times. Keeping silent while he told it was very difficult. As I listened, Lem's deviations from the versions of the story that I knew and considered correct, including my own, sometimes annoyed me so much that my emotions bubbled and seethed within me, producing a kind of re-actionary pressure that threatened to force an objection or correction from me. I stifled the urge, and instead I let the steam off in bursts of inoffensive interjections.

"Wow!" I said when I wanted to say "That's an outrageous fabrication, sir!"

"Amazing!" when I wanted to say "Totally unbelievable!"

"Astonishing!" when I wanted to say "You're full of it, Lem!"

In Lem's version of the invasion story, the men of Hopper's Knoll defeated the Martian invaders, but the Martians, routed and in full flight, blasted the village with a memory-eradication ray to erase any recollection of their ignominious defeat. The true story of Hopper's Knoll might have gone forever untold, even unknown, if Lem hadn't caught the flu a couple of years later. Fortunately for his career as local historian and raconteur (and unfortunately for the integrity of the tale as I knew it and told it myself) he *had* caught the flu, and in an influenza fever dream he recovered his memory of the battle. Through the agency of the story that he told, Lem's recovered memory became the catalyst for recovered recollections from other townsfolk, who—one by one and little by little—added bits of plausible detail to Lem's account, in an epidemic of fantastical recollective collaboration, until the whole town remembered what had happened, and their story had become full and rich and multifaceted, with a large cast of characters whose roles and remembrances reinforced one another. At last, "tetched by Mnemosyne," as Lem put it, they remembered in full how they had saved the world.

I remember Lem's story, and I remember that I was fascinated by his telling of it, and the way that the others who remembered having been a part of it contributed their bits on cue, clearly savoring the opportunity to strut onstage for a moment. Later that night, lying in bed in the spare room upstairs in the farmhouse at Gurney's place, I rehearsed the story until I fell asleep, so that I would remember it and be able to reproduce it and criticize it when I got the chance, but when I recall the story and the telling now, I find that the whole experience is dominated and somewhat obliterated by the memory, in the peripheral vision of my mind's eye, of a dark-haired girl on the edge of the listening crowd. I remember the story well enough, but it isn't what interests me now. She is.

IN THE MORNING, I soldiered my way through the endless farmhouse breakfast that Ma and Pa Gurney insisted I needed for the trials of the road ahead and then began preparing *Spirit* for takeoff. I was just about to say goodbye to the Gurneys when the man who had been my interrogator pulled into the driveway in a pickup truck, stopped beside *Spirit,* got out, and joined us.

"Son," he said, in a kindly but no-nonsense way, "I'd like a word with you before you leave."

"A word to the wise?" I asked.

He gave me that squinty-eyed look that I was getting used to, and took me aside, a few steps away from Ma and Pa.

"You know," he said, "a lot of people are suspicious of strangers, especially kids who come flying into town on motorcycles."

"So I've learned."

"On this trip of yours, I'm afraid you're always going to be the stranger riding into town."

"An object of suspicion."

"That's it."

"Strange as a Martian."

"Oh, folks may not think that you're a Martian in disguise necessarily—Hopper's Knoll may be unique in that respect—but they are apt to suspect your motives, and, once they have begun suspecting your motives, they're pretty generally likely to decide that the safest course is to regard you as a troublemaker, at least a potential troublemaker."

"That doesn't seem fair."

"Fair or not, that's the way it is."

"What do you think I should do?"

"It helps if you agree with them. Accept what they've got to say."

"Don't interrupt, you mean."

"That would be a start."

"But what if I've got something to say, too?"

"Best keep it to yourself. Just nod your head and say nothing."

"I guess, but—"

"I guess what I'm trying to tell you is, don't put your foot in it."

"In what?"

"In your mouth."

"You know," I said, shaking my head, "I've just got to say—"

He put a strong hand on my shoulder and gave it a cautionary squeeze. "What is it that you've just got to say, boy?"

"I've just got to say that you've really given me something to think about."

He narrowed his eyes, but he relaxed his grip, and I mounted *Spirit* and hit the road.

Chapter 6
The New Sheboygan

Humor . . . is almost never without one of its opposite moods—tenderness, tragedy, concern for man's condition, recognition of man's frailties, sympathy with his idealism.
  Ben Shahn, "The Gallic Laughter of André François"

'Tain't funny, McGee.
  Molly, to Fibber

Ha-ha!
  Bosse-de-Nage, in Alfred Jarry's *Gestes et Opinions du Docteur Faustroll*

"AS I ATTEMPTED TO EXPLAIN to *Spirit* so many years ago," I said, "I really do think that 'to put one's foot in one's mouth,' is generally misused. People use it to indicate that someone has made a gaffe, spoken out of turn, said what should have been left unsaid, or divulged a secret that should have been kept secret, right? Isn't that the way you hear it used?"

"Yes," she said, but she was concentrating more on highway traffic than on what I had to say, I think.

"That's the way I hear it used, too. People say, 'You really put your foot in your mouth,' when they want to point out a lack of circumspection when circumspection would have been a good policy. What they really mean, I think, is something more along the lines of 'You should have put your foot in your mouth' or 'I wish that you had put your foot in your mouth instead of blurting out all that stuff about Uncle Albert's checkered past' or 'Why, oh why, couldn't you have put your foot in your mouth when we got to the party and kept it there until we were safely back in the car?'"

I waited for a response. None came.

"In the course of its history 'put your foot in your mouth' must have suffered a semantic shift from its original cautionary meaning of 'shut up before you make a fool of yourself' to 'it's too late now, you jerk.' You want to know what evidence I have?"

As before, I waited for a response. Again none came.

"Well," I announced triumphantly, "here it is: the shift forced people to come up with an alternative that better expressed the original meaning, namely, 'put a sock in it.'"

I allowed her another moment.

"Foot, sock, they're clearly related," I pointed out.

Another moment.

"Don't you agree?" I asked.

"I'm sure I do, my darling," she said, "but I haven't really been paying close attention. The traffic is heavy, I'm playing dodgem cars here, and I'm trying to find our motel. Put a sock in it for a while, okay?"

I did.

THE PLACE that Albertine had chosen for our night's stop was not at all what I would have expected. It was one of the chain motels that line the major intersections of major highways and offer little more than a bed. When she turned off the highway, I assumed that she would hurry past the chaotic congeries of gas-food-lodging and send us down a winding lane to the only cozy inn in these-here parts. Enormous signs towered at the edge of the highway, urging the weary traveler to spend the night in a bed provided by the chains called It'll Do, Inn-a-Pinch, and Cheapo-Sleepo. I chuckled at them in a superior manner, but I choked on my chuckle when Albertine slowed and signaled for a turn into It'll Do.

"This is not at all what I would have expected you to choose," I said. "I'm disappointed, if you don't mind my saying so."

"It has a fitness center, a pool, a cocktail lounge, a restaurant, a free breakfast buffet, and the cheapest rate in a hundred miles," she informed me. "It was the best I could find."

"In these-here parts," I suggested.

"Right," she said, pulling into a parking spot with an abruptness that I didn't ordinarily see.

"Okay," I said with a shrug. "I guess it'll do in a pinch for a cheapo sleepo."

"Ha-ha," she said.

We took our bags from the car and rolled them to the entrance, where, as soon as the doors slipped open to let us in, a clerk at the desk looked up, bestowed on us a practiced smile, and recited a scripted greeting: "Welcome to the It'll Do experience! We hope your stay will be okay!" Then he shook his head and added with a weary sigh, ad lib, "Please—please—don't try any funny stuff."

"What?" I said, surprised.

"I've been checking you people in all day, and I've had all the gags I can take."

"I don't know what you mean."

"I've heard that one, too."

"I'm mystified," I said. "Is this the standard greeting across the entire It'll Do chain? If I walk into an It'll Do in Sheboygan—"

"You know," he said, holding up a hand, "just stop right there and let me ask you something—why is it always Sheboygan? What is it with you people that makes you choose Sheboygan when you're going to try to be funny?"

"I—"

"Is it supposed to be an announcement? 'Attention! Attention! A joke is coming!'"

"I—"

"Or is Sheboygan just supposed to be innately funny?"

"I—"

"Or is it the entire state of Wisconsin?"

"Please," I said, "stop. I don't know why you're asking me these questions, or what you mean about being funny—"

"You're here for the annual Humorists' Hoop-de-Doo, right?"

"No," I said. "Certainly not."

"Yes," said Albertine. "We are."

"We are?" I said, surprised again.

"By joining the Heartsick American Humorists' Association we got a tremendous discount," she informed me.

"But who's the humorist?" I asked.

"You are, my darling," she said, handing a membership card to the clerk. "You crack me up."

The clerk began to snicker as he tapped us into the computer. "You guys are pretty good," he said.

WE UNPACKED. We showered. We dressed for drinks and dinner. The cocktail lounge and bar were quite crowded, offering the possibility of an interesting conversation if we could pick the right people to sit next to, though the choice was likely to be forced because there were so few places available. Two stools were empty at the bar, but they were separated by two large men wearing black slacks and brightly colored shirts—one tangerine, one puce. Given the likelihood that the lounge was packed with humorists, the similarity of their outfits made it seem that they might be partners in an act.

"Let's sit at the bar," I suggested. "We can ask those two guys to move over."

We approached the bar and found the two bright shirts crying in their beer.

"It's over," groused one. "Never again will the kind of humor we grew up on, the kind of thing we enjoyed as kids, achieve the ascendancy, the cultural dominance, that it once enjoyed. Not in our lifetime."

"It was a golden age," moaned the other, "and this is an age of crap, comparatively speaking."

"Excuse me," I said to the one in tangerine. "Would you be willing to move one stool to your right, so that we could have the two vacant stools?"

He looked at me for a moment. He seemed genuinely puzzled.

"I don't get it," he said at last.

"Neither do I," said the one in the puce shirt.

"I was hoping you wouldn't mind moving over—"

"One stool to my right," said tangerine, with a puzzled look. "I got that part, but if I move one seat to my right, I'll be sitting in his lap. Is that supposed to be funny?"

"No," I said. "I was hoping that your friend would also move one stool to the right. That would leave two stools for Albertine and me."

They looked at each other, shrugged in the manner of two grumpy old men who are still willing to go along with a gag, and moved one stool to the right.

"Thanks," I said. Al and I took the free stools and ordered martinis.

"Well?" said puce, leaning around tangerine to say it.

"Thanks again," I said.

They looked at each other for a long moment.

"Impenetrable," said tangerine.

"Unfathomable," said puce.

"That's the whole problem today," said tangerine. "On the one hand, you've got this ineffable high-concept bullshit—"

"—and on the other you've got your lowbrow bathroom humor bullshit," said puce.

"—and the noble middle ground, where once we played—"

"—is vacant."

"Let's take these to a table," said Albertine.

AT THE ONLY TABLE with two seats empty, I stopped, indicated the empty seats with a nod of my head, and asked those seated around the table, "Are these available?"

"You see?" said a beefy man, bringing his hands together with a smart smack. "That's just what I've been talking about—a perfect example." To me he said, "A classic setup, classic. Thank you. You couldn't have arrived at a more opportune moment."

"By all means, join us," said a woman with hair that might have been dyed to match the puce shirt of the man we had left at the bar.

"I want to see where you're going to take this," said the beefy man.

"Take this?" I said. "Oh, I see what you mean. I don't really have any plans to take it anywhere. You see, I'm not a humorist."

"You're not?"

Albertine kicked me.

"Well, technically I am. That is, I am a member of the Heartsick American Humorists' Association—"

"Ipso facto," declared the beefy man.

"QED," said a small man beside him, who might have been the beefy man's professional sidekick.

"So give," said the woman with the hair.

I looked at Al. "How about helping me out a little here?" I asked.

"We're on the road," she said to the group, "bound for Corosso, New Mexico."

"Not bad, not bad," said the beefy man, rubbing his hands together in gleeful anticipation. "Corosso is the new Sheboygan."

"I think I see where this is going," said the woman.

"To New Mexico?" I suggested.

"Eventually," said Al, "but our immediate goal is to get back to the safety of our room and find out whether Bulky Burger delivers."

"Hilarious!" declared the beefy man, though he only chuckled.

ON OUR WAY OUT of the lounge, we heard another of the humorists saying this: "Ours is not an age for subtlety. It doesn't want a Wilde or a Parker or even a Wodehouse. It doesn't want wit; it wants the whoopee cushion. It's an age that calls for a Rabelais or the Balzac of *Droll Stories* or that old sniggering schoolboy Alfred Jarry. In an age when people think a bomb is an appropriate answer to an insult, a fart is a clever riposte."

"Well, I suppose he's right about that," said Albertine.

"I wish he weren't," I said.

"I know you do," she said. "So do I."

"I prefer the fart to the bomb, though."

"I'll take silence, thanks."

I STRODE THROUGH THE LOBBY with the purposeful look of a man who has left his toothbrush in the car. In the garage, I found an outlet, moved the Electro-Flyer to a spot one cord's length from it, and plugged it in for the night. Outside, I stood still for a moment, scanning the sky for the flashing lights of a helicopter. Nothing. I went back through the lobby. Passing the clerk, I patted my jacket pocket and said, "Toothbrush."

"Ha-ha," he said skeptically.

LYING IN BED that night, I had an insight, just before I fell asleep. It wasn't about humor; it was about Lem and his version of the Martian invasion story or, more accurately, my reaction to it. When I had objected to his altering the story, I wasn't taking offense on behalf of H. G. Wells or Howard Koch or Orson Welles. I was personally offended. The recorded version of the radio play that I had made with my friend Dan had been different from any of the sources we had used. It had been very similar to Howard Koch's radio play but not identical to it. We had made some changes out of necessity, others out of expediency, and others out of playfulness—changing some of the names of the characters to match the names of teachers in our school, for example—and the version that resulted was in a small way our own. That version had become in my storyteller's mind the version that I thought everyone ought to know and hew to, Lem included. It still is.

Chapter 7
A Banner Day

He was a bold man that first eat an oyster.
  Colonel Atwit in Jonathan Swift's *Polite Conversation*

IT WAS A DAY for rhapsodizing, one of those extraordinarily beautiful days when, under a sky pellucid and blue, you willingly fall victim to the illusion that life is good and nothing can go wrong. *Spirit*'s engine hummed, the air felt buoyant, and a couple of times when we crested a rise in the road, I gunned the engine and the road fell away beneath us. Oh, that exhilarating feeling of flight, the breathtaking thrill of being airborne for a few feet.

Toward evening, when the light began to thin, I found myself riding through a marshy area, and because the lack of trees or other concealing vegetation afforded me a long view of what lay ahead of me, I could make out a small town or village in the distance. Soon I came upon a road sign welcoming me to Mallowdale, and farther on, when I reached the edge of the village, I saw a bright banner strung across the main street. Because I was still too far from the banner to read it, I allowed myself to think that it might be a message of welcome for me.

"Oh, please," said *Spirit*.

"Why not?" I asked. "Word of my journey could spread by phone— and why shouldn't it? Why shouldn't people in the towns we've passed through telephone their friends and relatives along our route and urge them not to miss the daring flyboy when he passes through their town?"

Whatever the banner announced—and I still thought it might be my arrival—had certainly caught people's fancy. The whole town seemed to be in the street. I wished that I had taken the opportunity at the last rest stop to straighten my clothes a bit, comb my hair, and give *Spirit* a dusting.

"Am I dirty?" she asked.

"Not dirty, exactly. But both of us could use a little spiffing up."

"I know that I would look a lot better if you'd take that ratty banner off my tail."

I said nothing, but I had to admit that she was right. The banner advertising Porky White's Kap'n Klam restaurant had suffered from being dragged along the road through New York and New Jersey. It was battered and dirty and twisted, and the part that had initially read THE HOME OF HAPPY DINERS had been reduced to THE HOME OF HAPPY DIN.

Perhaps *Spirit* and I both understood how contentious an issue Porky's banner was likely to become, because we both stepped aside from any discussion of it with the simultaneous declaration, "This is an occasion!" and when I was close enough to read the Mallowdale banner, it told me that the occasion was the 97th Annual Marshmallow Festival.

Festive it certainly was, and the marshmallow theme was inescapable. Many of the citizens of Mallowdale had dressed themselves as the plump white confections, either just as they come from the bag, or in various stages of toasting, from barely beige through golden brown to singed to the fragile wrinkled skin of black that follows ignition. I felt conspicuous in my flyboy garb. It seemed as wrong as could be in a crowd where marshmallows were à la mode.

"You need an outfit," said a matronly woman at my side, taking me by the elbow. She wore a smile, but her brows were knit, giving her the air of someone taking pity on an unfortunate soul. In memory's eye, though, she seems not to be acting from spontaneous generosity but as part of a program. I see now that she was estimating in the back of her mind the benefit that would accrue from what she was about to do. "Here," she said. "Try this."

She offered me a crepe-paper hat that resembled a marshmallow somewhat. It was, I understand now, the Marshmallow Festival equivalent of the cheap jacket and tie that some restaurants keep in the checkroom for patrons who arrive dressed for dinner at a steel cart on the corner. The hat was enough of a marshmallow costume to make me feel that I could join the festivities. It was not nearly enough to allow me to fit in, but it was enough to make me stand out less. Still, as I walked around the center of the town, trying to mingle with the festive throng, I felt that the Mallowdalers considered me an outsider, someone suspect, possibly dangerous, a threat to their way of life, their beliefs, their young women. I liked it. I may have begun to swagger.

The flow of the crowd carried me to a parking lot behind the Marshmallow Museum where long tables and wooden folding chairs had been set up. From its resemblance to the Babbington Clam Fest's "Gorging Ground," I recognized this as a feasting area, and discovered that I was hungry. I joined the line for tickets. The price was reasonable, and the sign at the entrance said ALL YOU CAN EAT, a wonderful offer for an adolescent who had spent the long day piloting an aerocycle.

I paid the price. Not until I sat down and read the little menu card on the table did I understand that there would be nothing to eat that did not include marshmallows.

Of course, that made me feel tremendously nostalgic.

"This is just like the Clam Fest back home!" I said to the person sitting next to me, a woman I guessed, carefully dressed as an evenly tanned marshmallow on a supple stick cut from a cherry tree. "Back home in Babbington, on Long Island, in New York. It's just like this!"

"Oh?" she said, with none of the fellow feeling I had hoped for. "How is it 'just like this'?"

"Well," I said, still hopeful, "you're celebrating marshmallows, and we celebrate clams."

Across the table, a man in a charred head murmured to a neighbor, "Good lord, why?"

"We have a big feast like this," I went on, trying to ignore the offense, "but instead of putting marshmallows in everything, we have clams in everything—clam chowder, clam fritters, clams casino—"

The woman gave me, as well as a woman in a marshmallow getup can, a look simultaneously incredulous and dismissive. "Toasted clams?" she inquired icily.

"What?" I said.

"I was just thinking that since your clam fest is *just like* our marshmallow fest you must put clams on a stick and toast them over a campfire."

"No—of course not—we—"

"But certainly you put them in Jell-O, don't you?"

"No," I admitted.

"That would be really disgusting!" said the charred man. He sounded as if he might actually be ill, and I'll admit that the thought of clams in Jell-O makes me feel a little ill myself.

"I think that clams are disgusting any way you serve them!" said the charred man's companion.

This was an affront, and my first impulse was to respond in kind, to defend Babbington and its clams by attacking Mallowdale and its marshmallows. I looked at the plate of items I'd taken from the buffet, seeking inspiration there. For a moment, pride in Babbington and its esculent mollusk made me think of feigning revulsion to show these marshmallow boosters a thing or two, but the tidbits on my plate looked tasty to me. I sampled a marshmallow split open like a baked potato and stuffed with a scoop of peanut butter and found it good. I tried a melted marshmallow sandwiched between two golden crackers and found it even better. It wasn't long before I returned to the banquet table for another selection of the tasty treats. I was enjoying myself, just as I would have at the clam fest back home.

WHEN WE HAD FINISHED EATING, a hush began to settle over the crowd. People began shushing those who persisted in their conversations, poking their neighbors with their elbows, and nodding, sometimes even pointing, in the direction of the museum. Along with everyone else, I turned in that direction. There I saw a man standing at a lectern set in the middle of a table that ran along the rear of the museum, a table like all the others but distinguished by being set at a right angle to them and elevated a foot or so above them, and I realized with some excitement that I was about to hear an after-dinner speaker.

"This is another thing we have at the Clam Fest," I said, "an after-dinner speaker. Usually, it's the mayor. He spoke at the gathering on Main Street when I started my trip, too—just a few words, but—"

"Shhh," said my tablemates in chorus.

"We have gathered here today," the speaker began, "as we do every year at this time, to celebrate the roots of Mallowdale."

This opening was greeted with universal chuckling. Even I chuckled. Chuckling can be contagious.

"But seriously, we are quite literally celebrating the roots that give us the plump little confection that has made us what we are, the community we are, the neighbors we are, the people we are: we are celebrating the roots of the marsh mallow, the mallow that grows in our marshes. And we are here to listen to a story."

The hush grew deeper as the audience settled into the drowsy quietude that follows a big meal, even one with as much sugar as the one we had consumed, and accepted the pleasant invitation to return to the childhood habit of listening to a story.

"It is a story that begins with the couple we know as Ma and Pa Mallow, though their true names have been lost to history. Of course, when I attended these festivals with my family, when I was just a nipper, the story was about Mother and Father Mallow, but these are more relaxed times, so they have become Ma and Pa, and children—like those who are running around at the back of the crowd apparently beyond the control of their parents or guardians—are permitted a degree of disrespect that would have earned them a good hiding in my day."

He paused, and a number of embarrassed parents scurried to the back of the crowd to gather their children.

When the children were settled to his satisfaction, he continued. "Ma and Pa were out walking in the marshes one day, long ago, before any of us was born, sometime early in the last century, when our country was still young, younger than many of the people who lived in it, younger than Ma and Pa Mallow themselves. And it was much, much younger than the marshes."

"Which it still is and always will be," muttered a dark-haired girl in a chic marshmallow beret and a slim bamboo-stick shift. I looked in her direction, and her lips formed for the briefest of moments a trace of a mischievous smile.

"Ma and Pa almost certainly did not know that the Mallowdale salt marshes are what geologists call an anomaly. They didn't know that inland salt marshes like ours are so rare as to be almost unheard of. The few that exist, including one in the aptly named town of Saltville, Virginia, are spring-fed, and their springs originate in vast caverns of salt."

"I'd like to see those caverns someday," muttered the dark-haired girl.

"I certainly hope you are not questioning the veracity or accuracy of this account," said a stern voice from inside a charred marshmallow head below which the point of a carefully trimmed gray beard projected.

The dark-haired girl frowned slightly and shook her head, just barely.

"On this day, Ma and Pa weren't walking in the marshes for pleasure," the speaker asserted. "They weren't out for a stroll to look at the scenery. Ma and Pa had fallen on hard times. They were hungry, and they were searching for food. They were probably after meat, perhaps a water rat or a snake, but they didn't find anything so substantial, not that day. In desperation they were driven to pull the weeds that grew around them."

He paused for effect.

"And they pulled the mallow."

He paused again. The dark-haired girl rolled her eyes.

"They pulled the mallow!" the speaker almost shouted. "Why? Why did they pull the mallow? Why that plant? Perhaps there was an element of chance, of luck. It could be that they were attracted to the mallow by its delicate pink flowers. Perhaps they dislodged a mallow plant accidentally. Maybe they tripped over a plant, or snagged one on a crude boot, exposing its thick pale yellow root, and making them wonder whether, like the root of the carrot or the rutabaga, it was edible."

"The rutabaga is just barely edible, if you ask me," whispered the dark-haired girl, and she was whispering to me.

"We know many things about the mallow that Ma and Pa did not know. For one thing, we know that the mallow plants they found in the salty water of the Mallowdale marshes were immigrants. They were probably the descendants of stowaways, seeds that had traveled from the old world to the new world, possibly clinging to the shoes of a human immigrant, maybe also a stowaway."

"That's an interesting idea—" said the dark-haired girl.

I nodded in agreement. A low chorus of shushing arose around us.

"Ma and Pa didn't know that. Nor did they know that the roots of the mallow plant had been eaten for centuries in the fabled lands of Asia and

Arabia, that the food they were about to prepare and eat had once been reserved for the pharaohs of ancient Egypt, and forbidden to poor folk like Ma and Pa Mallow."

"I'd like to know how he knows what they didn't know," muttered the girl, right into my ear. Her warm breath tickled and thrilled me.

"That evening, they ate the mallow root," the speaker said, dropping his voice to underscore the import of that momentous occurrence. "We don't know how they prepared it, and we might ask ourselves about that, but there is a more interesting question: why did they eat it at all? Perhaps they already knew, from a friend or neighbor, that they could eat the roots of the plant, but if that was the case, then we must ask the same question of those friends or neighbors, and we can continue asking the question as far back in time as we care to travel, but still we must come to the first eaters of mallow root and ask why they ate it. As somebody said, 'It was a brave man who first ate an oyster.'"

"Or a clam," said the charred marshmallow with the stern voice.

"What if they were poison?" whispered a slight woman to her slight companion. Her pale marshmallow head seemed to wear a furrowed brow.

"Clams aren't poison," I said, annoyed by the suggestion.

The charred marshmallow raised an admonitory finger to the area of his head that I supposed hid his pursed lips.

"Necessity, we are told, is the mother of invention, and such was the case with Ma and Pa. They were driven by expediency, by their desperate hunger, to experiment. Their need was so great that they would have tried eating *anything* that they could harvest from the marshes. For whatever reason, they pulled as many of the mallow plants as they could carry, took them home, and prepared a humble dinner from their roots."

"They could have died in agony," the worried woman pointed out, glancing to her right and left for some support.

The shushing became insistent.

"From the desperate eating of the mallow root to the leisurely enjoyment of the puffy confection we know today is a long journey and a long story, a story that takes humankind from subsistence to luxury."

"Let's hope we're not going to make that journey," whispered the dark-haired girl.

"Where did the idea for the marshmallow confection come from? Or, to put that question in another, more far-reaching and profound way, what are the roots of human ingenuity? What insight inspires an invention? These are things we do not know, and perhaps never will know. They are part of 'The Riddle of the Marshmallow'—which just happens to be the title of the series of lectures I will be delivering on Wednesday evenings over the next six weeks, right here at the Marshmallow Museum. Tickets are going fast, but there are still places available. You will find the fee modest, and you can sign up—"

"I just think Ma and Pa were very, very brave," said the worried woman with the furrowed marshmallow brow.

No one bothered shushing her. Most of the people at our table—and at the others—were pushing their chairs back, rising, and making their way toward the exits.

I ALLOWED MYSELF to be moved by the crowd as it made its way toward the nearest exit. The dark-haired girl was in the section of the crowd that I was in, tantalizingly near but too distant for conversation. I would have had to shout to her. The flow of the crowd carried her little by little farther away, until I lost sight of her and I despaired of ever seeing her again. Making my way toward the exit, I grew increasingly depressed by the loss of the dark-haired girl and the thought that I had nowhere to stay for the night and might have a tough time finding a place in a community where I was so obviously an outsider. I began examining the crowd, searching for someone who looked accommodating.

"Excuse me—"

Miracle of miracles, it was the dark-haired girl, at my side, touching my sleeve.

"Oh, I'm sorry," she said. "I didn't mean to startle you."

"You didn't! I mean, well, you did, but I'm glad you did. I mean you surprised me, but it's a nice surprise—"

"You showed them a thing or two back there."

"I did?"

"You certainly did. You gave them a lesson in humility—and a lesson in generosity."

"I did?"

"Don't be so modest. You know you did. I think they treated you abominably."

"Well—"

"I felt as if I could actually see into your mind, and your heart, when you said that the Marshmallow Festival was just like the Clams and Oysters Festival—"

"It's—it's—Clam Fest—"

"—and I could feel your loneliness, the terrible isolation of an outsider in an alien culture, clinging for consolation to familiar rituals and customs, yet at the same time trying desperately to ingratiate yourself with the people around you by demonstrating that you had something in common with them, a culture of festivals and a reverence for local produce, for the harvest, a fondness for regional cuisine, and civic pride. But they rejected you, rejected your home town, your local comestible, everything you hold dear."

"Not everything—"

"I thought it was wonderful, really admirable, the way you held back, the way you restrained yourself from commenting on the food on your plate. You might have asserted the superiority of your home town, its customs and its cuisine, but you chose not to, you decided—or you knew—that it wasn't necessary. I thought that was fine and funny."

"Funny?"

"Yes."

"Why funny?"

"I'm not sure," she said. "You just seem funny to me. Of course, I recognize that the sense of humor, so called, varies enormously from one person to another, and that someone else might not think you were funny, but you just seem funny to me."

Before I could respond, she had bestowed upon me a parting smile and was gone, lost again in the moving crowd.

I SPENT THE NIGHT IN JAIL. It was a first for me, but there isn't much to say about it. After wandering around for a while, stopping *Spirit* when I saw a likely house, and knocking on the door to ask if I might spend the night, I was accosted by an officer of the Mallowdale police. He informed me that I had been alarming the citizens, which was a misdemeanor in

Mallowdale. I explained my situation. He offered the collective hospitality of the community in place of the individual hospitality of any of its
members. I hesitated, because I had hoped that chance might lead me to
the door of the dark-haired girl, where I would be welcomed. He noticed
my hesitation and offered the alternative of getting out of town "toot-
sweet." I chose a night in jail.

AFTER A MEAGER BREAKFAST of oatmeal and weak coffee the next
morning, I was escorted outside. I recognized the signs: the sheriff, or
whoever he was, intended to have a private word with me, to give me a
word to the wise. I was right.

"Son—" he began, "I think you know what I'm going to say."

"I do?"

"I would hope so," he said. "A fellow gets some time to think when
he's spending the night in a jail cell, and I hope that you used that time to
come to realize what a little egotist you were when you drove that weird
motorcycle into town."

"Piloted."

"Don't interrupt me, son."

"It's just that I was piloting, not driving. And it's an aerocycle, not a
motorcycle. It's got wings, and—"

"Perhaps you're interrupting me to demonstrate that you're still the
wretched little egotist you were when you rode into town?"

"No, sir. I mean, yes, sir. I think."

"You know that I'm right, don't you?"

"Well," I said, hanging my head, "the truth is that when I saw that
bright banner strung across Main Street, I thought that it might be a message of welcome for me."

"You don't say."

"I do say—but of course I was wrong."

"And during that night of introspection in my jail, did you discover
anything about yourself and your mistake?"

"Oh, yes. Definitely. I did."

"What?"

"I—well—"

"I would hope you discovered that a readiness to perceive the state of things as pertaining specifically to ourselves is one of the ways in which our senses are often deceived. I would hope you discovered that when we have insufficient data to know what is actually the case, we interpret the data that we have in a way that suits our predilections: optimists see good news; pessimists see bad news; the timid see danger; and a nostalgic booster such as yourself is apt to see in a crowd of strangers the eager ears of friends-to-be who want to listen to him describe each and every little detail about his humble home town and its queer customs. I would hope you discovered that, although we are all egotists to one degree or another, you have been an egotist to too great a degree. And I would hope that you discovered the desire and the will to control the tendency."

"That was pretty much it," I said.

Chapter 8
Egoists and Egotists

EGOTIST, *n*. A person of low taste, more interested in himself than in me.

Ambrose Bierce, *The Devil's Dictionary*

LITTLE BY LITTLE, as we motored along, avoiding the highway like good little shunpikers, enjoying the day and the air, I began to get an impression of chocolate. It began with a pleasant but elusive scent of chocolate, then thickened to a conviction that there was chocolate around somewhere, then thickened further until I thought that the air was filling with chocolate, then further still until I began to expect that a river of chocolate might come flowing down the road toward us like the river of porridge that had inundated an unfortunate village in "The Porridge Pot," one of the tales in *The Little Folks' Big Book,* the favorite book of my childhood.

"Call me crazy," I said, "but I think there's chocolate around here somewhere, lots of it."

"If you had been navigating as you are supposed to be, checking a map now and then, you would know that the next stop on our tour is Hershey, Pennsylvania."

"Watch out for chocolate, then," I said.

"Recent studies indicate that chocolate lowers one's blood pressure," Albertine asserted. "We are allowed to welcome it into our lives again. Chocolate is our friend."

"Not if it comes sweeping down upon you in a rushing river."

"Like porridge?"

"Yes! Did you read that story when you were a girl?"

"I think so. Or you told me about it."

"Hmm. Could be either. Our lives have come to overlap in so many ways, so thoroughly and completely, that we sometimes think we share even those parts of our past that we know we do not."

"But you cheat. You keep increasing that overlap artificially, pretending that you knew me before you actually did."

"Are you talking about those sweet and innocent days when we used to play together in the snows of Dayton, Ohio?"

"Yes, I am."

"When you were just a girl?"

"Yes."

"And I used to invent games that involved wrestling?"

"That's right."

"So that I could get you horizontal, wrap my little self around your little self, and bring us both to a state of bliss that our adult supervisors assumed we knew nothing about?"

"Exactly. Do you think there's a place around here where we could stop and make love?"

There was. There always is, Reader, if you look hard enough and are willing to make do.

OVER COCKTAILS THAT EVENING, in the hotel bar, Albertine paid me the compliment of saying, "I thought you displayed a really admirable degree of self-control back there in Mallowdale, not only at the marsh-mallow feast, but during the good talking-to that the sheriff gave you."

"Did you? Thanks."

"Unless you were hoping that the dark-haired girl had slipped out of her house in the morning to watch the birdboy take off and was lurking somewhere nearby, listening, and it was all a performance for her."

"It may have been," I admitted, "or it may have been a performance for the dark-haired girl at the wheel of the Electro-Flyer."

"I should hope it was."

A couple was sitting next to us at the bar, twitching with eagerness to add their two cents to our conversation, looking for some opening in which to insert themselves. (If you are part of a couple in love, Reader, you know what was happening. You have probably found it happening to you. It's a consequence of being in love. Couples who are not as much in love, or no longer as much in love, hope to inhale a bit of your happy state by insinuating themselves into your conversation. They expect to conceal the inhalation in the intervals between chatter, when they might seem merely to be pausing, catching their breath before the next utterance—but you know what they're up to, don't you?)

"Speaking of chocolate—" I said.

"That seems so long ago," said Albertine.

"Do you remember a function at the Boston Athenæum that featured a huge wheel or block of chocolate, or maybe it was several huge wheels or blocks of various types of chocolate, chaperoned by a charming Belgian who was offering very generous samples while enumerating its virtues and explaining its provenance?"

"Yes, I do. As I recall, it was an all-you-care-to-eat situation."

"I think you're right."

"So do I. Mmm."

"Do you also remember the way everyone who sampled it claimed an international history of experiences with chocolate, each of those experiences superior to the one we were having at the moment?"

"I do! I do! In fact, I recall that some people disdained to sample the chocolate at all, on the grounds that it couldn't possibly be up to their standards."

"Which they could tell merely by looking at it."

"Right!"

"It was a splendid display of egotism, the best I've ever seen."

"Egotism or egoism?" she asked.

"Mm?"

"You said it was a splendid display of egotism."

"Yes."

"But was it egotism or egoism?"

"I wonder, now that you ask."

"I know that in general use they both vaguely mean the same thing, but I'd like to know—"

Seeing his opening at last, the man in the couple beside us said, "I couldn't help overhearing. I think I can enlighten you a bit on the subject of egoism and egotism, if you will permit me." Without permission, he proceeded. "The older of the two terms is *egoism,* the sin of the egoist. It's a borrowing from the French *égoïsme,* from which *égoïste* is derived. The usual translation for that original term *égoïste* is 'one who thinks,' but I personally think that a more accurate expression of the idea behind the term as it was originally intended would be 'one who knows that he thinks,' that is, a conscious being."

"Ah!" I said. "You must be a relative of Angus MacPherson, my French teacher back at Babbington High quite a few years ago."

"No, I don't think so. I—"

"He's just kidding," said Albertine. "He's a card-carrying member of the Heartsick American Humorists' Association."

"Oh," the man said, with a slackness in his tone that said, simply but unmistakably, that however highly the rest of the world might esteem such status, he was unimpressed. "Well, the term *egotist* seems to have been coined by Joseph Addison, the essayist, to identify what he considered to be an annoying rhetorical style characterized by the too-frequent use of the first-person singular pronoun."

"Aye-yi-yi," I said.

"I always tell myself to use the *t* to remind myself of the difference between *egoist* and *egotist,*" the woman informed us. "Someone told me to do that long ago—but for the life of me I can't remember who it was."

"It was I, my dear," said the man.

"Was it? I don't think it was."

"I assure you that it was."

"Regardless of who it was who told me to do so—and I doubt very much that it was you—I remind myself that the *t* stands for *talking.*"

"I think you're getting ahead of yourself, dear," said her companion, with the appearance of good humor. "I think we've got to begin with a couple of definitions."

"Do you," she said icily.

"Yes, I do," he snapped. Then, to us, or perhaps to the room at large, he announced, "An egoist is a person who is guided by the principle of 'me first.'"

"I find that it applies in every circumstance, at every turn, whenever a choice must be made," the woman added.

"That was implied in my definition," her companion asserted.

"I had no way of knowing that," she asserted right back at him. To us she said, "I feel that I must point out that the principle of 'me first' is not quite the same as 'me only.'"

"Of course not," the man said with a sneer. "'Me only' is the solipsist's principle. For the solipsist, the notion of 'me first' is utterly superfluous."

"When you talk, all I hear is blah, blah, blah," she said.

"I wonder where the fault lies," he growled.

"What's your other definition?" asked Albertine with the subtlety of a diplomatist. "The definition of *egotist*?"

"An egotist is someone who is always talking about himself," said the woman.

"Or herself," the man suggested.

"I always remember the *t*," the woman said, almost wistfully, as if she were recalling a particularly poignant moment when she had used the *t* to remind herself of the difference between the words, sometime in the past, in other circumstances, in other company.

"I think a person can be an egoist and not realize it, don't you?" asked Albertine, intending a kindness, I think, drawing the woman back into our foursome. "There's a kind of egoism that is unthinking or passive."

"Yes," I said, doing my bit. "There's a kind of egoist who doesn't even consider other people and their needs, feelings, and desires."

"In fact," said Albertine, "I think that that kind of neglectful egoism is the most widespread, and the people who practice it are the egoists who are least likely to recognize their egoism."

"Could be," admitted the man. "Or else they're dissembling; they aren't quite assertive enough to put themselves first, but they are egoistical enough to be blind to the needs and rights of others — or deliberately to blind themselves to those needs and rights."

I began to wish that they would go away. I'd had enough of them. I wanted to be alone with Albertine. We two. Just we two. We two against the world, the whole yammering, battering, self-centered world.

"But if one's neglectful egoism, as you put it, is genuine," he went on, "it may be the worst kind of egoism. It's the kind that considers other people beneath contempt. What they think, what they do, what they feel, what becomes of them is simply of no interest whatsoever."

"My grandmother warned me against that," said the woman, with, again, that note of wistfulness.

"What?" he demanded of her.

"What you said," she said, from a distance.

"I said quite a number of things—"

"Must an egotist be an egoist first?" Albertine asked quickly, touching the arm of the distant woman. "Or can a person be an egotist without being an egoist?"

The woman didn't answer. Instead, with that odd distance still in her voice, she said, "I try to remind myself that talking must also be interpreted figuratively. It stands for many other ways of drawing attention to oneself or putting oneself forward." Then, suddenly bridging the distance, she squealed, "Oh! Don't get me started on the way my sister used to hog the camera when Uncle Jerry took those nudes of us in his 'studio'!"

Just to show that I was still in the game, I responded to Albertine's question with one of my own. "Must an egoist be an egotist or necessarily become one?" I asked. "Can one be an egoist without advertising it through egotism?"

"Oh, yes," said Albertine. "We saw it there at the Athenæum. The egotists were continually talking about their experiences with chocolate, demonstrating their superiority and the superiority of their experiences, while the egoists were quietly consuming all the chocolate they could get."

The distance had returned to the woman's voice when she said, "I think the saddest type of egotist is the one who is always telling you, or anyone she can find to listen, what she intends to do, because she doesn't have anything that she actually *has* done to brag about."

"Talking about the superb chocolate she intends to eat when she takes that tasting tour through Belgium, France, and Switzerland," said Albertine. A note of wistful distance had come into her voice, too, so I took her by the hand and led her away from all that.

AS SOON AS we were in our room, Albertine looked through all the drawers in our bedside tables, and then picked up the phone. "Front desk?" she said cheerily. "This is room four forty-five. There's no dictionary in our room. I think it might have been stolen. . . . What do you mean, you don't put dictionaries in the rooms? There's a Bible here. There ought to be a dictionary. All the better caravansaries supply them, I'd like to think. . . . Well, let me speak to the concierge. . . . Thank you." A moment passed, then she said, "This is room four forty-five. I need to know everything you can tell me about *egoist* and *egotist*. . . . No, they're not a band. They're words. . . . That's what I said: words. . . . I've just been talking to some people in your cocktail lounge, and I want to verify their assertions about them. I would have looked them up myself, but there's no dictionary in our room. If you would check the *OED* for me, I'd be very grateful. . . . What? . . . You're kidding. . . . Well, what's a concierge for, I'd like to know." She put her hand over the mouthpiece and said, "This is quite a hotel."

"Ask him to connect you to room service," I said. "I'm starving."

IN THE MORNING, when we were checking out, the couple we had met in the bar were also checking out. We exchanged pleasantries. After that, we stood in awkward silence. Then, inspired by the memory of my earlier trip, I broke the silence.

"Albertine and I are re-creating a cross-country trip that I made when I was a teenager," I said. "On that earlier trip, nearly every morning, someone in the town where I had stopped for the night would take me aside and offer me a bit of advice before I got back onto the road and resumed my travels. Would you care to participate in the re-creation of that trip by offering me a bit of matutinal advice?"

"Us," said Albertine.

"Would you care to offer us a bit of advice?"

"I gave you my advice last night," said the woman. "I told you to remember the significance of that little *t*."

"Actually," I said, "that was more like advice to yourself. You said that *you* always tell yourself to remember the significance of the *t*. You didn't actually advise *us* to do that."

"Well, I'm advising you now," she said.

"And you?" I asked the man.

"Don't talk to strangers," he said, and he turned his attention to the clerk.

When we were back in the car and on our way out of the parking lot, while we were paused for a moment, waiting for a break in the traffic, it took only a look to elicit the morning's advice from Albertine: "If they're giving out samples of chocolate, take all that you care to eat."

"Not all that you can eat?" I asked.

"No, no. You don't need a river of chocolate. Enough is enough."

Chapter 9
Frontier Justice

WHEN WE WERE ON THE ROAD AGAIN, *Spirit* coughed once to get my attention, then cleared her throat and asked, "'Piloted'?"

"What do you mean?" I asked, though I knew perfectly well.

"I very distinctly heard you tell the sheriff back there in Mallowdale that you 'piloted' your aerocycle into town."

I guess I was running out of patience with her. I pulled her to the side of the road, set her on her kickstand, took my copy of *Elements of Aeronautics* from the little luggage bin where it lay beside *Gestes et Opinions du Dr. Faustroll,* found the relevant passage, and read it to her:

> *Piloting,* as a general term, means merely steering a vessel or flying an airplane. The term *piloting* has been used technically, however, to denote the kind of navigating one does in getting to one's destination with the help of a chart or map; by following a highway, railroad, transmission line, river, or other such course; or by flying from one landmark to another which can be seen, as flying first to a mountain, then to a lake which can be seen from the mountain, then to a city which can be seen from the lake, and so on. Piloting as a method of keeping track of one's position and of getting to one's destination hardly needs comment as a science. It is like finding one's way by map while motoring.

"Or like finding one's way without a map while motoring," I said triumphantly. I stowed the book, mounted *Spirit,* and roared onto the road again.

"Just a minute! There is nothing in there that says that piloting *is* motoring, only that it is *like* motoring."

We might have continued in good-natured contention along those lines for some time, but we were interrupted.

Red light swept across *Spirit*'s wings, light from an old bubble-top cop car, a light with revolving innards like those of a lighthouse, primarily a mechanical device, not unlike the revolving light that I had made from a camper's lantern and an old windup record player years earlier, back in Babbington, back at home, for a game.

After I saw the light, I heard the siren, just a short burst or signal, a whine, briefly rising, quickly falling, to let me know that I was the object of the cop's interest, to tell me to pull over. I did. I twisted on my seat, and looked toward the rear, into the headlights. The car was black and white, clean, shiny. The cop, when he got out and walked toward me in the light, looked clean and shiny, too. He wore high boots, gleaming black.

"What kind of contraption is this?" he asked, examining *Spirit* with exaggerated contempt.

"It's an aerocycle," I said. "I built it myself."

He eyed me suspiciously.

"With help," I admitted, cracking under the force of his professional skepticism.

"You're going to have to see Judge Whitley," he said.

"Judge Whitley?" I asked, struggling to calm my twitching lips.

"That's what I said."

"That's an interesting coincidence."

"Oh, yeah?"

"Yes," I said, trying to smooth the waters. "You see, there was a Mayor Whitley in my home town. There have been several of them, in fact."

"You're probably making that up to try to get friendly," he said.

"No, honest," I said, as friendly as can be, "Mayor Whitley, Andy Whitley—"

"It's no use, kid. Judge Whitley has warned me against taking the statements of a prisoner at face value."

"A prisoner?"

"I'm going to lead the way to Judge Whitley, and you're going to follow me."

"Am I under arrest?"

"Just follow me—and don't try any funny business."

"Yes, sir."

He returned to his car, got in, and pulled slowly ahead of me. I started *Spirit* and followed, following him, following orders.

"Wow," I whispered to *Spirit*. "We're under arrest."

"You sound pleased by the idea."

"I may be. I'm not quite sure. I've already experienced my first road-block, and my first night in jail, and now I'm experiencing my first arrest. It's a momentous occurrence."

"Try to control yourself."

"I will, I will."

"And don't try any funny business."

"I won't, I won't."

I EXPECTED to be taken to City Hall. To be completely truthful, I expected to be taken to the Supreme Court building, if they had one in town. I expected the full treatment, and I expected to get it in a building with columns and a pediment and a Latin slogan chiseled in granite. Instead, the building that the cop led me to looked like a bar.

"It looks like a bar," I said to *Spirit*.

"It is a bar," she said, "judging from the sign that says 'Judge Whitley's Bar and Grill.'"

"It's not even chiseled in granite," I grumbled.

Judge Whitley's was a smoky den. The bar itself ran more than half the length of the narrow room, along the right side. Booths lined the left wall.

We entered and began slowly walking toward the back. The daytime drinkers and chatterers took note of the boy being urged along by the cop, but only in the most desultory way. Their heads turned, but then they lost interest. I had the impression, and recollection gives me no reason to change it, that the men in the bar were doing business of one kind or another, that a lot of business was being done there, that a lot of business got done there. I think that the experience of seeing all those smoking, drinking men bent to their business has stayed with me all these years, forever coloring my impression of—and my opinion of—the kind of business that involves meetings and deals: it made me feel that there was something furtive and dirty and dark about it. It was best done, if done at all, in hiding. And it was so distasteful, so bitter a pill to swallow, that it required liquor to get it down. I could see that it wasn't anything I wanted to be involved in.

In the rearmost area of the bar, in the left rear corner, there was one large booth with a round table. Seated there, on the far side of the table, in the deepest, darkest corner of the bar, was a large, florid man, smoking a cigar and squinting through his own smoke as he watched me approach. His size; his position; the lackeys who sat on either side of him; the sense that the others in the bar were there to speak to him, that they were supplicants waiting their turn, waiting to be called to an audience at the round table; the ambience of smoke and awe—all of that made me understand that this must be Judge Whitley, the big man, the guy who called the shots in Coincidence, Pennsylvania.

"What's this?" asked one of the lackeys, meaning me.

"Kid," said the cop. In his voice I detected deference—and concern. I understood that if he did or said the wrong thing it would not go well for him.

"I see that," snarled the lackey. "Whadja bring 'im here for?"

The cop looked at me. His eyes welled with regret. Clearly, he considered me one of his mistakes. He would have been better off if he had just sent me on my way, and he knew it. I gave him a reciprocal look. I felt sorry for him. I felt sorry for both of us. We were looking big trouble in the face, through a cloud of cigar smoke.

"Driving a motorcycle without a license," mumbled the cop, his eyes down.

"You got a license, kid?" asked the lackey.

"No, sir."

"And were you driving a motorcycle?"

"No, sir." I glanced at the cop, hoping he would detect the note of apology in my glance. I was sorry to contradict him, but if one of us was going down, it wasn't going to be me.

"You weren't driving a motorcycle?"

"No, sir. I was piloting an aerocycle."

"A what?"

"An aerocycle. It's a flying machine."

"An airplane?"

"Oh, no. No. Not an airplane. I'd need a pilot's license for that." I tried laughing, but what came out of me couldn't really be called a laugh, and it had none of the infectious quality that laughter ought to have.

"Are you trying to be funny?"

"Yes, sir," I admitted.

"This is no laughing matter."

"I was just trying to ease the tension."

Everyone found that funny, no one more so than the judge. From that response, and from the memory of that response, which has returned to me unbidden from time to time over the years, I learned that you never can tell what people will find funny.

"If I could go out to *Spirit,* sir—"

"You trying to be funny again?" the other underling asked.

"No, sir. Not this time."

"'Go out to spirit,' what is that, some kind of religious thing?"

"No, sir. *Spirit* is my aerocycle. That's her name."

"Oh, I see," said the judge, speaking for the first time. "You would like to go outside to your airplane—excuse me, your aerocycle—*Spirit.* Is that it?"

"Yes. If I could just—"

"If you could just go out to *Spirit,* hop on board and fly away, leaving us sitting here like a bunch of rubes, asking ourselves how we could have been so stupid as to let you go out to *Spirit,* when it should have been obvious that you were trying to escape, everything would be just swell, am I right?"

"No, sir! Honest! I wanted to get a book—"

"I knew it was a religious thing," said the second lackey. "There's always a book, *the* book."

"This book is—"

"This book is the truth, I suppose."

"Well, I think so."

My intention, as you will have guessed, was to use the passage on piloting from *Elements of Aeronautics* to convince Judge Whitley to release me on a technicality. "If I could just—"

I wanted to assert myself, and to assert the authority of Pope and Otis, but my throat was thick and my eyes were moistening, and I thought it wise to say nothing for a while.

The judge waited, and while he waited he stared hard at me, and then he snorted and said, "Officer Lockwood, you go get the good book."

"Yes, sir."

"It's in the small baggage compartment behind the seat," I explained. "Just twist the handle and you can open the door."

Of course Officer Lockwood brought the wrong book. Instead of Pope and Otis, he brought my copy of *Gestes et opinions du Docteur Faustroll*. When he dropped *Faustroll* in the center of the table, I thought I was doomed.

Everyone looked at the book. Then everyone looked at me. Then everyone looked at one another. Then everyone looked at Judge Whitley. Then Judge Whitley looked at me.

"Let's go outside, boy," he said, lifting himself up from his corner seat and occasioning a rapid shuffling of the underlings to give him passage from the booth.

He conducted me outside. The others must have known by his manner that they were not to follow. If you have ever been in a similar situation, you will know that I expected to be shot in the back of the head and dumped in a ditch.

Instead, he walked around *Spirit* a couple of times and then said slowly, deliberately, raising the book, raising his considerable eyebrows, "So you are one of the chosen few."

"Well—" I said, with a shrug, since I didn't know what he was talking about.

"You have sailed in the doctor's boat, across the Squitty Sea?" he asked, in a voice that I might have described as envious if it hadn't come from him.

"Um—I have done some sailing—"

"You have sojourned in the Land of Lace?"

"My great-grandmother was very fond of antimacassars—"

"And you have dallied in the Forest of Love?"

"Well—I don't want to brag—"

"You have spent the night in the Castle-Errant."

I caught the shift in his tone, a shift away from interrogation, but I wasn't sure how to respond to it. "Um—" I said, stalling, "—not yet."

"You have ascended the great staircase of black marble, felt the surge of the land-tide, and heard the musical jet!"

He was no longer asking me what I had done; he was telling me that he knew what I had done, even if I hadn't. I smiled noncommittally.

"You are a congregant of the Great Church of Snoutfigs!"

To my knowledge, I was not, but I wasn't about to contradict him.

"And you know the meaning of the words *ha-ha* as spoken by Bosse-de-Nage!"

At last I felt on firm ground. Boldly, confidently, with a comradely wink, I asked, "Are you trying to be funny?"

For a few horrible moments, I thought I had ruined everything. Then, at last, he said, as if he were passing sentence, "Ha-ha."

I said, "Ha-ha."

He said, "You'd better be on your way."

I was stunned. I was also a little disappointed. "You mean you're not going to throw me into the hoosegow?"

"No," he said. "I wouldn't want to stand in the way of the adventures of a young Panmuphle."

Panmuphle? Did he mean Panmuphle, the bumbling bailiff from *Faustroll*? Did all that nonsense about the Squishy Sea and the Forest of Lace and the Castle of Love have something to do with *Faustroll*? Maybe. Maybe all of that was in the parts I hadn't read yet.

"Before you go on your way, though," he said, "I'd like to give you a few words of advice."

Of course.

"Listen, son, I want to give you a warning, a word to the wise."

"Yes, sir," I said, trying to appear interested.

He took the cigar from his mouth. His hand was trembling. He waved the book at me and said, "You don't want to go waving this book around. People are going to take it the wrong way. They—they—they—"

For quite a while, he didn't say anything. Then he said, holding the book in front of him, "This kind of thing can get you into trouble. I think it would be best if I held on to it for you, kept it in protective custody, kept it in my custody for your protection. Do you have any objections to that?"

I had objections. It wasn't my book, for one thing. It belonged to my French teacher, Mr. MacPherson, and I was sure that he expected me to return it when the summer was over. For another thing, I had promised to translate it. How was I going to translate it if I didn't have it?

"Well?" he prodded.

"I don't have any objections," I lied.

"You're lying, aren't you?" he said.

"Yes."

He grinned. He handed the book to me.

"Keep it out of sight," he counseled.

"Okay. Thanks."

"You got any other subversive literature?"

"No," I lied again.

He gave me a long look. He snorted. He spat on the ground. Then he gesticulated with his cigar hand in the direction of *Spirit*. Gratefully, I mounted her and started her.

"Goodbye," I said.

"Ha-ha," he said.

Chapter 10
Caught

WE WERE CAUGHT IN A PACK, somewhere east of Friendsville, Maryland. We had been trapped in the pack long enough to get to know its cars and drivers. Ahead of us were the thoughtless, the witless, the thankless, clueless, and careless. Beside us were the blameless, harmless, and aimless. Behind us were the loveless, helpless, luckless, useless, and inconsolable. We felt boxed in, hemmed in, confined, imprisoned, as if society, symbolized or personified by the two dozen examples clotted around us on the highway, moving in lockstep, had decided to deny us our individuality, the full expression of our unique being, the opportunity to be all that we could be, a shot at the open road. We were impatient. They were inescapable.

I was on the verge of entertaining Albertine by expatiating along the foregoing lines when—eloquently, briefly, precisely—she rendered it superfluous.

"People!" she cried.

They couldn't have heard her, but they seemed to. Something disturbed the field. A bit of separation occurred, a space where there had been none, and the space began to grow as if it held within it an expansive force.

"Ooh, ooh, ooh," said Albertine, with undiminished eloquence.

The gap grew until it became an opportunity. Albertine rushed into it, through it, and into the open, out of the pack, free of the pack, ahead of the pack, in the clear, and climbing a long, gentle hill. Our Electro-Flyer hummed and sang. She howled with the pleasure of release, and her willing motor wound. We crested the hill at exhilarating, electro-flying speed—and there, on the other side of the hill, a couple of hundred yards ahead of us, was a police car. Standing beside it was a cop, holding a radar gun. Even at that distance I could see him grin when he glanced up from the radar readout to see us coming at him.

"Oh, shit," said Albertine, a woman who has her way with words.

She slowed, and she pulled over, just ahead of the cop car.

I began staring at the side of the road, and I continued to stare at the side of the road throughout the cop's interview with Albertine, because I knew that if I looked at her or at the cop I would burst out laughing and at least one of them would ask me what I thought was so funny.

"License and registration, please," said the cop.

"Is something wrong, Officer?" Albertine asked. I could almost hear her lashes fluttering.

"Wrong?" he said. "Let me check. Hmm. Well, golly, you seem to have exceeded the speed limit by quite a bit."

"I did?"

"Lady, you came over the top of that hill airborne. I thought you were a low-flying plane."

"Maybe there's something wrong with my speedometer."

"That could be, or it could be that sunspot activity made my radar gun wildly inaccurate."

"I think you're being sarcastic, Officer."

"Really?"

"I can't have been going as fast as you say. This is an old car. Technically, it's an antique.

"An antique."

"Okay, a replica of an antique."

"For a replica of an old car it's quite spry."

"I suppose it is, but I don't think that I could have been speeding. After all, I was just keeping up with the pack."

"Miz—ah—Gaudette—here comes the pack now."

I allowed myself a glance in the mirror. He was right.

Albertine sighed. She must have glanced in the mirror, too.

There was a period of quiet. Then I heard the cop click his pen closed and tear a ticket from his pad.

"Let me give you some advice," he said.

I bit my lip.

"Yes, Officer?" said Albertine.

"Get a radar detector," said the cop.

His boots crunched away. The pack rumbled by. The cop got into his car and trundled off behind them. Albertine flipped the switch and pulled the Electro-Flyer onto the highway.

"Don't you worry, honey," she said, patting the dashboard. "We're going to take that advice."

"Ha-ha," I said.

Chapter 11
Real Diner Cooking

Life is what we make of it. Travel is the traveler. What we see isn't what we see but what we are.
   Fernando Pessoa as Bernardo Soares, *The Book of Disquiet*

I CAN'T REMEMBER the name of the town. It was in West Virginia. I remember that. I also remember that the day's ride was a particularly pleasant one. I no longer had much hope that *Spirit* would lift me into the clear blue sky, but on that day I didn't particularly care whether she did or not. I was happy to roll along, feel the miles unroll beneath her wheels, watch the scenery slide by, and cover the day's distance.

   In the evening, riding into the light of the setting sun, I began to feel tired and hungry, as usual, so when I saw the sign welcoming me to the place I'll call Forgettable, West Virginia, "America's Home Town," I decided to stop and spend the night.

   Forgettable was an attractive little town. Though it was small, it seemed substantial and well established. Many of the buildings downtown were made of stone, including the handsome train station. All that stone impressed me. It suggested solidity, history, and permanence of an order beyond Babbington's. Forgettable seemed like Babbington's older brother, or a Babbington built by a wiser little pig, who knew that stone would resist a wolf's huffing and puffing better than wood could.

   Just across the street from the train station, there was a diner called Vern's. A sign in the window boasted "Real Home Cooking." How could I resist? I was a long way from home. Real home cooking might shrink that distance, might make me feel at least for a while the comforts of the home that now lay far behind me.

The entrance to Vern's was in the middle of its long front wall. A number of booths stretched along that wall to the left and right, a long counter with stools ran the length of the diner opposite the entrance, and the kitchen was on the opposite side of the counter, exposed to the view of the patrons. The layout and general appearance reminded me of Porky White's clam bar and the Night-and-Day Diner, back home in Babbington. Vern's was working for me. I hadn't eaten a bite, but already the place was reminding me of home. However, something wasn't quite right. I wasn't feeling the comfort that I had hoped I would feel. Instead, as soon as I was reminded of Porky's and the Night-and-Day, I began to miss them—and their setting, my home town—even more.

Standing in the entrance, I looked around, and I saw many happy diners, people who clearly felt at home there, who knew that in this place they were in their place, just as many diners back at home must have felt at the same moment, and I felt more acutely the distance between Forgettable and Babbington, the place where I belonged, where I would have been at home. There at Vern's, hesitating in the entrance, I suddenly recognized that the crepuscular melancholy I felt every evening on the road wasn't caused by hunger or fatigue, or by the gathering darkness, but by displacement, the feeling of being out of the place where I belonged, so far from home, awkwardly placed in someone else's place, in someone else's home.

"Welcome to Vern's," said a weary waitress. "Sit yourself down."

Still I hesitated. I wasn't sure that I could take any more of Vern's. I thought of returning to the parking lot, mounting *Spirit,* and heading back to Babbington, but I reminded myself that I was an adventurer, and adventurers pressed on; they did not turn back, not even in their thoughts. I did what the waitress had told me to do. I sat on one of the stools at the counter.

I chose a stool that would give me no neighbors, out of shyness, I suppose, or maybe because I already suspected that Vern's real home cooking was going to make me feel miserable, so miserable that I wouldn't want anyone to notice.

The waitress tossed a menu in front of me, and I began to feel more uncomfortable as soon as I opened it. Listed on it were many of the dishes that my mother made at home, from Salisbury steak and meat loaf to macaroni and cheese. Instead of the comforting warmth of familiarity, the names of these dishes brought the chill of loneliness. I allowed myself to glance cautiously around the room. No one seemed to take any notice of me at all. Maybe it was going to be all right. I could eat, keep my feelings to myself, and go.

A man sitting a couple of stools away had a different idea.

"Where you from?" he asked, leaning toward me. He was, I think, about fifty. He was smoking. A coffee cup was on the counter in front of him. He hadn't shaved in a day or two. His hair was stringy.

"Babbington," I said.

"Never heard of it."

"That's okay."

"So you came to Vern's to get some real home cooking, did you?"

"I guess," I said. I really didn't want to talk to him.

"What's it going to be?" asked the waitress, pouring more coffee for the man with the stringy hair.

"I'm not sure," I said, and I discovered that although I didn't want to talk to him I did want to talk to her. "You've got a lot of things here that make me think of home," I told her, "back in Babbington." I waited, hoping for some response, but she just stood there. "He never heard of it," I said, jerking my head in the direction of the man with the stringy hair, who had now moved two stools to his left, making himself my neighbor. "Maybe you've heard of it?" I asked.

"Nope."

"It's the Clam Capital of America. Are you sure that you haven't heard of it?"

"Yep. What're you going to have?"

"I don't know. Salisbury steak, I guess."

"Baked potato or mashed?"

"My grandmother really likes Salisbury steak," I said, speaking almost automatically, giving voice to my yearning for home. "She almost always orders it when we go out to dinner—I mean if my grandparents—I used to call them Gumma and Guppa when I was a kid—if they go out to dinner with my parents and me—which doesn't happen a lot, but does happen when we're driving to West Burke for our summer vacation and we stop for dinner on the way—"

"Baked or mashed?"

"Strictly speaking," said my neighbor, "the so-called Salisbury steak is not steak at all. It's ground meat—and notice that I am careful not to say 'ground beef'—formed into a patty in the shape of a cut of beefsteak and covered with a brown gravy, usually containing mushrooms."

"I know," I said.

He looked at me steadily for a long moment. I could see him out of the corner of my eye, though I refused to look at him directly.

"Gravy covers a lot of sins, son," he said. He pulled the ashtray from his earlier location and stubbed his cigarette in it.

"You know," I said to the waitress, "I think maybe I'll have meat loaf instead."

"Now, meat loaf can be made of many things," said my neighbor.

"Leave the boy alone," said the waitress.

"My mom makes it out of hamburger," said my automatic voice. "You know, ground meat—ground beef. And she puts bread crumbs and onions in it—chopped onions—and I think she puts some tomato sauce in it, too—the kind that comes in those little cans—and an egg—and then she mushes it all up and puts it in a glass pan—or I guess you'd say a glass dish—"

"Okay," said the waitress. "Baked or mashed?"

"Baked—no—I—"

The man pointed a bony, slightly trembling finger at the entry for meat loaf on the menu and said, "Many things qualify as meat. During the Great Depression, many people ate horse meat, and they were glad to get it. Others ate horse meat and never knew they were getting it. Many a family around here was kept alive by a ready supply of squirrels. I can imagine a clever housewife discovering that she could grind squirrel meat and make an appetizing loaf out of it. She probably called it meat loaf."

"I'm sorry," I said to the waitress. "I'm going to have macaroni and cheese."

She and I both looked at the man beside me to see if he had anything to say about that. He did.

"There are many kinds of cheese," he said, shaking his head at the horrible prospect. "Some are better than others, some are worse than others, some smell like a pen full of goats, and some—such as the abomination called 'pasteurized process cheese food'—are offered to us under the name of cheese though they are hardly cheese at all. What a weaselly nomenclature that is! It practically sneers at you, 'I'm not cheese, you poor sap. I'm just cheesy.'"

With a sigh, the waitress asked, "Peas, carrots, or peas and carrots with that mac and cheese?"

"On second thought—" I said.

"Fourth thought," she said.

"Huh?"

"Fourth thought. Your first was Salisbury steak, your second meat loaf, then macaroni and cheese, so whatever you're thinking of now is your fourth thought."

"Oh, yeah. Fourth thought. Sorry. On fourth thought, I'm going to have fish cakes and spaghetti. Back at home, my mother makes that for Sunday-night supper. Not all the time, but pretty often."

"This isn't Sunday," the man pointed out.

"That's okay. I'm going to have fish cakes and spaghetti anyway."

"Does your mother make her own fish cakes?" he asked.

"Um, no," I said. "She gets them at the fish store. In Babbington." As I said that, Mortimer's Fresh Fish seemed to reconstruct itself within Vern's diner. I could have been there. "Sometimes I get them for her," I said. "If I'm going downtown on Sunday—to see my friend Raskol—or my grandparents—not the ones we go to West Burke with, but my other grandparents—my mother will ask me to get some fish cakes for dinner." One of Mr. Mortimer's cats rubbed against my leg, the way it did when I stood in front of the refrigerated case and waited for the fish cakes. "Mr. Mortimer has six cats," I said. "They're named for the days of the week. But there's no Monday. That's because he's closed on Monday."

"And have you seen how the fish cakes are made at the fish store?"

"No. They're in the case when I get there. I mean, they're already made."

I had to struggle to keep myself from reaching down to scratch Sunday behind the ears.

"It's hard to know what kind of fish is in a fish cake," the man was saying. "There are many fish in the sea, and many of those fish aren't very appetizing if you see them as they are, before they get chopped and mashed and mixed with crumbs and floor sweepings."

"I don't think Mr. Mortimer puts floor sweepings in the fish cakes," I said—or, to be truthful, snapped. "I don't think he *would* put floor sweepings in the fish cakes."

"There are also many parts to a fish, many parts that you might not want to eat. Some of them fish got fangs, you know, like snakes, and spit venom powerful enough to kill a man. Who knows what's hidden inside that cake?"

"Can I have pork chops?" I said to the waitress.

"Sure. Mashed potatoes and peas?"

"Fine," I said. I closed my menu.

"Now what exactly do you suppose she means when she says 'peas'?" the man wondered aloud.

"Oh, good grief," she said. She bent down and opened a door in a steel cabinet, reached in and wrestled out a huge can, which she lifted up, then dropped onto the counter with a thud. "This is what she means," she said.

I reached out to it. I touched it. I turned it slowly, examining every side. The contents were, the back of the label declared, "Seeds of the variety of garden pea plant, *Pisum sativum*, known as Little Marvel, precooked, packed in water, and canned by Troubled Titan Foods."

The lump in my throat was so large and thick that I could hardly speak.

"We have—we—at home—we have these at home," I managed at last. I couldn't possibly have told them all the memories that the Troubled Titan had packed into that can, but I was willing to try, if only I could blink the water from my eyes and swallow that lump in my throat.

"You have to wonder about the quality of the water they pack these in," said the man.

"Oh, Vern, shut up," said the waitress.

I got up and in a blur I made my way to the door.

"What's got into him?" I heard Vern ask as I pushed my way outside.

"You gave him indigestion before he even ate," said the waitress. "Why do you do that?"

"I don't know," said Vern. "There's just something about strangers that makes me—"

WHAT IT WAS about strangers that made Vern treat them as he did, I cannot say, because I let the door close behind me, ran to *Spirit,* kick-started her, and drove a couple of miles down the road, where I found a garage whose owner was willing to let me spend the night on an old sofa in his office. I dined on candy bars. I don't know what was in them. I threw the wrappers away without looking at the ingredients. I fell asleep trying to figure Vern out and scanning my memory of the people who had been sitting in the booths while Vern was toying with me to see if I could spot a dark-haired girl. I did, in the last booth to the right of the entrance, far from where I had been sitting. She seemed to be having dinner with her parents. I couldn't tell what she was eating.

Chapter 12
Surprised and Delighted

Because a physical space in the world can always be returned to,
... we feel irrationally, somehow certain, impossibly certain, that
we should be able to return again to some often unfinished relationship ... back in the imagined inexistent space of the past.
　　Julian Jaynes, *The Origin of Consciousness in the Breakdown of
　　the Bicameral Mind*

ALBERTINE ANGLED onto the off-ramp. We could have been anywhere in the country where an interstate highway intersects a road that
may be important, even essential, to locals, but is to the speeding interstate voyager useful only for the short stretch in either direction that is
cluttered and clotted with franchise outlets and motorist services; we
might even have begun reliving the night when we stayed in an It'll Do
and met the egoists.

"I'm getting a strange sense of eye-eye-dee-vee," I said with a shiver.

"What's that?" she asked.

"Interstate intersection déjà vu."

"I see what you mean, but this time there will be no eye-dee-dee-vee, I
promise you."

"What's that?"

"It'll Do déjà vu."

"You mean this time you are going to drive past all of this and take us
to some cozy spot?"

"Well now, that little word *cozy* can mean different things to different
people," she said, "and *spot* can cover a lot of sins."

"Wait a minute—" I muttered, inspired by her performance.

"What is it?"

"Well, it's odd, but—"

"What?"

"Your imitation of my imitation of Vern has me thinking how odd it is that we feel something like nostalgia for even our bad experiences."

"Do we?" she asked, in a manner that made it clear that she, for one, did not.

"Apparently *I* do," I said, "because all of a sudden I yearn to return to Vern's."

"You do?"

"I think so. Maybe."

I scanned the road ahead of us, looking for a place where we could conveniently stop so that I could consult a map in search of some congruity between the past and present that would show me where Vern's ought to be. I could have asked her to pull into any of the fast-food joints or any gas station, or even into the parking lot of one of the motels. There was no reason not to pick the first one that she could have pulled into without causing a multi-car pileup, but my keen eyes saw, some distance down the road, toward the edge of the clutter, a Kap'n Klam. (As I suppose you know if you have not isolated yourself from the culture entirely, the Kap'n Klam Family Restaurants, America's only all-bivalve dining choice, rival some of the hamburger and pizza franchises in their ubiquity. "We're your korner klam shack," is one of their slogans. Reading those words now, you can probably hear the catchy Kap'n Klam jingle, I'll bet.)

"Why don't you pull into that Kap'n Klam?" I suggested. "That will give me a chance to study the map for a bit—"

"If you will turn your attention to our printed itinerary, item 12B, you will see that our dinner destination should be just a couple of miles along this road. Relax and enjoy the scenery. You don't really want to go back to Vern's."

I felt a sudden sense of relief. "Okay," I said gratefully. "You're probably right."

"I think you're going to enjoy the place we're headed for. According to their Web site, it's run by a young couple with a passion for food, life, and each other who found a tumbledown millhouse and converted it into exactly the kind of charming little restaurant that they would like to stumble upon if they were driving along the winding roads of vanishing small-town America."

"They said all of that?"

"They did."

"Including 'tumbledown'?"

"Keep your eyes peeled."

"How about the place up ahead? It's got that former-tumbledown-millhouse look."

"What's the name of it?"

"Jack and Jennifer's."

"That's the place."

"And Jack and Jennifer must be the young couple with a passion for food, life, and each other."

"I'd be willing to bet on it."

OKAY, IT WAS CHARMING. That is, it was charming if you are charmed by old mills converted into restaurants. Al and I are suckers for them. There must be something about the smell of old wood or the babbling of the old mill stream. We go into a state of receptivity that other restaurants in other styles and settings do not induce in us. Put us in a restaurant in an old mill and we are immediately predisposed to be pleased, even charmed.

A charming young woman greeted us when we entered. "I'm Jennifer," she said. Who else could she possibly have been? "And Jack is in the kitchen. We are delighted that you have chosen to join the narrative of our life together."

Uh-oh. I detected a whiff of something rotten in the enchanting aroma of the old wood.

"This is a charming place," said Albertine. She didn't seem to smell that hint of putrefaction.

"Oh, thank you," said Jennifer, seizing Al's hand and squeezing it. "Come this way—I have the perfect spot for you."

As we followed her, I whispered to Al, "Did you get a whiff of something—ah—malodorous—a little fusty?"

"Hush," she said.

"It's just that—something has made me wonder how long it's going to be before they turn this into a franchise—with Styrofoam wood and pre-recorded babbling."

"Behave yourself. Follow Jennifer."

The large dining room was more than half full, but Jennifer led us to one of the most desirable tables, beside a window, overlooking the mill pond. The charm began to return, and—if such a transsensual alteration is possible—that slightly off odor was sweetened by the babble of the brook below us and the play of evening light on the surface of the pond.

Another charming young woman came to the table and began pouring water for us. "This is Stephanie," said Jennifer. "She'll be your guide and interpreter this evening."

Uh-oh. Another whiff. I glanced out the window. The pond was still there. The brook was still there. Okay. Maybe.

With a winning smile, Stephanie handed each of us what looked like a slim paperback book, a novella, perhaps. The title of this little book was *The Story That Is Jack and Jennifer's*. Albertine and I, polite little fools that we are, accepted the book with thanks, opened our copies, and began to read. After a moment, we raised our eyes, looked across at each other, and exchanged the look that we refer to, privately, as "whassup wit dis shit?"

The little book had several chapters, with titles that matched the divisions of a conventional menu, such as "Appetizers," "Soups," "Salads," and so on, but the nod to convention ended there. This was the first item in the Appetizers chapter:

Yucatán Honeymoon Midnight Snack

When Jack and Jennifer met, they knew that it was the real thing almost from the start. I guess you could say they had stars in their eyes, because they never gave a thought to the serious side of life together as a couple, all they could see was happy times, and nothing but love and happiness ahead. Of course, they were broke, but did that matter? Not at the time. They had a dream, and they were the dream. It was the dream of Jack and Jennifer, 2gethah 4evah. Young and foolish, maybe, but they haven't changed one bit . . . except that they're not quite as young as they were, though lots of

people say they haven't aged at all, and they feel they owe it all to
the love they have for each other. Because they were so broke,
there wasn't any chance that they were going to have a big wedding
or an elaborate honeymoon. Instead, they moved into a small apartment and locked themselves in for a few days away from the world,
pretending that they were luxuriating at a lavish Yucatán resort.
That was their honeymoon. It wasn't really a honeymoon, it was
"playing honeymoon." Just like a couple of lovestruck kids. Call
them irresponsible, but they hadn't had the foresight to stock the
refrigerator for their adventure! They were determined not to leave
their honeymoon haven, so there would be no trips to the 24-hour
Kwikie Pickie for something to throw in the microwave. They had
to improvise with what they had. Just think about what's in your
refrigerator at home, and imagine living on that for a week. Toward
the end of that week, you're going to have to get pretty inventive!
That's the secret behind Jack and Jennifer's unique approach to cuisine — and that's how the Yucatán Honeymoon Midnight Snack
was born.

Stephanie was not hovering but she was lurking in a corner not far
from our table. I turned in her direction and smiled. She returned my
smile and stepped fetchingly to our table.

"Excuse me—" I began.

"Yes?" she said, turning on the charm.

"I've just started chapter one, and I wanted to know if I will eventually
find out what is actually in the Yucatán Honeymoon Midnight Snack."

With a coy twinkle in her eye, she said, "Why don't you order it and
see if you can guess? I'm sure you'll like it. It's really quite delicious."

"Is there meat in it?" asked Albertine.

"Are you a vegetarian?" Stephanie asked pointedly.

"Sometimes."

"Okay, well in that case, I will tell you that there is no meat in that
particular item."

"Can you tell me anything that is in it?"

"Jack and Jennifer feel that a meal is a story," Stephanie explained
with practiced patience, "and a story ought to surprise and delight. You

will enjoy your time with us so much more if you allow yourself to be surprised—surprised and delighted."

"What if I'm allergic to something?" I asked.

"What are you allergic to?"

"Penicillin."

"There isn't—ah—hmm—just a minute."

She walked off in a charming manner.

"Al, let's get out of here," I whispered.

"Shouldn't we let ourselves go and enjoy the experience?" she asked. "Surrender to the charm? Allow ourselves to be surprised and delighted?"

"We could go back to that Kap'n Klam."

She knit her brows and pouted. "Is this the man who wanted to travel without a map?" she asked. "Is this the bold venturer I married, erstwhile Birdboy of Babbington?"

"You know, Al," I said with the sigh that I use to signal that I have surprised myself with a profound insight into one of life's little mysteries, "reflecting on my feelings about Vern's—not just Vern himself and his habit of teasing strange kids—"

"You said it," she muttered, "not I."

"—but also the uneasy feeling I had standing there in the entrance, as soon as I had entered Vern's, I think I understand the popularity of chain restaurants like Kap'n Klam in a way that I never did before."

"We're not having dinner at Kap'n Klam."

"Okay, okay."

Tension crackled and snapped across the table, tension between the desire to follow a route—the comfort of the itinerary—and the impulse to roam farther afield—the romance of the open road. The surprise was that our poles had been reversed again, as the poles of the earth are said to reverse from time to time. I was supposed to be the one who wanted adventure, surprise, the uncharted; Albertine was supposed to be the one who wanted the plan, the itinerary, the strip map that doesn't even show the interesting area beyond the straight and narrow.

"Okay," I said again, "but—"

"I owe you one," she said.

And so we ate our way into the narrative of Jack and Jennifer. It was an experience that tasted like the last days of a winter that refuses to yield to spring, the last days before summer vacation when you're in the sixth grade, or the last few minutes before the dentist releases you from the chair. Take your pick.

LATER, IN BED, at one of the motels at the interstate intersection, after Albertine had paid her debt, she said, "Let's watch the movie."

"Aren't you sleepy?" I asked.

"Not yet."

"You're usually sleepy after we —"

"I know. But tonight I'm not. Let's watch the movie."

"Okay."

We had skipped dessert at Jack and Jennifer's, but we had been sent on our way with something like dessert. Jennifer herself had promised us, as she handed it to Albertine, that we would find it "sweet." It was a DVD entitled *Jack and Jennifer's Dream.*

"Do you think it's erotic?" I asked, peeling the shrink-wrap from it.

"I'm trying not to get my hopes up."

I loaded the video into the DVD player and hopped back into bed with Albertine.

The dream opened with a shot of Jack and Jennifer in bed, smiling out at us.

"Hi!" said Jack, giving us a hearty wave and squeezing Jennifer.

"Hi!" said Al and I right back at them. I gave her a squeeze.

"Jack and I wanted to thank you personally for becoming a part of the Jack and Jennifer Experience," said Jennifer.

"And we want to tell you about our dream," said Jack.

"It's a dream about making people feel at home," said Jennifer.

"Hmmm," I said. "I smell a pitch coming."

"Cynic."

"I bet I'm right."

Jack and Jennifer didn't let me down.

"That's right," said Jack. "At Jack and Jennifer's our goal is to make you feel at home in our home, as our guests."

"As our friends," said Jennifer.

"As our family," said Jack.

"And someday we want you to be able to 'Come Home to Our Home Wherever You May Roam,'" said Jennifer.

"That's our dream!" said Jack.

"Someday there will be a Jack and Jennifer's literally everywhere!" said Jennifer.

"Even in your home town!" said Jack, pointing right at me.

"We should have gone to Kap'n Klam," I grumbled.

"You see," said Jack, still apparently addressing me personally, "if there's a Jack and Jennifer's in your town, and you dine there—"

"—and we really, really, really hope you will—" said Jennifer.

"—then when you're far from home, traveling, journeying," said Jack, knitting his brows in sympathy for the lonely traveler, "and you come upon another Jack and Jennifer's, just like the one back home, you are going to feel as if there's a bit of your town, your rightful place, right there, wherever you are, wherever you happen to be."

"The warm, welcoming, and familiar coziness that is at the heart of the Jack and Jennifer Experience will make you feel as much at ease in the threatening world as you feel at home, not because you actually are at home, of course, but because you can retire for a time to a refuge, a little bit of home, an island of the familiar in the stormy sea of the strange," Jennifer assured us.

"And you can help us make this dream come true," said Jack.

"Yes!" squealed Jennifer. "You can get behind this dream!"

"You can literally buy into it," said Jack.

"The first Jack and Jennifer's franchises are available now. If you've ever heard people brag about how they 'got in on the ground floor' or 'happened to be in the right place at the right time,' this is what they were talking about," said Jennifer.

"You could be me," said Jack, again pointing that finger at me.

"And you could be me," said Jennifer, pointing at Albertine.

"This is getting scary," she said, pulling the covers over her head.

"I'm turning it off," I said. "You can come out now."

She peeked out cautiously, saw that the television screen was dark, then raised herself on an elbow and said, "By the way—"

"Mm?"

"I've been meaning to ask you something—"
"Mm?"
"Didn't Vern offer you any advice?"
"He didn't have to."
"You mean that it was implicit in everything he said?"
"Yes."
"'Beware of gravy'?"
"Exactly."

Chapter 13
Wireless

I sing the Body electric;
The armies of those I love engirth me, and I engirth them;
They will not let me off till I go with them, respond to them,
And discorrupt them, and charge them full with the charge of the
Soul.
    Walt Whitman, *Leaves of Grass*

I ARRIVED IN SWEETWATER in a bad mood. It was Vern's fault. In the morning, I was rolling along all right, thanks to *Spirit*'s sweet little engine—and I should say in praise of her, just in case she's listening, that her engine was strong and steady, and that she was remarkably stable for a two-wheeled winged craft on the ground. I could have said it to her then, and if I had I might have had a pleasant day, but the memory of Vern's teasing, taunting, and mockery spoiled it all. I'd lost face back there at Vern's. I knew it and I felt it. I was ashamed of myself for having been bested by the old bastard, and a part of me, not the best part, wanted to return to Vern's and take revenge. Throwing a brick through a window of his diner was the best plan I could come up with. It allowed for a quick escape, if *Spirit* was willing. The likelihood of my returning to Vern's and hurling that brick diminished with distance, but my shame and anger grew throughout the day. I turned my anger on the closest target: *Spirit*.

"What's the matter?" I asked her, leaning forward to make sure that she heard me. "Not in the mood for flying today? How unusual!"

"Why do you always talk to my engine?" she asked petulantly.

It wasn't what I had expected.

"I'm talking to you," I said.

"No, you're not. You don't talk to me—you talk to my engine."

"I do not," I said firmly.

"Yes, you do," she insisted. "You lean over and talk to my engine."

"It's just that when I lean forward—"

"You act as if my engine were all there is to me."

"Maybe it is," I snapped. "The rest of you doesn't seem to be good for much."

"That was cruel," she whimpered.

I was immediately sorry for what I had said, but I tasted blood, and I wanted more.

"Your wings are worthless," I said in a taunting voice that I hadn't heard myself use since I was a child. "I don't know why you even have them."

"Don't get nasty," she said plaintively. "Please."

I was winning—but I was beginning to feel like a heel.

"What's the matter?" I snarled, or attempted to snarl. "Can't take the truth?"

"No," she said, "I can't," and I would have sworn that I heard her sniffle. "I'm a failure, and I know it. I'm too heavy. I'm ungainly. I'm fat and ugly."

"No," I said, caressing her tank. "You're not. You're beautiful."

"That's all?"

"All? Beautiful? Isn't that enough?"

"I knew it!"

"What?"

"You do think I'm fat."

"No!"

"You said it!"

"I didn't!"

"You implied it. You said 'beautiful,' not 'slender and beautiful.' You think I'm fat. You hate me because I'm fat and I can't fly."

"No, no—"

"You're always talking about it, always teasing me about it, always—"

"It's just that—I wish—I wish I could feel the lift. Don't you? Don't you think it would be wonderful to be above the world, to be able to see far ahead of us, take the long view—"

Something like a sob escaped from her.

"Of course I do!" she wailed. "What do you think I'm made of? Can't you see that I'm more than metal and fabric and nuts and bolts, that I have feelings, desires, yearnings—just like you?"

"I—well—no—actually—"

"Don't you realize that you've given me all your emotions, that the yearnings I feel are your yearnings, the disappointment I feel is your disappointment!"

"I—"

"If you find me unsatisfactory, it's because you find yourself unsatisfactory. You project your failings onto me."

What the hell had happened? I'd hoped for a cathartic release of anger, a release that would serve as a surrogate release of shame, but my own anger had turned against me, or been turned against me. How had that happened?

Well, you've seen how it happened, but at the time I was mystified by the turn of events, and I was still furious, and so I entered Sweetwater fully loaded and cocked, on a hair trigger.

ANGER HAD SO BLINKERED MY REASON that I didn't even ask myself what Sweetwater's slogan might mean as I rolled past the sign that welcomed visitors to the town:

Entering Sweetwater
Population 8,700
"Someday We'll Be Wireless"

The day had advanced to that time when I ordinarily craved some human contact, when I hoped to find someone who would lend an ear to my story of the day's adventure, but not today. Because I was in no mood for conversation, I thought I would just buy a sandwich from a delicatessen and find some simple shelter for the night without having to persuade a family to put me up.

I rode *Spirit* up and down the main street, but I didn't find a deli. I did find Nielson's Museum of Wireless Power Transmission, though, and it resembled a deli. The signs in its windows promised, in addition to a "Thrilling Tesla Coil Demonstration," cold beer, bratwurst, and a lunch counter. When I entered, I found that Nielson's was a combination of a small grocery store and the promised lunch counter, run by a dour man with nearly no chin, assisted by a dark-haired girl of about my age, whom I took to be his daughter. Things were looking up. The girl was behind the counter, and the man was on a stepladder, bringing overstock down from a high shelf. I headed toward the counter. I knew that the man had spotted me, because I could hear him, behind me, scrambling down from the stepladder, and in another moment he was in front of me, rushing to interpose himself between me and the girl. Like two fighters, or two chess players, or a hockey goalie and an opposing forward—one a grizzled veteran, the other young, fast on his feet, looking for an opening, and eager to score—we danced our way through tactical maneuvers, feints, and adjustments. Though I had youth and will and lust on my side, he was practiced, he knew the territory, and he was more agile than I expected him to be. He won.

He took a stance behind the counter, nodded at the girl in a way that sent her scurrying off with a feather duster in her hand, and turned a look of triumph on me.

"I'd like a hero," I said, acknowledging defeat. "Ham and swiss, with mustard."

"A hero," he said. "I know what you mean, but we don't call it a hero here."

"What do you call it?" I asked, struggling to remain civil.

"A snake, a gut buster, a long lunch, or a cylindrical dinner."

"Okay. I'll have one of those."

"Which?"

"Aren't they all the same?"

"No."

"How are they different?"

"They have different names."

Behind me, the girl giggled. I wished that I could disappear, dematerialize, and then rematerialize outside, astride *Spirit,* on my way out of town.

"I'll have the ball buster," I said.

"What?"

"I mean belly buster."

"Gut buster."

"Yeah. That one."

He went to work. I could hear the girl behind me, going about the business of dusting, and I could feel my ears burning.

"Since you asked for a hero," said chinless dad, "I'm guessing you're from the New York area. That right?"

"Yeah."

"Where are you from exactly?"

Here we go again, I thought. "Babbington," I said, with anger that I couldn't conceal, "and you're right; it's in New York, on Long Island." I could have added, "You want to make something of it?" but even in the heat of the moment I realized that it would have made me sound like a kid on a playground.

Pretending that he was making idle small talk while working on the sandwich (and I could see that he was pretending), he asked, "Have you got electricity there?"

"Electricity?" I snarled. "Sure. Of course we've got electricity." What was this? A trick question? Behind me, the girl was trying to suppress her giggles, but failing.

"In your house?"

"Yes! In my house!" What kind of rube did he take me for? What kind of antiquated backwater did he take Babbington for? "Babbington's a modern place," I asserted. "It might look old-fashioned and kind of quaint, but that's just part of its charm. Actually—"

"How do you get it?"

"What?"

"The electricity. In your house. How do you get it?"

"We—um—it—I don't know what you mean."

"Comes through wires, doesn't it?"

"Of course it comes through wires."

"Ha! You think that's modern? You're living in an antiquated backwater, rube."

I'd had it. I spun around and made straight for the door, struggling to avoid looking at the girl, resisting the desire to take a mental snapshot of her to carry with me on the road, into the night. I ran down the steps and leapt onto *Spirit*'s saddle. I stood and brought my weight down on her starter pedal. She roared into life as if she were as irritated as I.

"Hey! Wait!" shouted the man. He was at my side, holding on to my arm. "What are you doing?"

"I'm getting out of here!"

"You're leaving? What's the matter? Was it something I said?"

"You're damn right it was," I shouted back at him.

Did I hear the girl gasp behind me?

"What was it?" he asked.

"You insulted my home town!"

"Insulted? Oh—that was nothing—"

"Not to me, it wasn't," I said. I wanted to hit him. I wanted to hurt him. I wanted to beat the shit out of him, if I could. I didn't say any of that. I growled. At least I think I growled. What came out of me sounds like a growl in memory. It might have been a howl, a howl of frustrated anger, wounded pride. I think the girl ran inside. I seem to recall hearing a door slam.

"Would you shut that thing off so we can talk?" he said.

"No! I'm leaving. And she's not a thing. She's an aerocycle—a slender beauty."

I started rolling toward the road. He trotted alongside me, imploring me to reconsider. I began speeding up. He began running. I speeded up some more. He grabbed hold of the remnant of the Kap'n Klam banner and tried to keep up, or to hold me back. I accelerated, thinking that I would force him to let go. He didn't. He fell to the ground.

"Hey!" he called. "Hey! Wait!"

"Let go!" I shouted.

I accelerated some more. He wouldn't let go. I was dragging him along. This wouldn't do. If I continued, I'd hurt him. Well, why not?

"Why not?" said *Spirit*. "Because if you did that, you would become someone very different from the boy you are now, someone I would rather not know."

"What's this? Are you my conscience now?"

"Maybe."

"Well, I don't want to hear you. I'm going to drag this guy till he bleeds."

"What fun! Revenge! A fine thing! How noble! Next you'll claim that he deserves it."

"Doesn't he? Didn't he hurt me? Didn't he slander Babbington? Didn't he call you 'that thing'? He does deserve it."

"That's what they all say."

"Ahhh, shit," I said. I stopped. I set *Spirit* on her stand and left her idling while I walked back to the father of the dark-haired girl. He had struggled to his feet and was checking himself for damage and dusting himself off.

"You okay?" I asked.

"Who invented the radio?" he asked right back.

"Guglielmo Marconi." There, I thought. That ought to show him.

"Wrong!" he said.

"Wrong?"

"Ever hear of Nikola Tesla?"

"Um—yes. I have. He invented the Tesla coil."

"And the radio."

"Are you sure?"

He snorted. I took the snort to mean that he was sure.

"You'll have to prove it to me," I said.

"Come on inside," he said, stretching his arm in the direction of the Museum of Wireless Power Transmission, some distance behind us. I looked in that direction. His daughter was standing at the entrance, holding her hands to her mouth in surprise and concern. "My daughter has prepared a presentation on Tesla, including a demonstration of the famous Tesla coil—you'd like to see that, wouldn't you?"

I had seen demonstrations of Tesla coils before. In fact, I had given demonstrations of Tesla coils myself. His daughter's presentation might share much with the others I'd seen and given, but it promised to be delightfully different. I would indeed like to see it, and I answered truthfully.

"Yes, I would," I said, and we began walking back to the museum.

"Tell him about the radio," he urged the girl as soon as we were within earshot.

"In 1943," she said, bright-eyed, "the United States Supreme Court declared that Guglielmo Marconi's patent on the radio was invalid and that Nikola Tesla was its true inventor."

"I didn't know that," I admitted.

"It's true!" she said. "We've got copies of the ruling right here, in the museum. Would you like one?"

"Well, I—"

"You can have it for free."

Mining the depths of my talent for humor, I said, "At that price, I'll take two."

"One per customer," said her father, whom I had forgotten.

"Come with me," the girl said. "I'll show you the museum. There's a Tesla coil."

"So I've heard."

"Have you ever seen a Tesla coil?"

"Yes," I said, offhandedly. "I've seen several, and I've even operated one."

"Oh," she said, disappointed.

"Back at home, in Babbington, that antiquated backwater," I said with a withering glance for her father, "I gave demonstrations for elementary school students, under the auspices of the high school science department, using a Tesla coil to make dramatic bolts of artificial lightning and a Van de Graaff generator to make my hair stand on end."

"That's wonderful," she said, "but—there are more practical uses."

"Oh. Of course. Sure. I'm sure there are. I didn't mean—"

We had made our way back into Nielson's, and she had led me to a back corner of the store, beyond a display of brooms and mops, where she began her demonstration.

"This is my Tesla coil," she began, beaming, "my pride and joy. I built it myself."

"Wow."

"Impressed?"

"I'll say. It's big. And it's different."

"Different from what?"

"From the little one I use for the demonstrations at home."

"What's different about it? Other than size, that is."

"The doughnut—"

"Torus."

"Right. I knew that."

"Ring torus, to be specific."

"The ring torus is—well—no offense—fatter."

"That's an excellent observation. There's a reason for the difference. You see, from what you've said I can tell that the coil you've been using was built for the purpose of entertainment. It's designed to inspire awe in the young and ignorant. Don't be offended by my saying this, but it's essentially a toy."

I wanted to say something along the lines of, "Nothing that came from your comely lips could ever offend me," and I was preparing myself to say—with a certain traveled suavity—something pretty much like that when she stopped me with a hand on my arm, then a finger to my lips.

"The small radius of curvature in your ring torus leads to loss of energy through coronal discharges and streamers," she said. Then she raised an eyebrow, inquiring whether I was following her.

I had been struck dumb. Her hand on my arm, her finger on my lips, were all I knew, all I needed to know.

"Sparks," she said in explanation.

"Mm—ah—yeah—uh-huh," I said with a certain traveled suavity.

"But as you can see my torus has a large radius of curvature—"

I nearly swooned. There was a definite danger of a coronal discharge. Or a streamer.

"—specifically to prevent such a wasteful loss of energy, because this coil does what Tesla designed it to do." She picked a lamp from a nearby table, a lamp without a cord, allowed herself a dramatic pause, then switched the lamp on, and with its light illuminating her face, she said, "It transmits power."

So did she. For the next hour or so, she was quite instructive on the subject of Tesla and the wireless transmission of energy; at least I have some memory of being impressed by her presentation, but nothing that she said about Tesla stayed with me. Later, when I reached Corosso, I had to spend hours in the library of the New Mexico Institute of Mining, Technology, and Pharmacy, reteaching myself what she had taught me, in order to understand why the radius of curvature was a factor in allowing a high electrical potential to develop on the surface of the torus, the area of which is defined by the equation $S = \pi^2 (R + r) (R - r)$ where R is the major radius of the torus and r is the minor radius of the torus, an equation that to this day makes me hot.

When she had finished, some time passed before I realized that she had. I don't know how long I stood there, dumbstruck, before she said, "That's it. That's the whole show."

"Oh," I said.

"I've got to go help my mom with dinner."

"Maybe I could—"

"Here you go," said her father's voice from behind me.

"Huh?"

"Here's your sandwich."

"Oh. Yeah. Great."

"You'd better be on your way before dark."

"On my way?"

"That's right."

"I was hoping—"

"Of course you were," he said. "You were hoping that you'd get to stay here for the night. You were hoping that after the missus and I fell asleep you'd manage to get a little—"

With the thumb and index finger of his left hand he formed a ring torus, and then he began poking the index finger of his right hand into it repeatedly, whistling wetly with each poke.

"Sir, I—"

"Let me give you some advice, kid: take the sandwich and make a graceful exit."

Reluctantly, I did.

Chapter 14
Retrospective Manifestations

WE HAD BEEN DANCING, and though we were now stretched out in bed we were still flushed with the pleasure of dancing. After an uneventful day of driving, we had showered, changed, eaten dinner, and then chanced upon a bar with one of those bands that seems to be able to cover every popular song in every genre from the last several decades. Now we were lying in the luxury of a queen-size bed apiece. I was luxuriating in mine. Albertine was luxuriating in hers. She was reading, carelessly, from a brochure about Blunderhaven, a mansion on an island in the Ohio River that we were thinking of visiting the next morning.

"'Blunderhaven,'" she read, "'is a showcase of priceless historical relics and objets d'art, blah, blah, a gateway to the past, blahbitty blah, antique weapons, household items, old clothing, farm implements, blah, blah, objects of yesteryear that now strike us with their quaintness.'"

She paused.

Breathlessly, I asked, "Why have you stopped, my darling? The tension has begun to mount."

"I was just wondering—oh, never mind." She took up the brochure again. "'Your enchanting day at Blunderhaven begins with a ride in a replica of a riverboat from days gone by.'"

She paused again.

I waited for a while. Then I asked, "How long does this replica ride last?"

"Twenty minutes," she said distantly.

"Let's say that twenty minutes have passed," I suggested. "We've disembarked. We're greeted by a docent or interpreter in period garb. What has she got to say?"

"'Welcome to Blunderhaven, a time capsule of bygone days and a monument to folly.'"

"'A monument to folly'?"

"That's what the brochure says, and I would expect the interpreter to stick to the script."

"Do I hear a little testiness in your voice?"

"Maybe."

"I suppose repeating the same script day after day would make an interpreter a bit testy sometimes. Please go on, though."

"'Nathaniel Hobson, self-styled Lord of Blunderhaven, was his own best friend and his own worst enemy, self-made and self-destroyed, worshiped and reviled, admired and ridiculed.'"

"Sounds like an interesting guy."

"'Although he rose from obscure beginnings to become one of the wealthiest men in western Virginia, his greed made him the compliant dupe of sharpsters and mountebanks, and he dissipated his entire fortune in pursuit of ever greater riches, backing every phantasmagorical scheme that was dangled before his goggling eyes, blah, blah, blah.'"

"He should have taken the sandwich and made a graceful exit," I commented, more to myself than to her.

She tossed the brochure aside.

"Am I to take it that the interpreter has quit and run off to Ohio with the riverboat captain?" I asked.

"The interpreter wants to know about those dark-haired girls who keep popping up in these memories of yours."

"They are you," I said.

"Oh, goodie," she said, abandoning the luxury of her own individual queen-size bed to join me in mine. "Now, in what sense do you mean that?"

"In what sense do I mean what?"

"I mean, do you mean that after we met you decided that our paths had crossed many times before in real life, in truth, in actual experience?"

"I—"

"Or do you mean that sometime after we met you came to believe that you had seen me many times before, that the dark-haired girl who had appeared so tantalizingly from time to time throughout your past must have been me?"

"No, I—"

"Or do you mean that, when we met, you became the compliant dupe of Mnemosyne, who played the trick of replacing your memories of all those other, earlier, dark-haired beauties with memories of me?"

"That's—"

"Or do you mean that now, in the telling, as a narrative device, a way to please, amuse, and seduce me, you are systematically placing dark-haired distractions in the scenes that you read to me?"

"Well—"

"Or do you mean that before you met me you saw many dark-haired girls that you desired and that I was merely the one you finally managed to seduce and snare? (You'd better say no to that one.)"

"Yes—"

"Yes?"

"I had to stop you somehow."

"Oh."

"They are there, those dark-haired girls, because they are retrospective manifestations of you."

"Retrospective manifestations."

"It's a technical term."

"I figured."

"I'll explain."

"Make me swoon."

"During my time in Corosso, I sometimes joined the paleontology group on their sallies into the desert, passing the time reading Tesla's *My Inventions* in the shade of an outcropping of rock while they learned how to use a pretended interest in fossils as a cover for espionage. The desert is a good place for memorization, so I can quote Tesla on manifestations, word for word."

"Mm?"

"Ready?"

"Shoot."

"'I instinctively commenced to make excursions beyond the limitations of the small world of which I had knowledge, and I saw new scenes . . . and so I began to travel—of course, in my mind. Every night (and sometimes during the day), when alone, I would start on my journeys—see new places, cities, and countries—live there, meet people and make friendships and acquaintances and, however unbelievable, it is a fact that they were just as dear to me as those in actual life and not a bit less intense in their manifestations.'"

"Simplify, simplify," she muttered, her eyes having taken on the glazed look of adoration with which she favors me nearly nightly.

"When I met you," I explained, "I realized that something had been missing in my life for all the years before I met you, though I hadn't felt the lack, and having met you I realized that what had been missing was you. When I began the methodical process of recollection that underlies my memoirs, my systematic cerebral excursions to bygone days, I felt the lack of you because I now knew what I had been missing back then, and I suffered for it as I never had the first time around. However, memory and imagination came to my aid, inserting retrospective manifestations of you here and there, and those are the dark-haired girls who—"

Reader, she snored.

Chapter 15
Held for Ransom

The Castle hill was hidden, veiled in mist and darkness, nor was there even a glimmer of light to show that the castle was there.
Franz Kafka, *The Castle*

WHENEVER I RECALL this journey that I'm recounting for you, when I take the trip again in my mind, it seems to be a journey of a thousand mistakes. As Lao-Tzu probably would have said if he'd thought of it, the journey of a thousand mistakes begins with a single misstep, and each of the thousand subsequent missteps can begin a journey of a thousand more.

"I think I made a misstep," I confessed to *Spirit*.

"You've been riding, not walking, so that is literally impossible," she pointed out pedantically, not at all in the chummy, inquisitive, and speculative style of Mr. MacPherson.

"I mean that I must have made a wrong turn," I said.

"Another wrong turn, you mean," she said smugly.

"Yes," I admitted irritably, "another wrong turn."

"Volumes could be written on the wrong turn as a metaphor for the human condition," she said. "Maybe they have been. You really ought to check. Perhaps when you get to the Faustroll Institute you could propose that as your thesis topic, if the Faustroll Institute requires a thesis. Does it?"

"How should I know?" I snapped. "I don't even know whether I'll ever get there. This isn't a journey—it's a disaster."

"I have an idea," she said, suddenly cheerier.

"What's that? Get a map?"

"No. No, I don't want you to do that. I want you to persist in your folly, fool."

"Thanks for the endorsement."

"What I want you to do is redefine the wrong turn."

"Redefine the wrong turn? What are you talking about?"

"Change your thinking. Change the way you decide what is a wrong turn and what is a right turn."

"How?"

"You set out to travel to New Mexico, right?"

"Right."

"But you also set out to have an adventure, right?"

"Right."

"So, any turn that puts you on the road to New Mexico is a right turn."

"Right."

"And any turn that puts you on the road to adventure is also a right turn."

"Hmmm."

"A turn that puts you on the road that leads to New Mexico *and* to adventure is doubly right, but a turn that leads to one or the other can't really be considered wrong."

"Gee, when you put it that way—"

"In order to be a wrong turn, a turn would have to lead you away from New Mexico *and* away from adventure."

"Then I haven't really made any wrong turns at all."

"Not yet."

BUOYED by *Spirit*'s redefinition of a wrong turn, I went on happily, making turns and choosing routes with new confidence, almost insouci-ance, until, at that crepuscular hour when my stomach began to tell me that the day's traveling should be brought to an end, I found myself in a place where the landscape seemed vertically exaggerated, stretched in the upward direction, as if a mathematical function had been applied to all its surfaces, exaggerating them along the y axis. The hills that I had been rolling through had become jagged peaks, the gentle winding road now clung precariously to the edge of a precipice, and there was something that seemed so unlikely that I thought it must be an illusion: at a turning a vista opened before me and I seemed to see, atop one of the peaks, a castle. It was veiled in mist and twilight, so I couldn't be certain, but I seemed to see a castle up there.

I stopped, removed my goggles, and rubbed my eyes. I blinked in the direction of the possible castle, half expecting it to disappear, but found that it was still there, looming in the mist above me, dark, cylindrical, crenelated, and threatening. At that moment it might have been wise to turn back, retrace my steps, and find an alternative route, but I was a headstrong boy on an adventure, and turning back would not have been in keeping with the new definition of wrong turns and right turns. A road that wound toward a castle seemed very likely to lead to adventure even if it wasn't likely to lead to New Mexico, and so I pressed on, making progress of a sort, climbing a little higher with each bend in the road, drawing a little nearer to the castle that now and then made a coy appearance through an opening in the tall pines.

Eventually, the road ended in a turnaround. There I left *Spirit* and began to climb a footpath that seemed as if it must lead to the castle.

After a long hike, I came to a small inn. Seeing the warm, inviting light through the windows of the inn, I remembered that I was tired and hungry. I decided to pause in my climb to the castle to have some dinner, perhaps to stay the night.

Entering, I found the front room of the inn, its dining room, empty of other travelers. I sat at a table. A waitress wearing a name tag that identified her as Frieda bustled into the room. She seemed not to notice me. Not at all. She put some linens into a cupboard, straightened them to her satisfaction, and bustled out. She bustled back in with a pair of candelabra. I cleared my throat. She still didn't notice me. I got up and walked around the room, trying the view from various windows, hoping that a boy in motion might be more noticeable, but still she seemed not to see me. Having lit the candles in the candelabra, she bustled out again. Shortly, she bustled back, carrying a load of plates. I refused to go unnoticed any longer. I spoke. "Frieda?" I said.

She dropped the load of plates and shouted, "Oh, my God in heaven!"

"I'm sorry," I said, squatting to help her pick up the pieces.

"Why did you sneak up on me like that? You scared the life out of me."

"I've been here," I said. "You didn't notice me."

"That's not my fault," she said. "You're not especially noticeable."

"I'm flying to New Mexico," I said, in an attempt to make myself more noticeable.

"That's ridiculous," she said.

"Honest," I said. "I really am flying—"

Something kept me from saying more. Frieda was on her hands and knees, making a pile of broken crockery, and I could see down the front of her dress, see the curve of her large breasts. The sight of her breasts, and the position that we were both in, brought a wave of nostalgia, because it reminded me of the crush I had had on Mrs. Jerrold, who lived across the street from my family home in Babbington, reminded me of the schemes I had hatched to visit Mrs. Jerrold, to get near her, and reminded me in particular of a rainy day when I had been playing marbles with her little boy, Roger Junior, in a ring of string that I had made on her living room carpet, and during my play had discovered a tape recorder under her sofa, which discovery prompted Mrs. Jerrold to get down on all fours to see for herself, which allowed me to sneak a peek down the front of her shirtwaist dress, which allowed me to see the curve of her breasts.

"What are you looking at?" asked Frieda.

"I—"

"You're looking at my breasts, aren't you?"

"Yes," I said with the frankness of an adventurer.

She gave me a swat and a smile and said, "I can't blame you for that; they really are quite magnificent. Do you want some dinner?"

"Yes," I said. "What have you got?"

"We've got dinner. You'll take what you get. It will be good. Sit down and wait. Be patient."

I sat. I waited. Frieda resumed her bustling in and out of the room, pursuing many little errands, none of which was the bringing of my dinner. I attempted to strike up a conversation with her, tossing out intriguing bits of information whenever she bustled in.

"I wasn't planning to stop here," I said.

"Uh-huh," she replied, not quite intrigued.

"I was going to hike up to the castle."

"What castle?"

"The castle at the top of this mountain. The one that's veiled in mist and twilight."

"Pfff," she said. "That's ridiculous."

"Maybe you're right," I said. "It's getting dark, and a hike like that could be dangerous in the dark. Still, I thought it would be an adventure, so I intended to make the attempt, but when I saw this little inn I realized that I was tired and hungry."

"Mm," she said, possibly just a bit more intrigued.

"I wonder if coming upon an inn at twilight has that effect on all travelers—makes them realize that they're tired and hungry—or maybe even makes them feel tired and hungry when they really aren't—through the power of suggestion. What do you think?"

"Happens all the time. Everybody knows that."

"Really?"

"Sure. That's how we get most of our business."

"Oh."

"It's not very interesting."

"It's interesting to me."

"If you want me to show you my breasts, you'll have to do better than that."

"Okay—I—well—what about the remarkable way that height distorts the perception of distance?"

"I never really thought about it."

"Here's the idea: we see something in the distance, and we make an estimate of the distance from us to it. More often than not, we make a simple straight-line estimate, without taking into account the likelihood that the way will be winding. We expect to go as the crow flies, but when we make an as-the-crow-flies estimate, we do not take into account the fact that we cannot fly. Over time, experience teaches us that we can't fly and that the way usually does wind, so we learn to correct our straight-line estimates—but only on level ground. When we look at something that is vertically distant—like a castle on a mountaintop—we forget that the way to it is likely not only to wind but to rise and fall, and that its ups and downs will make the way longer—and when experience teaches us that, then we really wish that we could fly, that we could go as the crow flies."

Here I paused. I thought of telling her about *Spirit*. When I say that I thought of telling her about *Spirit,* I mean that I thought of telling her everything about *Spirit,* from the inspiration to build her to the moment when I stopped her engine and left her in the turnaround down the trail, below the inn where I was pausing. That seemed like more of a story than I should be required to tell in order to see her breasts, so instead of telling it I said, hopefully, "That's pretty intriguing, don't you think?"

She stared at me for a long moment and then said, "I'll get your dinner." She bustled off. In a moment she bustled back and put a large bowl of stew in front of me. It smelled just wonderful, rich and hearty. She handed me a spoon. I tried a bite.

"Hooo!" I said.

"Not good?" she asked.

"Hot!" I exhaled.

"Oh," she said, and she leaned across the table and began blowing on the stew, allowing me another good look down the front of her dress. Was this the view she had suggested I might earn? Might I earn more?

"Unlike the crow," I continued, since I was at least as eager for a full view of her breasts as the next young aviator, "we foot travelers are going to have to hike up and down a rugged path, but we estimate the distance as the distance we see on a line of sight. Nor do we take into account the lets and hindrances that make the way seem longer, make it take longer to traverse than our simple estimate of distance would lead us to expect."

"I guess you're right," she said, but not in a way that suggested she was about to start unbuttoning the top of her dress.

"It's one of the habits of thought that make people think that life will be easier than it is," I said. "That's what my grandparents' neighbor, Mr. Beaker, used to tell me, back in Babbington. He was—"

"Eat your stew now," she said, as if I were her little brother.

"Okay," I said. I was hungry. Her breasts would have to wait. I fell to. Frieda stood there, across the table from me, with her arms akimbo, watching with satisfaction.

"Say, Frieda," I said, after I had eaten about half of the stew in the bowl, "do you suppose I could stay here for the night?"

"Of course you could," she said. "This is an inn, you know."

"I know—"

"We're always putting people up for the night."

"Of course—"

"You could say that it's our purpose in life, the means by which we justify our existence."

"That's great."

"I think we've got four rooms available. How much did you want to spend?"

"Ah," I said. "That's an embarrassing question. You see, I'm on my way to New Mexico—"

"You told me that already. You tried to make me believe that you were flying."

Chuckling like a kid who's been caught in a lie, I said, "Yes, I did."

"Then you went on and on with that business about crows climbing mountains—"

"Yeah. Well, I thought you would find that intriguing, but my point is that New Mexico is still a very long way from here, and I've got to watch my expenses. I have to buy food—and gas—and I'm on a pretty tight budget."

"Well then, I won't ask you how much you want to spend. I'll ask you how much you can afford to spend."

"Nothing."

"I think you're telling me how much you want to spend."

"Both."

She began a hearty laugh, as if I had delivered the punch line of a joke, but she suddenly stopped laughing and became perplexed. "I don't know what to do," she confessed. "I'll have to ask my father."

She left the room. I returned to my dinner, eating quickly. If I was going to be thrown out into the night, I'd like to be thrown out with a full belly.

A big man arrived. He might have been cut from a single block of granite. Everything about him said that he was not amused.

"You asked for a room," he said.

"No, sir," I said with a shiver. "Not exactly."

"What is that supposed to mean?"

"I asked *about* a room. I wanted to find out if a room was available, and what it would cost, just to see whether it might be possible for me to spend the night here on my limited budget."

"You had no right."

"No right to ask about a room? But this is an inn—as Frieda informed me—"

"You had no right to ask for a room if you were not prepared to pay the proper approved rate."

"I only asked *about* a room, not *for* a room."

"Don't quibble. You led my daughter to believe that you wanted a room."

"I did want a room, but I didn't know whether I could afford to pay the—ah—proper approved rate. I didn't know what the proper approved rate was."

"But Frieda tells me you wanted a room for nothing."

"If that is the proper approved rate, then I am prepared to pay it."

"Are you trying to be funny?"

"Yes," I admitted. "Just trying to lighten—"

"This is neither the time nor the place for funny business," he said gravely.

"Yes, sir."

"As far as I am concerned you entered this inn under false pretenses."

"No, I didn't," I said. "Honest."

"Come to think of it, if you entered this inn with the expectation of securing lodging at a rate below the approved rate, then you arrived here with the prior intention to commit fraud."

"This is all a misunderstanding," I said.

"I'm not sure whether to throw you out and send you on your way or call the authorities and have you locked up," he said. He brought his hand to his chin and wrinkled his brow, contemplating me and considering my fate.

Inspiration struck. "Suppose I pay for my dinner and a room by advertising this inn on a banner that I will tow behind my aerocycle as I fly the rest of the way from here to New Mexico?" I offered.

"Pfwit," he said. I decided that I didn't like him.

"I've already towed an advertising banner for Kap'n Klam," I said.

He looked as if he had been struck a blow.

"That is an odd coincidence," he said. "You have this banner?"

"Part of it," I said. "It used to say 'Kap'n Klam is coming! The Home of Happy Diners,' but now the last part just says 'The Home of Hap.'"

"Who is Hap?"

"Nobody. There is no Hap. The rest of the banner wore away, tore off, got left behind."

He narrowed his eyes.

"I can show you what's left of it, if you want me to," I added, with the shrug of a boy who hasn't even thought of the possibility that he might seize the opportunity to hop onto his aerocycle and make his escape without paying for dinner.

"I will call the owner," he said.

"Does he live in the castle?" I asked. "Up on the peak?"

"You saw a castle?"

"It was veiled in mist, but I could pick it out now and then, looming above me in the twilight."

"Yes, that's where the evil owner lives," he said thunderously. "He rules us with an iron fist. In ordinary circumstances, I would not call him. He does not like to be disturbed." He picked up the handset of a telephone on the counter that served as a registration desk and said, "Get me the castle."

He waited. I waited. Frieda waited. Of the three of us, Frieda looked best while waiting.

"This is the inn," he said after a long while. "I have a procedural question for Mr. Klam."

I shot a questioning look at Frieda. She turned aside quickly and began wiping a table with her sleeve. "Mr. Klam?" said her father, with an upward glance, as if he were speaking directly to the castle rather than through the telephone. "Forgive me for bothering you with this, but I have a procedural question. . . . Yes. . . . Of course. . . . I know. . . . Ordinarily, I wouldn't. . . . Yes. . . . No. . . . You see, here at the inn, there is a boy who has arrived on a small airplane—that is, that's what he claims— it's what he told Frieda—probably lying, of course—on his way to New Mexico. . . . I don't know why—but he says his budget is limited and he can't afford the proper approved rate for a room—instead, he offers to

tow a banner. . . . What? . . . Yes—yes—an excellent suggestion, sir. . . .
Yes—certainly—at once—thank you, sir."

He hung up and turned to me. "We can put you up for the night," he
said. "Get your things."

"This is all I have," I said, hefting my knapsack.

"Come with me," he said.

HE LED ME down a long corridor, turned into another corridor, went
down a flight of narrow stairs, passed through a door, went down an even
narrower flight of stairs into a dank cellar, and began walking along an
uneven floor between walls so close that my shoulders rubbed against
them and Frieda's father had to scuttle along sideways. We went up stone
stairs. We went down stone stairs. We turned to the right. We turned to
the left. At first, I tried to remember every turn we took, in case I might
have to retrace my steps, but I soon became too confused to remember the
route in such detail. Instead, I tried to retain a general impression. Did we
tend to turn right more often than we turned left? Did we descend more
often or ascend more often? I decided, after a while, that Frieda's father
was leading me through a tunnel that wound slowly up the mountain to
the castle. We came to a heavy door that he unlocked with one of the keys
on a large ring that hung from his belt. It groaned as he swung it open.
"Your room," he said, and he shoved me inside. I stumbled and fell to the
floor. When I got up, he had closed the door. Was I a prisoner?

I went to the door and asked, "Am I a prisoner?"

"A prisoner?" he said from the other side. "Of course not. You are a
guest at the inn."

A guest at the inn? Ha! I wasn't so easily fooled. I almost said so, but
just as I was about to speak the thought occurred to me that it might be
useful to conceal from him my realization that he had led me to the castle.
I decided to feign ignorance, to pretend that I really believed that we were
still beneath the inn. "Are all the rooms like this?" I asked.

"This is our most economical room," he said. "We reserve it for the
occasional guest who is traveling on a very limited budget."

"Could I have my things?"

He opened the door a bit and threw my knapsack in after me. Then he
locked the door.

"You didn't give me the key," I said.

"I'll keep the key," he said.

"How will I get out?"

"When your bill has been paid, I will let you out."

"How much does this room cost?"

"How much? Let's see—there will be the basic charge—the charge for cleaning—linen—the straw on your pallet—wear and tear—deprecia-tion—your dinner—water—air—"

"Air?"

"The air you breathe."

"Is it customary to charge for air?"

"Of course. Fifteen cubic feet per hour. Three hundred sixty cubic feet per day. It adds up. By morning, you will have run up quite a bill. You will owe us a considerable sum, and the owner is very strict about payment."

"I told you that I don't have much money—"

"If you cannot pay, you cannot leave."

"What am I going to do?"

"Perhaps you could telephone your parents back in—where was it you originated?"

"Babbington."

"They might be willing to wire you some money."

"Mmm," I said doubtfully. "They might."

"Or maybe you know some wealthy eccentric who would do so."

"Hmmm."

"You will have the whole night to think of someone who will pay."

"Okay," I said. "I'll try."

"Try very hard. Make a list of the people who like you enough to pay to have you released from your room."

"Is there a light in here?" I asked.

"I'll bring you a candle," he said. "It will be a dollar. I'll add it to your bill."

WORKING BY CANDLELIGHT, in the venerable tradition of impris-oned writers, I began to make a list of the people back in Babbington who might be willing to pay my ransom. My parents were at the top of the list, of course, but after I had listed their names I imagined myself calling them under the watchful eye of Frieda's father.

"Hi, Mom," I would say, as if nothing were wrong.

"Who is this?" I could hear her asking.

"It's me, Peter."

"Oh. What a coincidence. I used to have a son named Peter."

"This is your son named Peter."

"I haven't heard from Peter in ages. He's missing."

"Mom, I know I haven't written, but—"

"He said he would send me a postcard every night. I haven't received one for several days now, so I guess he's been eaten by a bear."

"Please, Mom—"

"Hello?" said another voice.

"Hi, Dad," I said. "It's Peter."

"I suppose you're calling to ask for money."

"It's funny you should say that," I would say, and I would lay the matter before him, tell him the whole story, and wait for his response.

"Well?" Frieda's father would ask after I hung up.

"He says they won't pay."

"Didn't you tell him you were rotting in a dungeon?"

"I did. He accused me of letting my imagination run away with me."

"Don't you know anyone else who can send you some money?"

I thought about it. Porky White might be able to send me some money. May Castle was supposed to have money. If she did, I supposed she would be willing to send me some. What about my grandparents? I'd never really considered what their resources might be. Did they have savings? Probably. They were frugal, or at least not foolish with their money. Then there were all my friends of my own age. They'd be willing to chip in. They might even be willing to canvas the town, take up a collection, go door to door. It might be exciting for them. It would make them feel that they were a part of my adventure, that they were with me in my hour of need. For a couple of minutes, I savored the thought of all of Babbington filling my friends' buckets with cash to ransom me, but then, with a deep sigh, I recognized the trouble with asking any of those people back home for money: I was going to be embarrassed. I would lose face. I'd be the butt of jokes for all the time that I was away, and when I came home the jokes would have been refined to a sharp cutting edge. I might not want to go home at all with that kind of reception waiting for me. The whole thing was becoming too disturbing. I was in an agitated state. I needed some distraction, something that would calm me. I decided to do my homework.

Before I left Babbington, my French teacher, Angus MacPherson, had assigned me the task of translating Alfred Jarry's *Gestes et Opinions du Docteur Faustroll.* When I began the translation, at a time that now seemed long ago, I found that I felt excluded from the book and from the world of Doctor Faustroll, as I might have felt excluded in a dream when I found myself trying to get to a place and discovered that I couldn't manage to get there, that the very air seemed too thick for me to part and pass through, or when I found myself moving along a wall, searching with my fingers for a door that would let me into a place where I knew that everyone was having a good time.

My habit as a reader, developed over the twelve years that I had been reading, was to find a way into a book, a way to insinuate myself into the goings-on. The obvious way in was through identification with a character, though there were other ways—playing the role of invisible spy, for one. Before entering *Faustroll,* I had expected to identify with Faustroll himself, the star. However, as I began my first attempt at translation, I found that another identification was urged upon me, almost forced upon me, as I made my way through the text, bit by bit, word by word, piece by piece, phrase by phrase. Faustroll remained distant, aloof, mysterious. Instead of identifying with him, I identified with Panmuphle, the vague and ineffective civil servant who first tried to serve him a warrant and later became his companion or sidekick, the guy riding shotgun on Dr. Faustroll's journey from Paris to Paris by sea. Within the book, or at least within my translation of it, my version of it, I was Panmuphle. Now, resuming my work, by candlelight, as Panmuphle, with frequent reference to my *Handy Dictionary of the French and English Languages,* I wrote:

On the Habits and Appearance of Doctor Faustroll

Perhaps it is because I was unable to serve notice on the elusive Doctor Faustroll that I have become somewhat obsessed with him.

I would not have used that word, would not have said that I was obsessed with him, but my wife, dear Madame Panmuphle, assures me that *obsessed* is the word that describes my state. I would have said that I was being assiduous in my pursuit of the mysterious doctor, and in fact I did say so, and suggested *diligent* as an alternative, perhaps even *sedulous,* but she assured me that *obsessed* is the word, and so I defer to her, as I do in all things not directly connected with my official duties, wherein I defer to Monsieur le Mayor.

I began my diligent investigation by interrogating his proprietères, Mr. and Mrs. Jacques Bonhomme. From Mr. Bonhomme I learned that Doctor Faustroll was born in 1898.

"You are quite certain of that?" I demanded of my informant, assiduous in my effort to obtain the facts, and nothing but the facts. "Oh, yes," he replied with ill-concealed annoyance. "It was when the twentieth century was minus two years old. The mysterious doctor was born at the age of sixty-three."

"I must not have heard you correctly," I said. "I thought you said that the mysterious doctor was born at the age of sixty-three."

"That he was," the gnome-like creature asserted, "and he has kept that age throughout his life. He is always sixty-three."

"I see," I said, though I most certainly did not. Because my experiences in the course of discharging my official duties have taught me the value of a skeptic's attitude toward the information the public gives to officials, I asked myself whether the person I was speaking to might be an accomplice of Faustroll, assigned the task of deceiving and misleading me. Even as I noted the age of sixty-three on my pad, I made the secret mark I use to indicate statements of questionable value.

"Please describe his physical appearance," I said.

Without even a pretense at labored recollection, the wizened man launched into a description, his rapidity leading me to wonder whether he had been rehearsed. "He is a man of medium height, or perhaps I should say average height, unless it is the median height that I mean; I am never quite certain about the difference," he said.

"Please, monsieur," I said, "try to be more precise."

"Very well," he said, "to be exact, his height is $8 \times 10^{10} + 10^9 + 4 \times 10^8 + 5 \times 10^6$ atomic diameters."

He intended to rush on, but I stayed him with an authoritative gesture and made him repeat the exact height. When I had it down, I bade him continue, employing another unambiguous gesture.

"His skin is the yellow of gold. His face is glabrous—"

"Glabrous?" I asked silently, through the medium of a raised eyebrow.

"Hairless, sir."

"Ah," I said. "Clean-shaven."

"Except for a mustache as green as the sea, like that depicted in the portrait of King Saleh—"

"King Saleh?" I asked, interrupting. "Who is this King Saleh? A crony of Faustroll's, perhaps?"

"Please, sir," said the doe-eyed daughter of the Bonhommes, who had until then remained silent, though hanging on my every word in evident awe of my office and person, "I know, sir."

"Yes, child?" I said, in the tone of an adored uncle.

"He is the ruler of one of the kingdoms of the sea in the Arabian Nights entertainments, sir," she said shyly, with a provocative pout.

"Thank you, my dear," I said, tousling the little darling's hair. "That reminds me: what of his hair?"

I STRETCHED. I rubbed my eyes. How long had I been working? I had no way to tell. I was tired, but that might have been the result of effort, excitement, and worry as much as the passage of time. I blew out the candle and stretched out on the pallet. I may have slept. I'm not sure. I may only have slipped into a state halfway between waking and sleeping without fully sleeping. I heard a scratching sound. I took it to be rats. I felt a certain satisfaction in the thought that there were rats scratching somewhere nearby. A dungeon ought to have rats. The rats would play a big part in the story of my imprisonment when I told it back at home, in Babbington—

"Boy!" said a voice, low but very near my ear. "Wake up!" I was being shaken. "Wake up!"

I blinked in the direction of the voice. Frieda was shaking me. She had a flashlight with her, and for a moment she shone it at herself, then snapped it off again.

"I wasn't asleep," I asserted.

"You were sleeping like the dead," she said.

"Did you come to lift my spirits?" I asked. I will confess, despite the fact that you may ridicule me for it, that my first thought was that she had come out of a spirit of charity to give me a slice of pie and show me her breasts.

"I came to help you escape," she whispered.

"Really?" I said, hiding my disappointment.

"Really," she said. "This farce has gone on long enough. I'll get you out of here and you can be on your way. Come on. Follow me."

She led me out of the room and we began edging along the narrow corridor. We came to an intersection and turned to the left. We came to another intersection and turned to the right. We came to another intersection, and she hesitated. I wondered whether she knew where she was going. I didn't want to ask. I didn't want to seem to suggest that she might be getting me into a situation worse than the one I had just left. I tried indirection.

"This is like Theseus trying to find his way out of the Labyrinth," I said. "Except that he was able to follow the string that Ariadne had given him. That's how Ariadne helped him find his way out—she gave him a roll of thread—a clew of thread—to unwind as he went in. In Mrs. Fendreffer's class, back at home—"

"Are you suggesting that I don't know where I'm going?"

"No! No, no. Of course not! I—"

"Boy, if you don't shut up my father is going to hear you."

"You don't have to worry about that, Frieda," I said. "Sound couldn't carry very far in a castle. The thick walls, the solid stone—"

She made a sound something like a snort and something like a laugh. "This is not a castle," she said.

"Aren't we all the way up the mountain, in the castle? Isn't this a dungeon?"

"It's a cellar. The cellar of the inn. And that thing you see up the mountain? That's no castle. It's a water tower."

"A water tower?"

"A water tower."

"And your father—"

"My father is my father. He's an imprudent man who has gambling debts. He needs money. When he saw you approaching the inn, he said to me, 'Frieda, here comes a little fool who could be the answer to my troubles.' He played you like a fish. At first, I thought, *Fine. Let the boy pay to get father back on his feet.* But then, tonight, when I was lying in my bed, I thought of you calling your mother, back at home, and I thought of my own mother, dead now for nearly two years, and I thought of the pain I would have brought to her if I had called her and said that I was a prisoner, and I knew that I couldn't let it go on."

"But—but—what about the tyrannical owner, Mr. Klam—"

"The only Klam I've ever heard of," she said, pushing against a door and opening the way into the dawn, "is the one you told us about, the one with the banner."

"Oh."

"There you are," she said. "Do you see the path?"

"Yes," I said. "It's veiled in mist, but I can see it."

She put a hand on my shoulder. "Let me give you a piece of advice," she said.

"I'd rather see your breasts," I said, under my breath.

"What?" she said.

"Never mind," I said. "What's the advice?"

"Don't go through life making water towers into castles," she said.

Chapter 16
Dreams of a Professional Fool

AS A WAY of making our trip more of an adventure for her trusty side-kick, Albertine had not told me where we would be staying for any of our nights on the road. It was her way of providing an element of surprise for me, while ensuring that there would be none for her. It was the way we both liked it.

"Tonight's lodgings should be very interesting," she said, speaking with the false coyness of one who has planted clues in what she has said and wants to be sure that her listener realizes that clues have been planted and can without too much effort be dug up.

"Fair Lady," said I, pretty sure of myself and the clues, "if there be any dragons hassling you, I'm your knight, Sir Peter the Errant."

I had guessed aright. The hotel loomed ahead. Of course, it would have been perfect if it had been a castle. It was not, though it had aspirations in that direction. It was wide and tall, and the lower floors were half-timbered, giving it the appearance of an Elizabethan inn enlarged beyond all regard for good proportion, with a bit of a castle stuck on top. It was one of the outposts of the Knight's Lodging chain, with a logo derived from—or (let's be frank despite the risk of a lawsuit) ripped off from—Picasso's drawing of Don Quixote and Sancho Panza.

We parked the Electro-Flyer in a dark corner of the garage just two long extension cords from an electrical outlet and trundled our rolling bags behind us to the entrance.

The entrance resembled the bridge over a moat. At the far side of the bridge stood a knight in shining armor. At our approach, he swung a massive oaken door open and said in an echoing, metallic voice that came from within his helmet, "Good e'en and welcome to the Knight's Lodging experience. It is a deep, rare, and much-anticipated pleasure to have you here. We hope your stay will be the stuff of legend."

We advanced on the desk like Una and the Red Cross Knight.

The desk was staffed by a jester. He was dressed in motley and wearing a cap-and-bells.

"Ha-ha!" he said, by way of greeting. "What's this? A lady and her lapdog? Beauty and the beast?"

"Let us move on, milady," I said to Albertine. "I suggest we find another hostelry."

"Thank you, sir, that is most gracious—" the clerk went on, shifting now to the detached tone people use when they're delivering the patter they've been trained to deliver, the tone you hear in the telephone voice of tech support, but then he seemed to realize that he had heard me say something he didn't want me to say, caught himself, knit his brows, looked at me sideways, and asked me, with genuine concern: "Why?"

"Are you going to tell me that it is the Knight's Lodging policy for the desk jester to insult the paying customers?" I asked, in a low and confidential voice.

"Well, yes," he said, whispering, in the same confidential mode, "it is—or—that is—it has been—and I have worked hard at it—playing the saucy jester, you know—impudent—exploiting his privileged position as the royal fool—but perhaps there has been a change in policy—perhaps you know something that I do not?"

How often does life open a door like that?

"Perhaps so," I whispered, knitting my brows as he had. "Do you know how to calculate the surface area of a ring torus?"

"Methinks we have two jesters here," he muttered, "where there is room for no more than one." Then he turned toward Albertine and asked, in the politest possible manner, "May I help you, fair lady?"

"We have a reservation," she whispered. "The name is Leroy."

The jester flipped open an ancient-looking book and began running his finger along a page. This surprised and—for a moment—impressed me. I wondered whether it could really be that Knight's Lodging used quill and ink for their reservation records. I leaned over the elevated portion of the desk, as if to help the jester spot our name on the page, and I saw that the book was illuminated by the glow of a computer screen hidden from the view of the registering guest.

"It's a fake," I whispered to Albertine. "He actually has a computer back there—"

"Sir," said the jester, his tone suggesting that he might call the security knights and have me tossed from the lobby like a cantankerous drunk through the swinging doors of Ye Olde Medieval Saloon.

"Sorry," I said, in a tone meant to suggest that I understood the value of illusion and that I really did regret having looked behind the curtain, lifted the veil, unscrewed the cover, and observed the operation of the springs and pulleys.

He cocked a skeptic's eyebrow at me and, turning away from me again, asked Albertine, "How are we spelling that?"

"S-O-R-R-Y," she said, the darling.

The jester regarded her from under beetling brows.

"I'm with him," she said with a shrug, as if it explained everything. "The name is Leroy, L-E-R-O-Y."

The jester said, immediately, "I am unable to find L-E-R-O-Y."

Albertine glanced quickly to either side of her, as if to ensure that she was not being observed, and then, beckoning with her raised forefinger, invited the jester to lean her way in order to achieve greater intimacy and confidentiality. He followed her lead, glancing from side to side, then leaning forward. I thought then, and I think now, that he was expecting a bribe, or a boon. "In that case, try Gaudet, G-A-U-D-E-T," she whispered.

Clearly disappointed, the jester flipped the pages of the book theatrically while manipulating the hidden keyboard with his other hand. I could see that his eyes were on the glowing screen, not on the book. After a moment, he announced, triumphantly, "There is nothing in my book!"

"Is there a room available?" asked Albertine.

"Oh, yes. We have many rooms available."

"Well, we'd like one."

"King, Queen, Knight, Lady, or" —a sneer flicked across his lips and wrinkled his nose— "Jester?"

"Knight and Lady," I said, disdaining to add, "of course."

"Sir Peter the Errant," Albertine said with a nod in my direction.

"And Lady Honey-Bunchy-Wunchy," I said with a nod in hers.

"Varlet!" the lackey cried.

A varlet scrambled forward at once and attempted to wrestle our luggage away from me. While we were struggling, the jester began shouting, "Stop that! Let go of those bags!" I assumed at first that he was telling the varlet to stop harassing the paying customers, but he ran around from behind the desk and laid hands on me in a way that made it clear that he thought I was the one at fault. "Will you let the poor varlet take your bags to your room, please?"

"I don't need help," I said.

"But he needs the money, you cheap fucking bastard!" the jester shouted—and then he caught himself. He stood stock-still for a moment, staring me in the eye. Then he swallowed hard and said, in his jester's voice, "I mean, you misbegotten whoreson knave."

I looked at the varlet. He was sniveling. He seemed more shrunken than he had when we'd been struggling over the luggage. I could imagine a starving family back at home, waiting for the scraps he stole from the kitchen. I felt like a misbegotten whoreson knave. I let go of the bags. I fumbled for my wallet, and I gave the varlet the first bill I pulled from it, from the back, where I keep the larger bills. "Sorry," I said, and I meant it.

I heard Albertine say to the jester, "May I ask why you're putting us through all this?"

"Oh, it's part of the Knight's Lodging experience," he said, "some of it—but I went a little overboard." He hung his head, and his bells jangled disconsolately. "I—I guess—if you get right down to it, I was making a pathetic attempt to salvage some dignity from a wasted life."

"Oh," said Albertine.

"Huh?" said I.

"There was something about you two—the moment you walked through the door—something that made me treasure the role I play here as I have never treasured it before. Please don't take offense at this," he said, turning to me, "but I think it was because I saw in you another like myself, a jester, a fellow fool, if you like."

I didn't care to reply to that. I regarded him quizzically, as if I didn't have the slightest idea what he might be talking about.

"I had the feeling that you were going to try some kind of funny busi-

ness. Maybe you were going to try to obtain lodging under false pretenses, or perhaps perpetrate some fraud, bilk the guests in some way,
steal the silverware, something like that, or—and this is what sent the
chills through me—that you were going to audition for my position. I
thought—I feared—that you might have come here to replace me. I
thought that you were going to take from me the only thing I have, the
only thing that is left to me from a lifetime of striving and failing—my
status as a fool."

"Well," I said, with the disarming shrug and grin of a guy who has an
uncanny knack for saying just the thing to brighten the mood in a room, "I
am a card-carrying member of the Jesters' Guild, one of the ancient guilds
established to prevent the mysteries of the craft from falling into the wrong
hands."

"Please," he said, "don't try to make light of this. The time for jesting
is past. I'm baring my soul to you here. Have a little respect."

"Um, sure," I muttered. "Of course."

"I don't know why," he went on, resuming his soul-baring, and examining my face at the same time, "but there is something about you that
reminds me of someone, someone who played a powerful part in my life."

I stood a little taller.

"He made me what I am today—a fool, a franchise jester, a clown, a
buffoon."

I stood a little less tall.

"It began when I was a kid. I grew up here, in the town down the road.
The family house is still there, though—well—I don't live there. I
haven't gone anywhere. I'm still stuck in the same town, though I once
imagined that I would go everywhere. You see, I had dreams—dreams of
flying."

"Ah, yes," I said sympathetically.

"When I was a boy, another boy, a boy about my age, came into town
one summer evening on an outlandish kind of airplane, a motorcycle with
wings."

"What?" I said, surprised and thrilled.

"I was in awe immediately. It was awe at first sight. I don't mind
admitting it. I was in awe—but there was something else, too. I was
inspired."

"Wow," I said. "This is just amazing—"

"Seeing that kid, just seeing him on that amazing contraption, made me think that life was full of possibilities, and not just life in general, or somebody's life, or that boy's life, but my life."

My heart was racing.

"May I ask you something?" I said.

"Peter—" said Albertine, counseling caution.

"I just have to ask this one thing." I turned to the jester. "Did you actually see this contraption fly?"

"Did I see it fly?"

"That's what I'm asking."

"Of course I saw it fly. It was a beautiful machine, and it flew like a dream."

"Okay," I said. "Sorry for the interruption. Please go on."

If I had caught sight of myself in a mirror at that moment, I know what expression I would have seen. I've seen it on my face before. It's the look of one who possesses secret, and satisfying, information.

"That boy brought with him, when he flew into town, a great gift."

Pride swelled my breast. What a noble little lad I had been.

"The gift, the gift that he brought me, as if it was a gift for me alone, was a license to dream, and to dream big."

"Gosh," I said, reverting to the lingo of my boyhood. "I can't tell you how much it means—"

"I never thanked him for that gift," he continued. "I never even spoke to him, because I was too much in awe of him, but when he flew out of town I waved goodbye and I whispered my thanks to him."

If my grandmother had been there she would have told me that I looked like the cat that swallowed the canary. I was grinning from ear to ear. In another moment, I would reveal my identity, and—

"Now, of course, so many years later, I curse the day when that boy flew into town and made me dream!"

"What?" I said. "What did you say?"

"He ruined my life, the little bastard. I could have been a contented man today, living a little life, with a sweet little wife, in the little town where I grew up, just down the road—but no—no—I had to dream—I had to reach for something bigger—I had to go chasing the dream of flight."

"It's getting late," I said with an elaborate yawn. "You're looking tired, Al. Maybe we should go to our room."

"Please, please don't go," he said, grasping Albertine's hands. "I see that you have a sympathetic soul. We fools have our faculties, you know. In my case it's a talent for sympathy, and I can see that you have it, too. Please hear me out. Please suffer this fool."

"Gladly," she said, drawing him to her and wrapping her arms around him.

"What do you say we get a drink?" I suggested.

"I can't leave my post," he said. "It would cost me my job."

"You can go if you like, Peter," said Albertine.

"Oh, no, no," I said. "I'll stay." To the jester I said, "I have a sympathetic soul, too. Ask Al. She'll tell you. Many people say that I—"

"Go on," she urged the jester, with deep compassion.

He released a long sigh, shaking his head, jingling his bells, and said, "In the years that followed, while I was finishing high school, I kept the example of that boy in my mind, as a reminder of what I could do if I put my mind to it, if I stuck to the job at hand, if I didn't ever lose sight of my dream, and I tried to build a plane."

"Oh, no," said Albertine. I could see the tears welling up in her eyes.

"Not an easy thing to do," I said, as one who knows.

"I bought plans," he said. He was beginning to sniffle. "I bought supplies and tools. I bought parts. I worked after school and weekends to earn the money, and then I worked at night, in my family's garage, trying to build the thing. I gave that plane everything I had. I had no girlfriend, no pet, no spending money, no friends. I gave myself entirely to my pursuit—my fool's errand." He looked at Albertine. Tears were running down his cheeks. "And I failed," he said.

"You poor man," she said. She brought his hands to her lips and kissed them.

"Nothing to be ashamed of," I muttered.

"I didn't give up," he said. He stood a little taller. "I told myself that the boy who had flown into town hadn't quit, and I wasn't going to quit either. So, as some fools do, I persisted in my folly. I worked my way through college, and I went into the family business, becoming my father's partner in our little pharmacy in town. I had no wife, no children, and no real future, but I always had the same dream. I bought more plans, more materials and tools. And again I failed."

"Darn that dream," said Albertine.

"Dreaming can be a positive thing," I asserted. Albertine gave me another look. "Not while driving, of course," I added.

"I bought kits," said the jester, shaking his head in disbelief at the extent of his folly and making those damned bells jingle again, "kits that were supposed to be so easy, so complete, so carefully designed that they were—foolproof!" He began to laugh. It was a sharp, giggling laugh, like a naughty child's. "Foolproof! They were foolproof!" He did a little dance in place, playing the fool for us now, doing his job, entertaining us. "And every time I tried to build a plane from a foolproof kit I proved that there could be no kit so simple that it was proof against the efforts of *this* fool!" He took a few steps, side to side, like a hopping crab. "Whatever it took, however hard he had to work, *this* fool could find a way to fail!"

Albertine was dabbing at her eyes. The jester went on dancing as he spoke, taking little hopping steps that jingled his bells.

"I hit bottom," he said. "I got the idea that if I took the latest kit plane apart completely and put it back together again, I could make the damned thing fly. I won't tell you how many times I did that. If I told you, you'd think I was insane. Let's just say that I tried and tried and tried. And failed and failed and failed. But that's not all. I let the business go. So I failed at that, too. I lost the pharmacy. I lost the family home. I turned to drink. I wandered around town all day, aimlessly, drunk, and slept in the park at night. I was as low as I could go."

The jester stopped dancing and hid his face with his hands.

From behind his hands he said, "I'm sorry to burden you with my troubles. I shouldn't be making you listen to my tale of woe—after all, it's not your fault."

"Well," I said with a sigh, "in a way it is, because you see, I was—"

Albertine shot me a look. I shrugged and shut up.

The jester grinned at us suddenly. "But here comes the good part," he said. "Here comes the story of my success!"

"Great!" I said. "Let's hear it."

"Every now and then, when the weather was bad, the local cops would throw me into jail for the night, clean me up, give me a hot meal, and try to 'get me on my feet.' I'd gone to school with some of those cops. We'd grown up and grown old in this town. Some of them were nearing retirement. They knew about my obsession—my dream of flight—and I couldn't help feeling that they were laughing at me. All it took was a word, a look, a certain tone of voice. One day, I knew it beyond any doubt. It was a miserable day, cold and wet, and I was willing to endure the shame of their charity and their ridicule for the warmth of a cell, so I let them take me in without protest. After dinner, the chief of police himself paid me a visit. 'They're building a big new resort hotel in town,' he said, casually. 'Out by the highway. One of those Knight's Lodgings places. You might be able to get a job there. It looks like you're just what they're looking for.' He handed me the local paper, folded to an ad, and he left me alone with it. I could hear him snickering as he walked away. I picked up the paper and read the ad, and I knew he was right. I was just what they were looking for."

He began that dance again.

"And that's how I became a professional fool!" he shrieked.

Albertine and I looked at each other.

"If it's any consolation," I said, reaching out to him in a comrade's way, "I too have been a fool at times, and I—"

A look of terror came over his face.

"But," I said hurriedly, forcefully, "I assure you that I have no designs on your position. None whatsoever. I'm not a professional fool. Honest. Just an amateur. I shall neither usurp you nor make the attempt. When I play the fool, it is in private, in milady's chambers, exclusively for her entertainment."

"Let's go to bed," said Albertine.

YOU MIGHT THINK that I lay in bed, restless, wracked with guilt. No, I didn't. I owe it to Albertine that I fell asleep quickly and slept through the night. Before we turned in, she threw her arms around me, hugged me, kissed me, hugged me again, and said, "It really wasn't your fault. If it hadn't been flying, it would have been some other dream, inspired by some other traveler. It wasn't your fault."

IN THE MORNING, at breakfast, where a different jester was cutting capers, pulling eggs from the ears of male guests and pinching their ladies' bottoms, I thanked her for the consolation she had given me, and I asked her, "Did you sleep well?"

She burst into tears.

"My darling," I said, rising from the table and rushing to her side, holding her. "What's the matter? Is it the jester? His story? His dream?"

"No, no," she said. "It isn't that. It's just that—last night—after you fell asleep I found that I couldn't sleep—because of the jester, I guess—so I turned the TV on."

"I never heard it—"

"I muted it—and turned the captions on."

"You are the sweetest."

"That's me," she said, smiling through her tears, "but—like a fool—I watched the news."

"Oh."

"What a species," she said, shaking her head, huddling in my arms. "It was as if I had been condemned to watch the whole bloody history of human viciousness."

"Let me guess," I said. "Pride, avarice, envy, wrath, lust, gluttony, and sloth, right?"

"That's the news in a nutshell."

"And this morning you're feeling the tug of gravity."

"Yes, I am."

"Let me lift you," I said. "Today I promise you humility, liberality, friendship, kindness, temperance, and diligence."

"And chastity?" she asked, wrinkling her nose in that adorable way she does when she's invited to eat fish.

"How about tempered lust?"

"Fine with me—but can you really deliver?"

"I can. Come on. Let's get into that Electro-Flyer and flee, and while we're en route I'll read you the chapter I call 'Poppy's Pockets.'"

Chapter 17
Poppy's Pockets

The storyteller: he is the man who could let the wick of his life be
consumed completely by the gentle flame of his story.
    Walter Benjamin, "The Storyteller," in *Illuminations*

THE GOLDEN LIGHT dominates my memory, light that saturated the
sky and the air around *Spirit* and me. That golden light was everywhere,
as if it came from all directions, casting no shadows. It was as bright as,
but different from, the beach light I was accustomed to at home. That
beach light also came from above and below, but it was whiter from below because it was reflected from the water and the sand. This light was
yellow, reflected from the golden plants that grew alongside the road.
Even now it coats my memory like a sticky liquid, like honey. It's pleasant, warm, and coddling, if a little cloying.
    I thought that these golden plants might be wheat, and so I was filled
with a poignant nostalgia, because, years earlier, my grandfather had
thought of growing wheat in the back yard of my family's suburban tract
house, back in Babbington, and though he had never succeeded, I had got-
ten it into my head that I knew what a field of wheat looked like.
    "This is the famous waving wheat," I informed *Spirit*.
    "Really?" she said. "It looks like waving weeds to me."
    "It's wheat," I said assuredly.
    I came to a crossroads settlement, just a mile or so of shops and houses
stretching along each of the arms of the intersection. How should I choose
from among the houses the one to approach, the one where I would ask to

be taken in, fed, and sheltered for the night? Should I choose the largest? The smallest? The best maintained? The most neglected? I would choose the most welcoming. Of course. One of them stood just a bit apart from the others, with those yellow plants in abundance around it, and there was something about the light of the late afternoon sun on the rail fences and the dust in the yard, the long driveway to the house, that made me think that I would be welcome there. I wasn't particularly tired, but I wanted a warm welcome. I wanted to be taken in.

"That's the place for us," I whispered to *Spirit,* hushed by the golden radiance of it all.

I turned into the driveway, and something changed. I detected a stillness now that made me feel like an intruder. I felt that I was violating the privacy of the people who lived there, that I was trespassing, not only on their property, but in their lives, and I changed my mind about the welcome I would be given.

"Maybe not," I said.

"I see what you mean," said *Spirit.* "We don't belong here. They won't want us here."

I had begun the awkward process of turning *Spirit* around when I heard the wheezing hinges of a screen door and turned again toward the house. There, in the doorway, was a grandmotherly figure. She was wearing an ample dress, and she had an ample bosom. Everything about her spoke of amplitude and comfort—not opulence, but a reliable sufficiency. She shaded her eyes with her hand and gave me a long look. Then she went back into the house.

"She's probably got a pie cooling in the kitchen," I muttered hungrily.

"Cherry," said *Spirit.* "Tart and sweet. With a crust as golden as the evening air."

The woman returned, holding a plump pie in both hands. She was followed by a man dressed in a black suit.

I set *Spirit* on her stand, wiped my hands on my pants legs, combed my hair with my fingers, wiped my hands again, and began walking toward the house. As I approached it, other people began emerging from it, each of them making the screen door wheeze and bang. They ranged in age downward from the old woman, and all of them were dressed in black. One by one they lined up along the porch as if they expected me to take their picture, a portrait of the family on their porch. One of them, a boy about my age, came down from the porch and walked out to meet me.

"Are you the photographer?" he asked in a subdued voice.

"No," I said, "but it's funny that you should ask."

"Funny? Why?"

"The way everybody came out of the house and lined up along the porch made me think that somebody was going to take their picture—"

"My grandfather died," he said.

"I thought that they were expecting me to—what?"

"My grandfather died."

"Oh—your grandfather—oh—I'm sorry."

"It wasn't your fault."

"I—no—it wasn't my fault—I meant I was sorry for you—for your loss—but—I should go."

"No, no. Don't go. Having you here will turn us aside from our misery and mourning. You will take us out of ourselves."

"I should go."

"You should stay."

"No—I really should go."

"My grandfather would have wanted you to stay, to meet everybody, have dinner, and even stay the night if you need shelter. He was a generous man. Hospitality was important to him."

"Well, okay."

"Come on," he said, turning toward the house, leading the way, "we're just about to have the period of remembrance. It's an old family tradition."

"That sounds like something private," I said.

"No, it's good to have a stranger at the remembrance because it gives everyone an excuse to speak at greater length about the deceased than they otherwise would."

"You mean because the stranger doesn't know anything about—the deceased?"

"Exactly. You'll be doing us a big favor."

I followed him to the porch. There was a round of introductions and a little awkward small talk. Someone asked me about *Spirit*. Someone else asked me about my travels. And someone asked me where I was from.

"Babbington," I said. "It's in New York, on Long—"

"I remember!" thundered a voice from the other end of the porch.

"Really?" I said, surprised. "You've been there? That's—"

"I remember!" said everyone else, in voices not quite so thunderous.

"All of you? Wow. I—"

"They're remembering Grandfather," the boy whispered. "The reminiscence has started."

"Oh," I said. "I thought—"

He put his finger to his lips, and I shut up.

"I remember the way my brother Richard taught me to fish when we were boys," said an elderly man at the far end of the porch, sitting near the thunderer who had announced the beginning of the period of reminiscence. "I wasn't very good at it." A good-natured, familial chuckling animated the comfortable crowd. "Richard taught me that fishing is an occupation for the patient. 'The rewards may not come soon, and they may not come often,' he said, 'but if you've got bait on your hook, and your hook is in the water, and the line is in your hand, you'll catch your fish sometime or other.'"

Everyone smiled a bittersweet smile. Everyone murmured approval. I joined them. I may have been a young fool in many ways, but I had a sympathetic soul.

"I remember—um—the candies," said a little girl in a black velvet dress. I remember thinking that the dress must be new, bought for this occasion. Judging from the way she rubbed the nap of the velvet, the girl was nervous, and she was worried that she might have said the wrong thing. Everyone chuckled. One or two sniffled.

"Do you want to say anything more about the candies, honey?" asked a woman beside the girl, a woman who had to be her mother.

"Um," said the girl. She thought for a moment, then turned to her mother and asked, "What?"

"About Poppy's pockets?"

"Oh. Yeah. Poppy would say, 'Better look in Poppy's pockets. You never know what Poppy might be hiding.'"

We all sniffled.

"I think we all remember Poppy's pockets," said the girl's mother, dabbing at her eyes, "any of us who were invited to go hunting for candy in Poppy's pockets."

"Or money," said a man seated across from the girl's mother.

Everyone glared at him. Me, too.

"Well, I was never actually *invited* to hunt for money in Poppy's pock-ets," the man explained, "but I did *find* money there one time, when I was hunting for candy."

There was some snorting and a bit of harumphing.

"Well, I did," the man insisted. "Wads of it. Crumpled balls of cash. I can remember it to this day. I thought it was for me. But it wasn't. Poppy stuffed it back in his pocket and bought my silence with a candy mint."

There was an awkward silence. It lengthened.

"What I'm always going to remember about Dad is his optimism," said a man near me. All the rest of us, including the man who had found the wads of cash in Poppy's pockets, sighed with relief, glad to have the awk-ward silence broken.

"He was an incurable optimist, that's for sure," said the little girl's mother.

"A cockeyed optimist," said the thunderer at the far end of the porch.

"We all know about Dad's wonderful sermons," the man who had bro-ken the silence continued, "and to me they were his way of trying to turn his optimism into a new era of humility, liberality, friendship, kindness, temperance, and diligence."

"Yes, sir," said one of the elders.

"A noble, if futile, effort," said the thunderer.

"Yes, a noble effort," said the younger man, "and I suppose you're right about its being futile, and I suppose that there is really no reason for me to talk about it any further, since all of us know all about it—but—"

He looked at me. Everyone looked at me.

"Wait a minute," he said. "It's not true that all of us know about it—there is one among us who knows nothing about it—our guest." He ex-tended his arm toward me. "And so I'm going to tell him." Speaking directly to me now, he said, "Our family has been a part of the warp and weft of this town for generations. My grandfather was mayor for many years. My brother is assessor and collector of taxes. Even I, in my modest way, serve the town. I run the local paper, *The Oracle*. My father—may he rest in peace—was pastor of the Little Church on the Hill—and he was widely—universally—admired for his sermons."

There was murmurous approval for this way of putting it, and I nodded my head and made a bit of a murmuring sound myself to show that although I was not one of them I was as one with them.

"His sermons were not about sinning, and they were not about sins. Nor were they imprecations to his parishioners to mend their ways. They were never admonitions to behave. There were no threats in them. There was no cajoling in them. They were, instead, predictions. They didn't ever ask people to shun error and do right, instead they showed people what their lives would be like if they actually *did* live as they *ought* to live. I wish I could convey to you how exhilarating it was to hear these evocations of the truly good life, not the shallow so-called good life of tawdry pleasure, but the real thing, the rich life that goodness would bring. It's—it's beyond my power—I—"

In a soft, almost distracted voice, his mother, Poppy's widow, said, "Why don't you read one of your father's sermons to the boy?"

There was a stunned silence.

"You mean—go into his library and—go into his files—and get one of his sermons?" asked the son.

"That's what I mean," said his mother.

"But—I—I've never been in there." He looked around the porch. "No one here has ever been in there. It was Dad's sanctum sanctorum. It would feel like a violation."

"It's time the door was opened," she said. "The place needs a good airing. Besides, you'd like the boy to hear one of your father's sermons, wouldn't you?"

The thunderer said, "I'd be pleased to hear you read one of them myself."

One by one, the others voiced their agreement with him.

"Mom—" said the son.

She reached into her bosom and drew out a key.

"Okay," the son said. He took the key. "I'll be back in a minute."

He left, and he left behind him the silence of anticipation.

The widow broke that silence, saying, "Why doesn't everybody get something to eat while we're waiting? Everything's laid out in the dining room."

We trooped into the dining room, took plates, circled the table, heaped our plates high, and returned to the porch, where we fell to. The food was hearty and delicious, and the conversation was warm and lighthearted. I could see that everyone missed Poppy, that he had been well loved, and that the mourners' loss was great, but I could also see that their affection for one another was a powerful palliative. I wondered, and for a moment even thought of asking, whether one of Poppy's predictive sermons might have taught them, in the exemplary manner that his son had described, how to endure this day.

Only when we had finished eating did the group begin to wonder what was keeping Poppy's son.

"Better send out the dogs," said the old man whom Poppy had taught to fish.

"I'll go," said the widow.

"No, no, you stay there and rest yourself," said the thunderer. "I'll go."

When he didn't return after a few minutes, the widow said, "I'm going," and this time no one objected when she rose and left.

Time passed. None of the three returned.

"I'll go," said the mother of the little girl in velvet.

"Hell, let's all go," said the old man. "At my age, I can't afford to wait much longer."

Laughing, we all headed for Poppy's library.

When we got there, the laughter stopped. I think the notion that we were violating Poppy's privacy overwhelmed and hushed us. We crowded silently around the open doorway, peering in, the ones in the back standing on their tiptoes to try to get a look.

Inside the room, Poppy's son and widow and thunderous friend were hard at work. They were tearing the place apart. The files had been pulled open. Desk drawers lay on the floor. Papers were everywhere. The thunderer had tipped an armchair upside down and was reaching into its underside. The widow was groping inside the open case of a grandfather clock. The son was emptying a cigar box onto the floor.

In the middle of the massive desk was a heap of cash. Most of the bills were rumpled and crumpled, squeezed into wads and balls. All of us recalled the reminiscence about finding money in Poppy's pockets when rummaging for candy, and the man who had made the claim recalled it, too. "See?" he cried. "I told you! I told you there were wads of cash!"

The three in the room turned from their work, startled. They looked at us. They looked at one another. They looked at the wads of cash. They looked at us again. Their faces fell.

"Poppy—" said the son.

"It seems that Richard—" said the thunderer.

"My dear husband—" said the widow.

"Money—" said the son.

"In the files—and the desk—" said the thunderer.

"It's everywhere!" said the widow.

"Poppy had his hand in the till!" sang the man who had found the wads in Poppy's pocket. "He was skimming the collection cash!" He erupted in a cackling laughter that I can hear in memory as I write these words. "He was lining his pockets!"

Everyone but the cackling man was embarrassed into silence. People hung their heads. They drifted away from the library. They distanced themselves from one another. They licked their wounded illusions.

The boy took me aside. "I think you should go now," he whispered. "Go away. You can sleep in the barn if you want, but no one is going to want to see you in the morning. Seeing you would remind them of their shame. Please—go on out to the barn now—and go away in the morning—before first light."

SPIRIT AND I retired to the barn. Sleep did not come quickly, so I got out my copy of *Faustroll* and my *Handy Dictionary,* and I resumed my interrogation of the Bonhommes, as Panmuphle. Their daughter had just informed me that King Saleh, who had worn a mustache like Dr. Faustroll's, was the ruler of one of the kingdoms of the sea in the Arabian Nights entertainments:

> "Thank you, my dear," I said, tousling the little darling's hair. "That reminds me: what of his hair?"
>
> I had hoped that the girl would respond, but her mother stepped forward, interposed herself between the girl and me, and declared in a businesslike manner, "His hair is ash blond and very black."
>
> "Forgive me, madame," I said, "but I do not see how it can be both blond and black."
>
> "It alternates hair by hair," she explained, as if to an imbecile, "in an auburnian ambiguity that changes with the hour of the sun."
>
> I regarded her a moment with incredulity. "You have the soul of

a poet, madame," I said at last, when I had recovered myself. "Perhaps you will continue."

"His eyes are as two capsules of simple writing ink," she said without hesitation, "prepared like the eau-de-vie of Danzig, with golden spermatozoa within."

This, I must confess, did not make any sense to me, though the mention of spermatozoa made me flush crimson, which in turn made the Bonhommes' fetching daughter giggle in a way that made me redden even more.

"He is beardless," said Mr. Bonhomme, apparently eager to have his contribution weigh as much as his wife's, "except for his mustache."

"Does he shave himself, or does he visit a barber?" I asked, thinking that a barber might be an additional source of useful information, since barbers are famous for interrogating their clients while they are under their ministrations.

"Neither, monsieur," said the little man.

"You said that he was beardless," I reminded him.

"Through the use of microbes of baldness, of course," he said.

"Hmmm," I said, while surreptitiously making a note to inquire of the neighbors whether the Bonhommes might be insane.

"They saturate his skin from groin to eyelid," he explained, with the same air of addressing an imbecile that I had found so annoying in his wife, "and they nibble and gnaw at the—the little bulbs."

"The follicles," his daughter corrected him shyly.

"Yes!" he said, with a papa's pride. "The follicles."

"I must ask you, sir," I said, "how you know these things, which, it seems to me, are of a rather intimate nature."

He shrugged in the way that everyone does to indicate that the answer must be obvious. I raised an eyebrow to indicate that I would like more of an answer than that shrug.

"Sir," lisped the comely daughter, "we have all done some services for Doctor Faustroll from time to time. My father has performed the duties of a valet, my mother has cooked for him, and I—"

"Mademoiselle," I said compassionately, "you do not have to—"

"My daughter has performed the duties of a maid, sir," said Mrs. Bonhomme.

"I see," I said. "As a result of this work, then, you have all had an opportunity to observe the mysterious doctor."

"That is correct."

"Pray, go on," I said. "Tell me more."

"In contrast to his smoothness from groin to eyelid, from groin to feet he is sheathed in satyric black fur," said the wife.

"My goodness," I said. Involuntarily, I glanced at the Bonhommes' toothsome young daughter before noting the word *satyric* on my pad.

"That morning—" said Mrs. Bonhomme.

"The morning of his disappearance?" I asked.

"Yes, sir. Of course, sir. That morning he took his daily sponge bath, using paper painted in two tones by Maurice Denis, depicting trains—"

"I must interrupt again," I said. "Do you mean that he substitutes paper for sponge in his sponge bath?"

"No, sir," said the daughter. "He substitutes paper for water."

VERY EARLY in the morning, the boy came and shook me awake. I was asleep on my notebook, with my books in the hay beside me.

"Time to go," he said.

"Mm-hm. Okay. I'm awake. I'm going."

I got up and started to mount *Spirit* in the dark.

"If you don't mind," he said, "could you push it out to the road before you start it?"

"Huh?" I said sleepily.

"The noise," he explained.

"Oh. Yeah."

I began pushing her. He walked along beside me.

"Do you have any advice for me?" I asked when we neared the road.

"Advice?"

"Yeah. It seems that just about everybody I meet has some advice for me. I thought you might."

"No. I don't have any advice for you."

"Okay. In that case—" I mounted *Spirit*.

"I guess I have a request, though," he said.

"Yeah," I said. "I know. Don't worry. I won't tell anybody."

"Thanks."

"You don't have to thank me—but—I have a question for you—is this wheat?"

"Wheat?"

"All this golden stuff growing all around."

"Nah, that's not wheat. Just weeds."

Chapter 18
Tomorrow's News Today

The sense for projects—which could be called aphorisms of the future—differs from the sense for aphorisms of the past only in direction, progressive in the former and regressive in the latter. . . . One could easily say that the sense for aphorisms and projects is the transcendental part of the historical spirit.
  Friedrich Schlegel, *Literary Aphorisms*

BEFORE WE BEGAN OUR TRIP, I had hoped that here and there in our travels, during our reiteration of my aerocycle journey, Albertine and I would stumble upon some of my personal landmarks from the original trip, rediscover some of the places where I had experienced significant adventures on the way to New Mexico years earlier. I had hoped that revisiting some of those places would allow me to reflect upon the changes that time had wrought on the landscape and culture through which I had journeyed. I had also hoped to impress Albertine, or at least to convince her that the trip had actually occurred. To ensure that we would stumble upon at least one of my landmarks, I had done something, well, sneaky. I had gone looking for one of them on the Web, and I had found it. So it was with mounting anticipation that when a certain highway exit approached I suggested that we take it and see if we could find a small town where we could have lunch.

"I have a hunch," I said.

"A hunch about lunch?"

"A hunch about a town. It ought to be around here."

"You mean the town where Poppy lined his pockets?"

"We'll see," I said.

The town hadn't changed much. There was more of everything—there were more shops, more houses, more cars—but still no more than the two main streets, and still the waving yellow weeds along the roadside. We drove slowly along the street that ran east-west, and near the center of the town, I found the institution I'd been looking for.

"Look," I said. "That's the newspaper office."

"Where?" she asked.

"There, on the right. *The Oracle*. See the lettering in the window?"

The Oracle
"Tomorrow's News Today"

"Oh, my gosh," she said, braking and then angling into a parking slot at the curb.

"You didn't believe me, did you?"

"Of course I believed you," she said. She switched the Electro-Flyer off and reached behind her for her handbag.

"How much?" I asked as we got out of the car and started toward the office.

"How much what?"

"How much did you believe me?"

"Pretty much."

I swung the door open and held it for her. The office was quiet, and nearly empty. There was one young woman at a desk, tapping softly at a computer keyboard. She glanced up when we came in, smiled in greeting, and went back to her work. Albertine and I stood for a moment just inside the door, expecting that as soon as she came to a point in her work when she could pause she would ask us what we wanted. We continued to wait, but after a while we began to feel that we might wait as long as we chose to wait without ever having the woman pause and ask what we wanted, so I decided to come right out with it, more or less.

"Is the editor in?" I asked.

"Oh," she said, apparently surprised by the question. "Yes, he is. Do you want to see him?"

"Yes," I said. "We'd like that."

She got up at once and came to the railing that separated the front of the office from the area that was crowded with desks, though she seemed to be the only worker.

"I'm sorry," she said as she swung the gate open for us. "I thought you had just come in to watch."

"To watch?" asked Albertine.

"To watch me work."

"Does that happen a lot?" I asked.

"People coming in to watch me work? Yes, quite a lot. It's a way to pass the time. People drop in to watch me write the news."

"You mean to watch you invent the news, don't you?"

"Yes, I do," she said. "So you know about *The Oracle?*"

"I was here years ago," I said. "I was a teenager at the time. I—ah— flew into town on an aerocycle. I was on my way to New Mexico—from Babbington—my home town—back in New York—and someone every- body called Poppy had just died."

"Oh," she said, dropping her eyes to the floor. "Poppy. He was—"

"Quite a character," I offered. "I was there for the remembrance cere- mony, at Poppy's house, on the porch."

"The house is still there," she said, "but—it's not a home anymore."

"Funeral parlor?" I asked.

"Not quite," she said with a giggle. "Medical center."

A man wearing rimless glasses emerged from a door in the back, read- ing a sheet of paper but addressing the young woman. "Candace," he was saying, "would you see what you can do with this mosquito business? I've been banging my head against it for an hour and—oh—hello." He stared at Albertine and me.

"Peter Leroy," I said, extending my hand, "and Albertine Gaudet."

"They came to see you," the young woman explained. "Mr. Leroy was at the remembrance for Poppy."

The man bent his head forward and looked at me over his glasses.

"I remember you," he said.

He didn't seem to relish the memory. He took the glasses off and rubbed the indentations they had left on either side of his nose.

"What brings you here?" he asked.

"We were passing through—"

His look was so full of suspicion that it was nearly audible.

"Really," I said. "Albertine and I are retracing the route I took all those years ago, for the sake of my memoirs, and to correct certain misimpressions—back at home—in Babbington—"

"It's true," said Albertine.

"How could I possibly have kept myself from dropping in for a visit?" I said.

"Mm," he said. "Did you expect to find my father here?"

"He would have to be eighty or ninety now, wouldn't he?"

"He would be eighty-eight, but he's—no longer with us."

"I'm sorry to hear that," I said. "The fact is, though, that I had a hunch I'd find you here."

"Why's that?"

"Just a hunch."

"Mm," he said again, in that suspicious way of his. "You say you're writing your memoirs?"

"Constantly," I said. "I often say that the wick of my life is being gently consumed by the flame of my memoirs."

The editor of *The Oracle* looked at Albertine and raised an eyebrow.

"Believe me," she said, "he says it more often than I can tell you."

"And I suppose you're here to tell me that you're going to write about my grandfather—about Poppy."

"I'd like to," I said, "but not if you'd rather I didn't. That day, years ago—or actually the next morning—you asked me not to tell anybody about what had happened, what Poppy had done—and I've kept silent about it until this morning, when I told Albertine while we were on our way here."

"A memoir is a history," he said. "It's a story with a debt, a debt to the past. You pay the debt in the coin of truth."

"Hmm," I said, nodding thoughtfully but noncommittally.

"All I would ask is that you remember all the people who were on the porch that day, for the remembrance, and think about the Poppy they remembered, rather than the Poppy we—ah—discovered—later—"

He broke off. He looked at Candace. He looked at Albertine and me.

After a while, he said, "Sorry. I'm not talking about truth, am I? What

I guess I mean is that I wish you knew more than what you learned that day. If you did, you might—look, have you got a while? I'd like to tell you about Poppy, and my father, and myself, and *The Oracle*."

The young woman cleared her throat.

"And about my family," the man said. "This is my youngest daughter, Candace." He drew her to him and hugged her, then said, "If you've got a little while—"

I looked at Albertine, asking, with my eyes, whether we had a little while.

"We've got more than that," she said. "We'll spend the night in town if there's a decent hotel."

"There's a hotel," said Candace, "but I wouldn't ask you to stay there. Come home with us."

We did go home with them. It wasn't far. Albertine and Candace rode in the Electro-Flyer, and I walked with the editor, Edward Hemple. The house that he and his daughter lived in was modest but solid, unassertive, a good refuge for a father and daughter who spent their days at the taxing and audacious task of predicting the future.

Edward's story didn't come until after dinner, when we settled into the plump furniture in the front room and listened in the gentle light of two dim lamps.

"My grandfather died in disgrace," he said, addressing this preliminary to Albertine. "He stole from the church where he was pastor, literally taking the cash from the offering tray."

"I know," said Albertine. "Peter told me about the remembrances on the front porch and the discovery of the hidden—ah—"

"Loot," suggested Candace, with a giggle.

With a smile for his daughter, Edward said, "You see how time has diluted the shame—for some people. Candace thinks of Poppy's thefts as a joke—"

"Not a joke, exactly," she protested. "More like a single picaresque escapade in a narrow, conventional, and essentially honorable life."

"Maybe it was that for Poppy, too," Edward said. "An escapade. And maybe he did it for the little thrill that it may have given him, for the spice that it may have added to his life. He certainly never seems to have spent any of the money. Maybe he never intended to. But for my father it was a heinous crime, and he lived the rest of his life under the shadow of its disgrace."

"He ran *The Oracle* then," I said. "I'm curious to know how he handled the story."

"He didn't," said Edward.

"He didn't report it?"

"He arranged things so that he wouldn't have to."

"How?"

"The next day, after you had left, he came to breakfast late, and he had a plan. He summoned all the family and friends, everyone who had been on the porch that day, to the house, and he distributed the cash among them. Their job was to return the money by putting it into the collection plate, little by little, a small amount added to their usual offerings, Sunday after Sunday. It took years, but eventually it was all returned."

"The debt was paid," I suggested.

"The financial debt," he said, "the debt to the parishioners of the Little Church on the Hill. But not the debt to the past."

"The one that you pay in the coin of truth," I said.

"Exactly. My father never wanted to pay that debt. He never wanted to acknowledge it, didn't even want to think about it. He wouldn't talk about Poppy, and his silence and denial drove a wedge between us, because my curiosity about the man was boundless. I wanted to understand him. I wanted to know how he had come to do what he did. I mean, in this little town, especially in the little town that this used to be when he was stealing from the collection plate, or the little town that everyone thought it was before they discovered that its pastor had been stealing from the collection plate, the enormity of that theft was—it was staggering."

He got up and went to a cabinet. From it he took a bottle of cognac and four glasses. The look of surprise on Candace's face said that this was an event. It portended revelations.

"I kept pestering Dad to tell me things about Poppy that he didn't want to discuss," he said as he poured, "and I pestered him and pestered him until he ordered me out of the house and struck me from his will."

He raised his glass to a portrait of his father.

"I moved into an apartment over the grocery store downtown. Fortunately, my mother was sympathetic. She used to visit me every Thursday, and she'd bring me a roasted chicken. I wonder if my father knew. One

Thursday, she brought me—in addition to the cold roast chicken—a paper bag with some of Granddad's papers in it. Week after week, she brought more, until I had them all. I read my way through them, and I began to understand him. I began to see that Poppy had had one very good idea in his life—and I don't mean skimming the collection plate."

"I'm glad to hear that," I said.

"I mean what I've come to call the power of positive predictions."

"You mean his sermons telling people what life would be like if they lived as they should?"

"I do, but at first I got it backwards."

"How so?"

"I couldn't help wishing that my grandfather's history had been different in the one essential way that would have made it better."

"No wads of cash," I said.

"No wads of cash," he said. "I'm sure you can understand how I wished I could rewrite that history, changing only that one thing, making my grandfather again the innocent that we had all thought he was, making his life end the way it should have instead of the way it did."

"Did you?"

"I tried. I couldn't do it. I couldn't make it convincing. I couldn't even convince myself. It was as if the truth was there, between the lines, and anyone would be able to see it."

"Sometimes," I said, with conviction, because this was a subject I actually knew something about, "we say much, much more than we mean to say, because what we want to hide reveals itself in every word that we say about everything else."

"That's it," he agreed. "The thing that I was leaving unsaid announced itself on every page."

"It was the past reminding you of your debt," said Albertine.

"It was," he said, and with a sly smile he added, "but when my father retired I found a way to stand that debt on its head. Instead of paying the debt to the past, I began investing in the future."

He paused, and I knew he was waiting for Albertine to urge him on.

"Go on," she said obligingly. "I'm fascinated."

"Well," he said, "when I thought about it, I realized that a newspaper is like a serial history."

"History in daily installments."

"Right. Exactly that. But my grandfather's good idea was about influencing the future." He got up and opened the briefcase that he had carried home with him. From it he pulled a copy of *The Oracle*. "I've turned *The Oracle* into a serial prediction. Take this copy to bed with you. Let it lull you to sleep. You can tell me what you think of it in the morning."

Candace showed us to a comfortable room, and we got into bed as quickly as we could. We read *The Oracle* with fascination, passing sections of it back and forth. The issue we read was dated ten years ahead of the current date. The town we read about was a place where people got along with one another. They were humble and modest, not pushy or demanding. They were generous with one another, eager to give, eager to help. They respected their differences, but they cultivated collaboration. They were friendly. They were neighborly. They were welcoming. They were quick to praise and slow to condemn. They had sympathetic souls. They were moderate in what they asked of one another, and of the earth. They were diligent in their work, and they were unswervingly optimistic.

"It's going to be a nice place," I said.

"We might want to return in a decade and see how it turns out," suggested Albertine.

"Maybe," I said with a yawn.

AT BREAKFAST the next morning, Ed and Candace were silent, but I could see the eagerness in their eyes. They wanted to know what we thought of *The Oracle*.

"It's a fascinating idea," I said, "but let me ask you something: have you thought of going beyond local predictions?"

"Beyond?"

"Yes. How about—let me see—world peace, international brotherhood, the triumph of reason over superstition, an end to vengeance—"

He laughed, but it was a bitter laugh.

"Sorry," I said. "I didn't—"

"Mr. Leroy," he said, rising from the table with a look that I remembered from years ago, when he had told me to spend the night in the barn and leave before dawn, "I may be every bit the cockeyed optimist that my grandfather was, but I am not a fool."

Chapter 19
Homesick and Blue

Cut grass. Work fast.
  Dersu Uzala, in *Dersu Uzala*

IT WAS A BLACK, tempestuous day, a day more night than day. I had been riding through rain since morning. Rain was ahead of me, rain was all around me, it was rain without end. The coming of evening was a gradual darkening, from dark to darker to black and wet, but now and then, in place of the enveloping darkness, the world was lit by lightning.

Spirit coughed.

"What's the matter?" I asked. "Are you okay?"

"I can hardly breathe," she said. "I feel as if I'm drowning in this rain."

She began to wheeze. Then she made an alarming noise that I had never heard from her before, "Pitipootipit."

"What?" I asked.

"Pitipootipit," she said again. She hesitated a moment, as if she had something else she wanted to say. "Sorry," she said at last, "but I think I'm—"

She stopped.

I tried to restart her. I couldn't do it. "You'll have to push me," she said.

I dismounted and began pushing her through the rain. I was wet and miserable, and I couldn't see a single light from a single house where we might take shelter. In the brief illuminations I saw that we were in what seemed to be cattle country, or cow country, with fenced fields of grass on either side of me and, here and there, a tree.

I knew the folly of taking shelter under a tree in a thunderstorm, but, as I said, I was wet and miserable, and I wanted a few minutes when I could sit quietly and eat a soggy sandwich. That, I thought, would cheer me up, embolden me, inspirit me, and give me the strength to resume my journey.

In a flash, I saw a sheltering tree, venerable and welcoming, its branches stretching out like the timbers of a low ceiling. This tree had stood there for so long, I reasoned, through so many storms, that it wasn't likely to be struck by lightning now, and I would be safe and dry beneath it, I hoped. I pulled off the road and stopped *Spirit* in the shelter of the old tree.

"What are you doing?" she squealed.

"Stopping here to get out of the rain, eat a sandwich, dry off—"

"—and get fried to a frazzle by a bolt of lightning."

"Oh, that's not likely to—"

"I want you to get me out of here."

"Don't you want to be out of the rain for a while?"

"Of course I do, but not if I'm going to end up as a twisted mass of smoking metal."

"Oh, pitipootipit," I said.

"In the morning you'd be found lying beside me, a crackling corpse, sizzling and smoking like a bird on a spit."

"If there were anyplace else, I'd—"

"You could build a shelter from supple saplings woven into water-proof mats and lashed together into a simple structure like a pup tent."

"How could I—oh—I know what you mean. I could build a shelter like the one those guys built in *Bold Feats*. I could probably do that."

"It would be fun."

"Maybe."

"And your father would be so proud of you."

She was right. My father undoubtedly would be proud of me if I did something that might make it into *Bold Feats,* a magazine that he subscribed to despite my mother's objection that it was "not the sort of thing that Peter should find lying around." The magazine's slogan, printed below the title on the cover of every issue, was "No Kidding"; if it were around today, I suppose its slogan would be "No Bullshit." It was full of stories about adventures that men had when they left their families behind for a weekend and went fishing. Some of the adventures were pretty exciting. I used to read an issue now and then when I found it lying around, but some of what I found in it puzzled me. I didn't understand, for example, why the voluptuous women that these men encountered when they stopped for coffee on their way to fishing holes of legendary abundance vanished from the stories entirely after a single tantalizing appearance. I was younger than the target audience, so perhaps I didn't understand what made middle-aged men tick, but I knew that if I found myself in a diner staffed by "babes" and "hot numbers" it would take much more than a "fishing hole known only to a lucky few" to lure me away.

As I headed into the woods to find some straight and supple young saplings, I tried to recall the adventure story that had included the weaving of the saplings into a simple structure like a pup tent, struggling, as I meandered through my memories of issues of *Bold Feats,* against the distracting babes and hot numbers and against my tendency to indulge in nostalgia, which kept grabbing my memory of a particular issue and putting it into the context of my home life back in distant Babbington.

"Peter, have you seen the latest issue of *Bold Feats*?" my father asked in one of those memories.

"I sure have," I said. "In this issue, two guys on their way to the 'legendary lair' of a 'monster wall-eyed pike' stop at a 'sleepy beanery' for a couple of mugs of 'hot joe' and they are served by a 'smoldering blonde' wearing a dress that fits her 'like a coat of wet paint.'"

"Where is it?"

"The 'legendary lair' or the 'sleepy beanery'?"

"*Bold Feats.*"

"Oh. It's—ah—well—it's in my room. I'll get it."

I dashed upstairs. The magazine was under my pillow, and I wanted to retrieve it without having my father see where I was keeping it. Starting downstairs, I flipped through it quickly, hoping for one last look at the illustration of the smoldering blonde in the dress of wet paint, and I came upon—I can see it now—the illustration of the simple structure made from saplings.

"What's keeping you?" called my father from the living room.

"I was just—ah—looking at the illustration that accompanies one of the adventures."

"Peter," said my father, frowning and running his hand through his hair, "I think you should know—I mean I think it's my duty to tell you—as your father—that—those illustrations are—well—let's say they're exaggerated."

I looked hard at the illustration.

"I think I see what you mean," I said. "It's not likely that these guys would come upon so many young, supple, pliant—"

"Peter," he said, "give me that."

I handed the magazine to him and—

"What are you doing?" asked a deep voice from close beside me in the dark woods.

"Holy shit!" I shouted in greeting. I leapt back and peered in the direction of the voice. I saw the shape of a man. He was hugging himself and shivering. "Where the hell did you come from?" I asked him.

"I'm not sure," said the man. "I don't really feel as if I've come from anywhere. I have a vague feeling that I was on a fishing trip—I remember stopping for coffee—there was a waitress—"

"A smoldering blonde?"

"Yes. How did you know?"

"Just a guess."

"But then suddenly there was all this rain—and I was in the woods here—and someone was thrashing around in the brush like a madman—and that was you."

"I'm not thrashing around like a madman. I'm cutting saplings."

"What for?"

"To weave together—to make a shelter—from the rain," I said, returning to the work.

"Why don't you just take shelter under that big tree?"

"Lightning," I explained.

"Lightning?"

"You're not supposed to take shelter under a tree in a thunderstorm because—"

An illustrative bolt struck the big tree, cleaving it in twain.

"Yeeeow!" cried the fisherman, apparently impressed.

"What are you doing?" asked a sweet voice, a girl's voice.

"Cutting saplings," I said.

"Who are you talking to?"

"Some guy who was on a fishing trip and got lost in the rain," I said.

"I don't see anybody."

"You don't?" I said.

"No," she said. Lightning struck again, farther away. In its light I saw that she was a dark-haired girl. Actually, I saw that she was *the* dark-haired girl. I didn't see any sign of the fisherman.

"He must have run from the lightning," I said.

"It cleft that ancient oak in twain," she said.

"I like the way you put that," I said.

"I have a way with words," she said.

"You do," I said. "You would be an excellent companion on a journey—on life's journey."

"You're making me blush," she said.

"I know you," I said, standing straight up to give my aching back a break. "I saw you one day, back at home, in Babbington, one summer day when I was stretched out along the bulkhead on the estuarial stretch of the Bolotomy River with my friend Raskol."

"That's possible," she said.

"We were both younger," I said, "just kids, really, but I remember you. I was on the Babbington side of the river, and you were across the way. You were sunning yourself on the foredeck of a lean blue sloop. Even though you were just a girl, I could see that you were—"

"What are you doing?" asked another voice. It was my father's.

"I—um—well—I—" I said evasively.

"I asked you what you're doing."

"Cutting saplings," I said, relieved to remember that I was doing something that would make him proud of me. "I'm going to weave them together to make a shelter because taking shelter under a tree would not be wise, as you probably know from that issue of *Bold Feats* that had the story about the two guys who were on their way to the legendary lair of a monster wall-eyed pike but became stranded in a violent storm and—"

"I don't think those are saplings."

"You're right," I said. "They're not. Whoever planted this bit of woods apparently never thought about the needs of a young adventurer on a rainy night. There are no straight young saplings." I hacked at the brush. "There are bushes. There are brambles. There is poison ivy. It wasn't like this in the pages of *Bold Feats*."

"You talking about the men's magazine?" asked the fisherman, materializing out of the rain again.

"Yeah," I said. "My father gets it. This is my father—"

I turned toward my father, intending to introduce him to the fisherman. He wasn't there.

"He's around here somewhere," I said. "He must have wandered off in search of saplings."

"It's funny you should mention *Bold Feats*," said the fisherman.

"Why is that?"

"Because I sometimes get the feeling that my life is an adventure straight out of the pages of that magazine. I don't mean to brag, but—"

"Hey, buster, what do you think you're doing?"

"Huh?" said the fisherman and I in unison.

An obliging lightning flash illuminated a smoldering blonde in a rain-soaked dress that clung to her like a rain-soaked dress.

"Wow," said the fisherman and I in unison.

"Don't give me that," said the blonde. "I've heard it all."

She waved a soggy piece of paper under the nose of the fisherman.

"What's the idea of running off without paying?" she demanded.

She turned to me and explained. "This four-flusher here comes into the high-class diner where I'm a waitress, see, orders the He-Man Breakfast—three eggs, sausage, bacon, pork chop, home fries, grits, toast, a short stack, and our famous bottomless cup of joe—chats me up pretty good, and then when I go to hand him the check, he's gone. Just like that! Nowhere to be seen. Disappeared."

"I must have blacked out," the fisherman said.

"I have been known to have that effect on guys," the blonde admitted.

"One minute I was in that sleepy beanery—"

"Hey!" said the blonde. "I resent that remark."

"Are these your friends?" asked the dark-haired girl.

"You're back," I said.

"Was I gone?"

"I think so. I lost sight of you. I'm glad you're back."

"That woman—" she said, with a tilt of her head in the direction of the blonde.

"You can see her?" I asked.

"Yes," she said, a suggestion of annoyance in her voice. "I can see her."

"And the fisherman?"

"The man beside her? Are you asking whether I can see him? Yes, I can."

"This is pretty amazing."

"Is she your—girlfriend?"

"The smoldering blonde? My girlfriend? No, she's—"

"I'll take a turn at that work if you want," said my father.

"I knew you must be around here somewhere," I said.

He held out his hand. I gave him my knife. He started cutting brush.

"Where was I?" I asked.

"You were bringing me that issue of *Bold Feats,*" he said, "but you were dawdling over it, drooling over the illustrations of loose women in tight dresses."

"'Loose women'!" cried the blonde, running her hands over her tight dress. She elbowed the fisherman and said, "Are you going to let him get away with that?"

"See here," said the fisherman to my father, "I think you owe the lady an apology."

"Well, *is* she your girlfriend?" asked the dark-haired girl.

"Hey, toots," said the blonde, putting a hand on her shapely hip, "do I look like I've got to go robbing the cradle to get a date?"

"Perhaps you and I should return to the—ah—high-class diner," the fisherman suggested, daring to put a hand on the blonde's shoulder.

"That's a great idea," I said. "The dark-haired girl and I have a lot to discuss, and—"

"This was the best I could do," said my father, staggering into view under the weight of an enormous armload of cut brush. He dropped it on the ground, looked up, caught sight of the smoldering blonde, and said, "Oh, my god, I've died and gone to heaven!"

"Dad!" I said.

"I'm Bert Leroy," said my father, advancing on the blonde with his hand extended. "Has anybody told you that your dress fits you like a coat of wet paint?"

"Gee, thanks," said the blonde.

"See here, pal," said the fisherman. "The lady and I resent that remark."

"Speak for yourself," said the blonde.

"I'm going to build a simple shelter out of that brush," my father said to her confidently, "and when I'm finished I hope you will join me in it, get out of this rain, and—"

"Dad!" I said. "Go home! Mom is waiting for you. She must be worried."

"You're married?" asked the blonde.

"Well," said my father, "in a way."

"What kind of girl do you take me for?" she asked him, cocking that shapely hip, tossing her wet hair, and thrusting her chin at him. She grabbed the fisherman's arm and said, "Come on, sweetie, let's go. I do not choose to consort with these people any longer." They walked off in the direction of the road, dissolving as they went.

"Dad," I said, "you should go back home."

"Yes," he said with a sigh in the direction of the vanished babe, "I guess I should." He started on his way. After a few steps he stopped and said, over his shoulder, "You won't tell your mother about—"

"It's our secret," I said, and he slipped from sight.

"I should go, too," said the dark-haired girl.

"Please stay," I said.

"My parents will be worried. They'll wonder where I've gone."

"Will I see you when I get back home?"

"I hope so," she said.

"Maybe you'll be in the crowd that gathers along Main Street to greet me when I come flying back into town."

"I suppose I could manage that," she said, already evanescing, adding a laugh that lingered long after she was gone.

IN REALITY, I lay beneath *Spirit*'s right wing, huddled in the tent I'd made by draping my poncho over the wing, shivering in the rain, warming myself with memories of home and wishful visions of the dark-haired girl. I hadn't invited the fisherman and the smoldering blonde into my simple shelter. They had arrived courtesy of *Bold Feats*. I hadn't invited my father, either. He was there because he was a subscriber, I guess.

Chapter 20
Sound Effects

CUE THE LIGHTNING. "Crrrrr-ack!" Cue the thunder. "Brrumble. Thuboom." Cue the rain. "Pitat. Pitatat." More rain. "Shlapalap. Rushalap." More rain. "Blububduba—"

"What are you doing?"

"Trying to re-create the atmospheric conditions and the 'atmosphere': the rain, the lightning, the thunder."

That was true. But it was not the whole truth. I had thought that I heard, in the distance, but keeping pace with us, the sound of a helicopter, *whup-whup-whup-whup,* and I was obscuring that sound, muffling it with a blanket of atmospheric effects, so that Albertine wouldn't hear it. There was the chance that if she did she would bring the Electro-Flyer to a screeching halt, jump out into the road, and begin waving her arms above her head, signaling the flyguys to swoop down and carry her off.

"It's getting late," she said. "I think we ought to head for our motel."

"Just a little farther, okay? I have a feeling that we're very close."

"Peter, we're looking for a patch of ground with a couple of twisted trees, a field—"

"Or meadow."

"—a wooded area off in the distance, and a rail fence at the roadside. I don't think we're going to find it."

"I just have a feeling that—"

Was that the helicopter sound again? Cue that alarming noise that had come from *Spirit*'s engine years earlier. "Pitipootipit, pitipootipit." Cue the stuttering, the hesitation, the shuddering, the—

"Now what?"

"I'm trying to reproduce the sound poor *Spirit* made when she began wheezing and coughing, just before her gradual collapse, when she became too weak to go on."

"You're scaring me," she said. "I'm heading for the motel. Directly for the motel."

"Probably a good idea."

"You're going to love it. It's the Paradise Pines Motor Court, an amazing piece of 'motel moderne' architecture, a place that once promised the touring motorist 'everything that is new and ultra-modern' and tonight promises this particular pair of touring motorists a comfortable retreat—uh-oh."

We had arrived at the motor court. Under towering pines lay a cluster of tiny bungalows that had once been new and ultra-modern. Now, they were old and ultra-decrepit. In front of the bungalows was a small office in a separate building with an angular roof and a soaring sign that still held some of the neon tubing that spelled the name, but it was dark. The whole place was dark.

"It looks closed," I said. "As in out of business."

"Do you think maybe they just forgot to turn the lights on?"

"No, I don't think so."

"Why don't you check?"

"I can see that it's closed—"

"Just check, okay?"

"Okay." I opened the door and stepped out from under the shelter of the Electro-Flyer's clear plastic top. "Crrrrr-ack! Brrumble. Thuboom. Pitat. Pitatat. Shlapalap. Rushalap. Blububduba—"

"Stop that!" she said.

I tried the door to the office. It was locked. I peered inside. The office was nearly empty. It had been deserted long ago. I felt Albertine's disappointment, and I felt a bit of disappointment myself, because I would have enjoyed staying there if it had been in good repair or nicely restored. For a moment, I thought about our taking the place on as a project, restoring it, and running it, but I shook the thought off with a shiver and banished it forever. As I started back toward the car, I realized that I was smiling.

"They're out of business," I said.

"Oh," she moaned.

"Let's hit the road and see where chance leads us," I said.

We started off, into the night and the unknown. I began rubbing my hands in gleeful anticipation. We were going to have an adventure.

Struggling to find our way back to the highway, both of us peering into the dark, I could feel the tension rising in the car. Albertine was not happy about this turn of events, and I was. I admit it. The dark night, and the dark road, made the perfect setting for a breakdown or a slide off the highway into a ditch. What fun! I was on the edge of my seat, and enjoying the perch. The only thing lacking was a storm, but life has taught me that one cannot have everything.

When I glanced at Al, though, and saw her knuckles white with the pressure of her grip on the wheel, I felt the difference in our situations. She was doing all the work. I was having all the fun.

Then I seemed to hear that damned helicopter again, its relentless *whup-whup-whup-whup,* behind us. It had to be those flying EMTs in pursuit of Albertine, or Giggles, as they had taken to calling her.

Thinking quickly, with the resourcefulness of a desperate man, I remarked in a lighthearted way, "If we were in an old movie now, something black-and-white and grainy, there would be a storm, in addition to all this darkness. We would turn the car radio on and hear a report about an escaped killer on the loose, believed to be wandering the dark roads near the area of the ultra-modern Paradise Pines Motor Court." I reached for the radio. "Kkkhhhshhwaukkhh," I said, in a fine imitation of static. "We interrupt this program to bring you a police bulletin: be on the lookout for an escaped lunatic with an irrational animosity toward electric cars—"

"Turn it off!"

"Click!"

"Whew."

"As soon as we heard that report," I said, "lightning would split the sky—crrrrr-ack—thunder would rumble over us—brrumble, thuboom—and our low-battery warning light would begin to flash, intermittently illuminating our faces with an eerie glow."

"You mean the way it is now?"

"Pretty much like that."

"It would make us extremely anxious," she said.

"So I would say, 'Let's stop at the next place we see, whatever it's like, even if it's—crrrack—brrumble—thuboom—that place.'"

IT WOULD BE a large Victorian house, dark and imposing. A sign on the lawn would advertise it as

The Scary Old House
Bed and Breakfast

We would park in front and climb a long series of loose steps to the front door. A busy little woman in a mobcap would answer our knock.

"Oh, my goodness," she would say when she saw us standing there with our suitcases in our hands, "more travelers seeking shelter from the storm. Come in, come in. There's always room for one more."

"We are two more," I would point out.

"What?" she would ask, nonplussed.

"He's trying to be funny," you would say. "It's best just to ignore him."

"Oh. I see," the woman would say. "Ha-ha."

You would give me one of those elbow pokes in the ribs that you've perfected, and we would begin hauling our bags inside.

"Don't bother with those," the woman would say. "You just take yourselves into the parlor, warm yourselves by the fire, and get acquainted with the other guests. I'll have my son Snort take your bags upstairs. He's a bit of an idiot, but he's strong as an ox, and he's not dangerous unless he gets out of sorts. Snort! Snort, you idiot bastard, get out here and carry these folks' bags upstairs."

A large young man would lumber out of a room at the end of the hallway. Beetle-browed and hulking, he would growl, grab our bags, and stomp up the stairs.

"Did he seem out of sorts to you?" I would ask you as we entered the parlor.

"Hard to tell," you would say. "Maybe he was just trying to be funny."

"Ha-ha," I would retort.

There would be quite a little crowd in the parlor, and they would be engaged in an agitated conversation. You and I would slip in as quietly and unobtrusively as possible, so as not to interrupt the congenial social intercourse of strangers thrown together by a storm, seeking comfort in friendly companionship, a warm fire, and sherry. Our stealth wouldn't work. The conversation would stop as we made our way through the group to get near the fire. By the time we had claimed a couple of warm spots for ourselves, we would have the feeling that we were not as welcome as we might have wished to be.

A buxom woman, fiftyish, dressed in a long velvet dress accessorized with a diamond necklace that spread across most of her imposing front, would turn to a wild-haired old fellow in a baggy suit and say, "Please go on, Professor. What you were saying was so very interesting. I hope the interruption hasn't derailed your train of thought."

"Please accept our apologies," I would say. "We were forced to seek shelter from the rain, very much as I was forced to seek shelter in this area many years ago when I was traveling to New Mexico—"

"I was saying that I have been studying the caramba-mamba," the professor would say.

"Gosh, that's the world's deadliest snake, isn't it, Professor?" a fresh-faced lad with sandy hair would ask.

"Indeed it is, young man," the professor would say. "Are you interested in herpetology?"

"Nah," Sandy would say with a flip of his hand, "I just like snakes."

"I see," the professor would say with a chuckle, sending a wink in the direction of the buxom woman. "If the caramba-mamba is a snake that interests you, I have a specimen in my room that you might like to see."

"In your room!" the buxom matron would squeal. "Oh, Professor! What if it escapes in the night? We might all be killed in our sleep!"

"My dear woman," the professor would say, "I assure you that there is no cause for alarm. The creature is quite safely enclosed in a cage that can only be opened with this key." He would produce a key from his pocket, hold it up for all to see, return it to his pocket, and pat the pocket to show everyone how secure the key was on his person.

Outside, a bolt of lightning would strike a tree in front of the house, splintering it with a ripping sound like the scream of a small, furry animal being disemboweled by a goshawk—something like eeaghhhgrackouukirsch. It would be followed by a clap of thunder—drubbleduboom-buh—that would rattle the windows and rumble the floor beneath our feet.

A blonde in a white satin dress clinging to her like the paint worn by the blondes in *Bold Feats* would wail, "Make it stop! Somebody make it stop! It's driving me insane!" She would throw herself across a sofa like an invitation.

I would take a seat on the sofa beside her and say sympathetically, "I know how you feel. When I was on that trip that I mentioned, years ago, I thought of taking shelter under the spreading branches of a large tree—"

"Did the woman in the mobcap mention sherry?" you would ask.

A big, snarling man would rise from an overstuffed chair behind a plant, where he had previously been invisible, and demand in a deep snarling voice, "What's that you said?"

"I was hoping that it might be cocktail hour," you would tell him.

"Oooh, Francis!" the blonde would squeal. "There you are! Did you have a nice nap?"

"Nah," Francis would say with a shrug, rolling the shoulders of his double-breasted suit and patting the gat in his shoulder holster. "It's hard to sleep with a gat digging into your ribs and that storm raging outside. It's enough to drive a guy nuts."

"I was just telling everybody that the thunder is driving me crazy," the blonde would explain.

"And I was telling her how much the storm reminded me of a night years ago," I would offer, "when I was flying—well, taxiing—to New Mexico and—"

"Yeah, I heard ya," Francis would say, flicking the ash from his cigarette into a potted aspidistra.

A brilliant bolt of lightning would catch us all in its sudden silver light.

"Stop it!" young Sandy would scream. "Somebody please make it stop! If one more bolt of lightning freezes us in its light like that, burning our startled expressions into my brain, I'll go mad! I tell you I'll go mad!"

You would turn suddenly and slap him hard across the face, then again, and again.

There would be a moment of stunned silence. Then Sandy would slump into a chair, subdued and whimpering.

"Say, that was quick thinking, sister," Francis would say.

"I've been to the movies," you would explain.

I would have found the bar by then. I would pour a couple of shots of brandy into a tumbler and hand it to Sandy. "Here, drink this, kid," I would say, "and pull yourself together."

"I thought there was going to be sherry," Francis would say, pouting.

"I couldn't find any," I would explain, "but there is gin, and I am prepared to make a martini for anyone who would like one."

It would be martinis all around, with the exception of Sandy, who would stick with the brandy.

When Francis had a drink in hand, he would say to the professor, "I heard what you said about the caramba-mamba, Professor."

"Yes?" the professor would say.

"Maybe you'd like to bring the snake down here, so that we can all get a look at it."

"Oh, I don't think that would be wise," the professor would say sagely.

Francis would pat the bulge in his double-breasted jacket and say slowly, "I do, Professor. I think it would be very wise."

"Oh, yes, Professor," the buxom woman would say, all aflutter, "please do bring the snake here for us to see—if you think it's safe."

"Yes, well," the professor would say, with a wary eye on Francis, "perhaps I will," and he would start upstairs.

Suddenly Snort would burst into the room from the hallway. "Is that an electric car outside?" he would shout. "Is somebody here driving an electric car?"

You would say, "Yes, we're driving an Electro-Flyer, the only Electro-Flyer in the world, in fact."

And I would say, "We're driving to New Mexico, re-creating the trip that I made in an aerocycle when I was a teenager—"

Snort would begin tearing his hair, throwing the furniture around, and screaming, "I hate electric cars. I hate them! I hate them!"

The professor would appear at the top of the stairs and call out, "Stay where you are, everyone! Don't move an inch! The caramba-mamba is missing!"

The lights would go out.

"Come on, Al," I would say, "in the darkness and confusion we can make our getaway."

We would grope our way along a hallway until we came to the kitchen, where we would slip out the back door, tiptoe down the driveway to the front of the house, get into the Electro-Flyer, switch it on, and slip away from the Scary Old House, silently, with electro-flying swiftness.

"That was a close shave," I would say, "close as wet paint."

"You're enjoying this, aren't you?" you would say. It would be an accusation, but you would be smiling as you made it.

"Well," I would say, "it *has* become more of an adventure than it would have been if we had been able to stay at Paradise Pines."

"I wish that it would stop being an adventure," you would say, "and start being more of a—"

"OH, LOOK!" she said. "Up ahead. There's a motel." She gave a sigh of relief. "There seem to be quite a few cars parked out front—and it doesn't look scary at all."

We took our bags from the trunk, registered, and found our room.

"Thanks for keeping me entertained," she said.

"I'll just check under the bed for snakes," I said.

"Please do."

"I'll also go out to the parking lot and find a way to plug the car in."

I slung my extension cords over my shoulder and slipped into the night. I found an outdoor outlet not far from the car, ran my cords, made them as discreet as possible, and then stood to listen. There was no helicopter, no *whup-whup-whup*. The night was as silent as it was dark.

Chapter 21
The Ideal Audience

Truth is appalling and eltritch, as seen
By this world's artificial lamplights.
    Owen Meredith (Edward Robert Bulwer-Lytton), *Lucile*

DURING THE DAY, while I was riding along, I composed a song, in my head, and my song quickly became one of those songs that one cannot get out of one's head. In fact, I'm hesitant to include it here because I fear that I may be doing you a disservice, Reader, by introducing it into your head, from which I fear you may not be able to drive it. However, in the service of completeness, I must include it, and so I do:

O, Babbington, my Babbington,
You know I love you dearly.
When I'm abroad, you're with me still,
And I can see you clearly.
The people who don't live in you
All live their lives so queerly.
Where'ere I roam, I yearn for home,
And I mean that most sincerely.
Ooo, bop, sha doobie doo wop.

I was very proud of myself for addressing the song to the town itself, as if it were a sentient being, an entity vibrant and alive, capable of comprehending and appreciating my paean to it.

"You are driving me crazy with that song," claimed *Spirit*.

"I think it's pretty good," I said, frankly and honestly.

"I might have agreed the first time I heard it."

"I've got to keep repeating it so that I can memorize it."

"I've already memorized it."

"I hear the rhythm of the road in it."

"I keep hearing 'Ooo, bop, sha doobie doo wop,' and if I hear it one more time, it's going to drive me insane, totally, irreversibly insane."

"Okay," I said. "I get the point. I'll be quiet."

We rolled along. I memorized my song, subvocalizing instead of singing. As usual, at the predictable time, evening came on. As usual, I began looking for a good place to stop for a meal, a shower, and a bed. I came to a crossroads where there was a sign that pointed the way to two towns: Happy Valley to the right and Eldritch to the left.

Much has been written on the effect that the names of places have on our predisposition toward them, nearly all of it by Marcel Proust. Consequently, there is nothing left for me to say on the topic, in general. Specifically, though, I can add my bit to the grand conversation by noting that the two names had immediate and contradictory effects on me. Eldritch sounded to me like a place that would be weird, strange, and eerie. Happy Valley, on the other hand, seemed likely to be jolly, its populace welcoming and complaisant.

"It's Happy Valley for us!" I said, steering *Spirit* to the right.

We went on our way, but I soon began to doubt that it was the right way to go. So did *Spirit*.

"If we're on the way to Happy Valley, then Happy Valley must have fallen on very hard times," she said.

"I'm going to turn around," I said, "and I hope that you won't invoke the rule that adventurers do not retrace their steps."

"This might be a special case," she said.

"Wait a minute," I said. "We may not have to break the rule after all. There's a fork in the road up ahead."

At the fork, there was another sign, like the one we had seen farther back, but this one claimed that the road to the left continued on to Happy Valley, while the road to the right would take us to Eldritch.

"That's funny," I said innocently. "I thought Eldritch was on the left back at the other fork."

"It was," said *Spirit*. "Or at least the sign said it was."

We went to the left this time, still heading for Happy Valley, we hoped.

We hadn't gone very far when we came to a third fork. The sign at this fork pointed to Eldritch on the left and Happy Valley on the right.

"Hmmm," I said, bearing right. "I'm getting suspicious about this."

"Hmmm," said *Spirit*. "So am I."

A little farther on, we came to another fork. Again, the directions had reversed, with Eldritch now on the right and Happy Valley on the left. I stopped, puzzled and a bit apprehensive. Not only did the relative locations of Eldritch and Happy Valley seem to shift with each fork we encountered, but regardless of whether we took the right or the left fork, we seemed always to be heading to a place more eldritch than happy. Then my apprehension turned to terror. A memory had returned to me. It was the memory of a night when I was sitting on the beach, "Over South," on the barrier island that separated Bolotomy Bay from the Atlantic Ocean. I was sitting on the sand, in a ring with other members of the Young Tars, listening to our leader, Mr. Summers, tell us a tale from the bygone days of old Bolotomy, and the tale he was telling was sending a shiver of fear down my spine, making me hug myself for comfort and warmth and lean toward the fire. It was a story about a gang of thugs in Babbington in the nineteenth century who used to lure—

In the light from *Spirit*'s headlamp, something moved. My heart began racing. I swung the lamp from side to side, slowly, and I saw something move again.

I took a deep breath and, drawing on the afternoons I'd spent at the Babbington Theater, called out, "We've got you covered! Show yourself!" I heard a tremor in my voice, but it was hidden but a snarling roar from *Spirit*. I looked at the throttle. I hadn't realized that I had twisted it, but I must have.

"We've got you surrounded," I said, adding another snarl from *Spirit*. "You might as well give up."

"Don't shoot!" cried a voice. A pair of hands shot into the air from behind a bush on the edge of the light from *Spirit*'s headlamp. I turned the handlebars in that direction, turning the full light on whoever was hiding there. I was still terrified, but I was emboldened.

"Come out with your hands up," I said, "and if you know what's good for you, you won't try any funny business."

"Yes, sir," said the voice. Slowly, a head rose above the bush, and then, very cautiously, with his hands held straight and high, a skinny, frightened boy about my age took a few steps toward the light.

When he reached the edge of the road, I said, "Stop where you are."

"Yes, sir."

"And keep those hands up. I'd just as soon shoot you as look at you."

"My hands are up. I'm keeping them up. I'm going to keep them up."

"One false move, and I'll—"

"No false moves," he said, quickly, nervously, blinking in the headlamp light. "You won't get any false moves out of me, none at all."

"Let's hear what you've got to say about the signs," I said.

"Signs? What signs?"

"You know what signs—the signs that point the way to Eldritch and Happy Valley."

"What about them?"

"They're confusing, wouldn't you say?"

"If you find them confusing, maybe it's just because you—"

"Listen, kid," I said in the manner of a movie tough guy, "if you are about to suggest that I find those signs confusing because I am easily confused, I would suggest that you remind yourself who has got the drop on whom."

"Sorry!" he said, and I could see the fear run through his body, the same fear that was running through mine. "I didn't mean to say that—it—it just came out."

"In that case, I'll ignore it," I said.

"Thanks," he said, shading his eyes to try to see who was behind the blinding light.

"This time," I snarled, "but not next time."

"There won't be a next time. Honest."

"Peter, let's get out of here," whispered *Spirit*.

"We can't go yet," I told her in a hasty whisper. "This is some kind of ambush—we've got to find out how many other thugs are in the gang—and where they're hiding—if we're going to get out of this alive."

"Ambush? Thugs? Gang? G-get out alive?" she wailed.

"Are you talking to me?" asked the skinny kid.

"Just giving some orders to my men," I said. "Now about those signs. The way I see it, somebody's playing tricks with those signs."

"Tricks? What kind of tricks?"

"Somebody's been switching the signs back and forth, changing the direction of them at every fork, so that first Eldritch is one way and Happy Valley is the other way, and then it's the other way around, and then it's the other way around again, and then—"

"I'm not sure I follow you."

"Are you trying to be funny?"

"Me? No! No. Certainly not."

"That's good, because funny kids make my trigger finger itchy."

He swallowed hard and said nothing. He opened his mouth, then closed it. Again he shaded his eyes and tried to see beyond the screen of light.

"Who do you suppose did that to the signs?" I asked.

He blinked and swallowed again.

"Did you do it?"

"M-me?"

"Yeah, you."

"You're accusing me of tampering with road signs to confuse travelers—lead them astray—?"

"I was just thinking that you're stuck out here in the middle of nowhere—you must get pretty bored. You might be looking for something to enliven your existence. In your desperation, you might turn to pranks."

"P-pranks?"

"They might be harmless pranks—or they might be something worse."

The boy's eyes grew wide. "L-look," he said, "this wasn't my idea, honest. I—"

Suddenly, looking at him there, in front of me, trembling, squinting into *Spirit*'s headlamp light, I realized that chance had given me something I had always wanted, something that I had heard of but had never actually seen before—

"Can't we just get out of here?" pleaded *Spirit*.

"Not now," I said, "not when chance has given me what every storyteller longs for."

"What's that?"

"A captive audience," I said. Then, to the skinny kid, I said, "I'm going to tell you a story."

"A s-story?"

"Yes," I said, "and you are going to listen closely, because this is a story about what happens to people whose pranks are not so harmless."

"Is it a long story?"

"Not too long."

"Can I put my hands down while you're telling it?"

"Okay, but keep them where I can see them, and remember what I said about no false moves."

"No false moves. I remember."

"Long ago," I said, "in Babbington, New York—where I—where I grew up—and lived until I became a special agent—"

"Special agent?"

"That's right—Special Agent—ah—Panmuphle."

"Pan . . . what?"

"Panmuphle. It's my code name."

"Oh."

"Anyway, as I was saying, long ago, in Babbington, there was a gang of young punks who called themselves the Bolotomy Pirates."

"Bolotomy?"

"That's what the name of the town was before it became Babbington."

"Oh. I see. Probably an old Indian name."

"That's right. The bay is still called Bolotomy."

"Oh, so it's on a bay."

"Look, kid, shut up and listen. This is my story."

"Yes, sir."

"The Bolotomy Pirates started out as pranksters—just a bunch of bored kids looking for something to put a little spark in their lives—you know what I mean?"

"Well—I guess—"

"Back in those days, a lot of shipping passed by the part of Bolotomy called Over South. That's a little settlement on a barrier island across the bay from the town itself, just a strip of sand that separates the bay from the Atlantic Ocean."

"Mm-hm."

"The Bolotomy Pirates often visited Over South because it was a place where they could get cheap liquor and easy women."

He muttered something.

"You got something to say?" I growled.

"I said I wish there was a place like that around here," he said.

"Yeah, well, the Bolotomy Pirates fell in with some hard types Over South. They took to gambling, and it wasn't long before they were deep in debt to people who didn't like waiting to be paid."

"Gosh."

"One of those hard types told the gang that if they didn't want to end up gutted like flounders, they'd better come up with the money they owed."

"Gutted like flounders—gee—"

"Then he suggested a way that they could get the money."

"Yeah?"

"He reminded them that a lot of ships passed by on their way to New York. This was long ago, remember, in the days of sailing ships. The ships would pass Bolotomy, and then, farther west, they'd turn into a channel where there was a break in the barrier islands and head into the sheltered waters of the bay. Then they'd have smooth sailing all the way to New York Harbor."

"Mm."

"The channel entrance was marked by flags during the day, and at night it was marked by a primitive sort of lighthouse, not much more than a signal fire."

"Like a road sign—" he said, more to himself than to me.

"The plan that the hard type offered the boys was this: they would wait for a night when the sea was rough, and then build a false signal fire on the beach Over South. When the captain of a ship saw the fire, he would think it was the fire that marked the channel, but that would actually be miles away. The captain would steer a course toward the false signal fire and run the ship aground in the surf off Over South. In that rough surf, it wouldn't take long for the ship to break up. The idea was to steal the cargo as it washed ashore, of course, but the gang wouldn't be able to do that right away. They would have something else to take care of first. They would have to make sure that there were no witnesses, no one who could report being deceived by a false signal fire. That meant that there couldn't be any survivors. A good number of the crew were likely to drown in the surf, of course, but anyone who managed to swim to shore—well, the boys were going to have to kill those."

He had been holding his breath. He let it out now and gulped another.

"One of the boys was given the job of lighting the false fire and keeping it burning bright, while the rest of the gang hid in the dunes and waited until the time came to do their grisly work."

He swallowed hard again.

"The one who tended the fire told himself that his part in the scheme wasn't nearly so reprehensible as the part the others were playing. After all, he wasn't actually going to kill anybody."

"That's right," he said. "He was right. He wasn't actually going to kill anybody."

"That's just what his friends, the other Bolotomy Pirates, got to thinking. They got to thinking that he wasn't actually going to kill anybody— and that might be a problem."

"A problem—" he muttered.

"A ship came. They couldn't be sure at first, because they couldn't see it, and they couldn't be sure that they were hearing the wind in its rigging over the sound of the surf, but then they began to hear the sound of its masts groaning and cracking, and its sails shredding, and its hull being torn asunder, and the screams of its crew."

"I don't want to hear—"

"The cracking and shredding and rending and screaming went on and on, as the waves tore the ship apart. It wasn't long before a couple of sailors came staggering through the surf, trying to make it to the safety of the shore. The gang swept out of the dunes and down upon the sailors, swinging their clubs and bludgeons. The boy who had charge of the fire stayed at his post. He tried not to hear what he was hearing, and when he found that it was impossible not to hear it he tried not to recognize what he was hearing. He tried to tell himself that what he was hearing was not the sound of living people being battered to death by the boys he thought of as his friends."

"Oh," said the boy.

"But then out of the dark came two of those friends, and between them they were dragging the nearly lifeless body of one of the sailors. They dragged the poor wretch into the firelight and dropped him at the feet of the boy who was tending the fire. Then they handed the boy a club and told him to finish the job that they had begun."

"They wouldn't do—"

"The boy stood there, holding the club, and one by one the rest of the gang came out of the night and formed a circle around him. There was no way out. He turned this way and that, looking into the eyes of his friends, looking for some sign that they were his friends, that they weren't going to make him do this, that they were going to allow him to be the one among them who didn't do anything more than change the road signs—"

"What?"

"—that he would be the only one who didn't do anything more than light the false fire—"

"You said 'change the road signs.'"

"—that there would be no blood on his hands."

"There wouldn't be. I mean, technically, if I just changed the—I mean—if he just lit the fire—"

"The circle began to tighten around him. The other boys advanced on him, step by step, swinging their clubs, with fire in their eyes."

"No."

"He remembered what the hard type had told the gang: there must be no survivors."

"Ahhhh," the boy cried. He fell to his knees. He clasped his hands together and extended them in imprecation. "Help me. Please help me. You've got to help me."

"Where are your friends?" I asked.

"At the old quarry."

"Where's that?"

"Not far. Half a mile. That way." He jerked his head to the right.

"What's the plan?"

"We—I—switch the signs so that anybody who comes along ends up at the old quarry. Eldritch or Happy Valley, it doesn't matter. If you follow the signs you'll end up at the old quarry."

"And there?"

"It's dark. You wouldn't see the quarry's edge until it was too late. You'd fall—to the bottom."

"And then?"

"The gang is hiding in the woods—and they—just like what you said—" He hung his head. A moment passed. He lifted his head and looked into the light. "What are you going to do?" he asked.

"Yeah, Special Agent Panmuphle," said *Spirit,* "what are you going to do?"

"I wish I could turn you around and get out of here, without looking back, without ever giving another thought to this skinny kid or his friends lurking around the old quarry—"

"Great. Me too. Let's go."

"—but I can't do that. I know too much."

"Don't say that!"

"Maybe we could—make a deal—" said the skinny kid, shading his eyes again, trying desperately to see who he was dealing with.

"The right thing to do would be to take him to the police," I said.

"Oh, sure," said *Spirit,* "and spend hours telling them the story and waiting while they check it out, search the woods around the old quarry, round up the gang, bring them in, and question them."

"Suppose I turn myself in—" the kid suggested.

"Then there is the matter of your driver's license," *Spirit* continued. "That is, the matter of your not having a driver's license. Why should the police believe *you,* a kid without a driver's license? Why shouldn't they throw *you* in the clink instead of a fine upstanding local lad like Skinny?"

"I'm on the horns of a moral dilemma," I said.

"Come on, mister," Skinny wailed, "gimme a break!"

"Huh?" I said.

"Help me out of this jam," he pleaded, "and I'll go straight, honest. I'll never do anything wrong again. All I've really done so far is change the signs. And the rest of the gang hasn't done anything yet, either. There's still time for us. I've seen the error of my ways, and I can reform. I know I can! So can the others. When I tell them that story, they'll see the light. I know they will. They're good kids at heart. Honest they are. We were just bored—you know, like you said—just bored. That's what got us up to this mischief. You know, idle hands are the devil's playground. Or workshop. How does it go? 'Idle hands—'"

"Shut up, kid," I growled.

"Yes, sir. I was just trying to recall whether it's 'Idle hands are the devil's playground' or—"

"Can it!"

"Yes, sir."

"Here's the deal."

"Yes?"

"I'm going to let you off—this time."

"Oh, thank you—"

"But—"

"But?"

"If I ever hear that you or any of the other young punks in your little two-bit gang of would-be pirates has strayed from the straight and narrow I will track you down—and when I find you I will shoot to kill."

"'Sh-shoot to kill,'" he said. "I understand."

"Don't forget it, and make sure the others don't forget it, either," I said, mounting *Spirit*.

"'Shoot to kill,'" he said. "I've got it."

I made *Spirit* growl again. Then I took off, heading back the way we had come, flouting the rule that adventurers do not retrace their steps.

WHEN WE WERE well on our way, *Spirit* asked, "How on earth did you come up with all that?"

"A few years ago, when I was in the Young Tars, we went on an outing Over South—"

"Yeah, yeah, yeah," she said.

Together, we began to sing:

> O, Babbington, my Babbington,
> You know I love you dearly.
> When I'm abroad, you're with me still—

Chapter 22
Eldritch, Redefined

WE ARRIVED AT THE MOTEL just at that time when the optimism of
day is beginning to yield to the gloom of night. The neon sign was sput-
tering. The 'No' in 'No Vacancy' flickered on and off. The office was lit,
dimly, but there was no sign of anyone inside. We pulled under the porte
cochere and sat there for a moment or two in silence. The air was heavy
with the smell of cheap booze and stale cigarettes.

"What do you think?" I asked.

"I think that the flickering sign is trying to send us a message," she
said.

Another car pulled into the parking lot and under the porte cochere.
The couple in the car looked at the office and then at us. We looked at
them. They grinned sheepishly. We grinned sheepishly. They shrugged.
We shrugged. They got out and headed for the door. I gave Al a look.
She gave me a look.

"Shall we move on to someplace else?" I asked.

"Come on, bold venturer," she said. "If they can take it, so can we."

We got out of the car and walked to the door. I swung it open for her
and indicated with a sweep of the hand that she was free to enter.

"After you," she said.

"Okay," I said.

The woman in the couple that had preceded us turned and gave us a
wink. Then she smiled and shrugged the small swift shrug of one who
expects a good time. Al and I exchanged another look, a puzzled look.

"Hello?" the man called.

Nothing.

"Hello?" called the woman. "We'd like to check in."

"I'm not sure about that," I muttered.

From somewhere behind a wall or two, there came the sound of a chair scraping on a floor and then the sound of a door being opened and closed. Presently a door in the wall behind the desk opened and a surly man with a limp came through it. He had tired eyes, a nasty grin, and a day's growth of beard. A cigarette hung from his lower lip. He was shrugging into a wrinkled sport jacket, probably to hide an automatic in a shoulder holster.

"Who the hell are you?" he asked.

"What's it to ya?" snarled the woman.

"I gotta put somethin' in the register," he said. "I'm gonna need two names."

"Bonnie and Clyde," said the woman, cocking a hip. "He's Clyde."

"Last name?"

"I'm Parker and he's Barrow."

"Whoa," said the clerk. He put the pen down and gripped the edge of the counter. "Whoa."

"What's the matter?" the man asked.

"I'm not sure I want to check you in."

"Why?"

"Because—look—I guess you're not aware of this, but you've got the same names as two of America's most notorious criminals."

"Oh, I know," said the woman. "We hear that from people all the time."

"Still, how's it going to look?"

"What?"

"Well, suppose you two go on a rampage while you're here, robbing, killing, looting, maybe torching the place to hide the evidence, and then in the charred rubble my boss finds the registration book and sees that I allowed you to register as Bonnie Parker and Clyde Barrow?"

"Mmm. I see what you mean."

"He'll have my ass."

"Okay. Suppose we register under other names?"

"Now you're talking."

"For me, how about Connie Barker?"

"Not great. A little lame, to tell you the truth. But it'll do."

"And for me," the man said, "how about Clarence Darrow?"

"Excellent. Yeah. Clarence Darrow. Excellent. You've got a knack."

Clarence smirked at Bonnie—I mean Connie—and she stuck her tongue out at him.

"Be right back, folks," the clerk said to Al and me, "soon as I show Miss Barker and Mr. Darrow to their room."

He led them out the door and into the night.

Albertine and I looked at each other.

"What do you say?" I asked.

"I'm game."

I tried not to allow myself to grin in anticipation of the pleasure of playing someone else for a night, but instead I had to turn aside and study the paint on the wall.

The clerk returned and said, "Well, folks, what's it going to be?"

"Just tonight," I said. "We're on the road."

"I getcha," he said with a wink, spinning the register so that it faced us.

I hesitated for only a moment, then wrote "Panmuphle."

I handed the pen to Albertine and watched as she wrote "Giggles."

The clerk spun the register back in his direction and scrutinized the entry. "You got eye-dee?" he asked.

"I—ah—well—" I said, patting my pockets.

"Ah—let me see—" said Al, rummaging in her purse.

"Ha-ha," said the clerk. "Joke's on you. Do I look like the kind of guy who's going to care if you register under a phony name?"

"Ha-ha," I said.

"Ha-ha," said Al.

"Speaking of phony names—" I said.

"Phony names? Who said anything about phony names?"

"No one," I said. "Of course not. No one said anything about phony names. I don't know how the idea came into my head."

"He gets these attacks," Albertine explained. "Ideas come into his head."

"He's not gonna get violent, is he?"

Cue the rain. Cue the lightning. Cue the thunder.

"Oh, shit," said the clerk, hurrying around the end of the counter and rushing to the door. "I didn't know it was supposed to rain tonight. It's Manager's Bar-B-Q Night. This is gonna piss people off." He scanned the sky anxiously. "It might blow over," he said hopefully. "You better get to your room, though. If it does rain, it's gonna be in buckets."

"You know," I said, taking our bags and following him as he led the way out the door, "for some reason, I've been wondering whether I haven't been here before."

"Uh-oh," he said. "Spooky."

"Yes," I agreed. "It is kind of spooky. You see—"

A bolt of lightning.

"—I have the odd feeling that I was here when the town was called—"

A rumble of thunder.

"—Eldritch."

"Oh, yeah. It used to be Eldritch."

"Really?"

"Yeah, but we went through a community redefinition."

"A community redefinition? Did I hear you right?"

"Yes, you did. You most certainly did. We redefined ourselves as Hideout Hollow, 'The Place to Get Away to When You Make Your Getaway from Someplace Else.'"

"Hideout Hollow?" I said. I was puzzled. "That sounds—well, forgive me for saying this, but it sounds derivative."

"Derivative?"

"Yeah. Isn't there a Happy Valley around here somewhere?"

"Just over the hill. Oh, I see what you mean. You're right. They were our inspiration."

"I thought so," I said. "Happy Valley, Hideout Hollow. It's pretty obvious."

"No, no. That wasn't it. They redefined themselves as Terror Town, 'Your First Choice for a Vacation That Will Make Your Flesh Crawl.' Did wonders for them. Nobody was interested in a place like Happy Valley anymore. Old hat. Too soft. No edge. Terror Town, though, that was an instant hit. Did you know that before we redefined ourselves Terror Town was getting nearly ten times the tourist business that Eldritch was getting?"

"No. I didn't know that."

"You didn't? I thought it was pretty widely known. You don't keep up with the tourist industry?"

"Not as much as I should—"

"Basically, Eldritch was going broke. It got so bad that some desperate town councilpersons would sneak out at night and switch the road signs, so that people who intended to vacation in Terror Town would find themselves in Eldritch instead."

"I think some of that was already going on when I passed through here as a boy, quite a few years ago, on my way to New Mexico, piloting an aerocycle that I had built in my family's garage back in Babbington, my home—"

"What are you talking about?"

"About the first time I passed through here."

"Yeah, but what's the point?"

"Perhaps you've heard about the night when Special Agent Panmuphle passed through here years ago."

"Not that I remember, and I still don't see your point."

"The point is that a kid was switching road signs when I came through here years ago."

"Oh. Okay, now I see what you're getting at. That doesn't surprise me. In fact, it wouldn't surprise me at all if some of the very same councilpersons who tried sign-switching as a way of steering tourists to Eldritch hadn't done a little sign-switching as a prank when they were kids and that's what inspired them to undertake their desperate program of misdirection later in life. I mean, how many original ideas does anybody get in a lifetime? You can't really blame someone for mining the rich lode of youth during the mental doldrums of late middle age, can you?"

"No. Certainly not. I didn't mean to imply—"

"Anyway, it turned out the problem was the name. We hired consultants, they surveyed a sample of the populace and found that something like ninety-two percent of people who planned to take a vacation within the next twelve months had no idea what *eldritch* means."

"Ninety-two percent?"

"Ninety-two percent."

"So you changed the name."

"Changed the name, came up with a good explanatory slogan that tells you what kind of experience you're going to have when you visit, trained the townspeople how to behave when they're interacting with visitors, re-modeled our attractions and accommodations—"

"Redefined yourselves, in short."

"You got it, Panmuphle. We redefined ourselves. Here's your room."

"Thanks, I—"

"Anything else?"

"What time is the Manager's Bar-B-Q?"

"Called on account of rain."

"Aw, gee," said Albertine.

"Well, Miss Giggles, if you and Mr. Panmuphle—Special Agent Pan-muphle, I mean—would like to come back to the office after you get set-tled, I'll give you a beer in consolation."

Giggles was all for it. That's why we found ourselves, a little later, drinking beer in the office and discussing the difference between night and day.

"I KNOW HOW IT IS," he was saying. "I've been there. It's like day and night. Or night and day, I guess I should say. That's what people say, isn't it? It's like night and day? Well, it is. Rolling through the day, the bright American day, you feel something big, and strong, and—what? Uplifting! That's what. Up-fucking-lifting."

"Like the lift on an airplane wing," I suggested.

"Sure. Whatever. I wouldn't have said that. In fact, I didn't. I didn't say anything about an airplane wing. Didn't even say anything about an airplane. I said 'uplifting,' as you may recall. I had in mind something spiritual. That's the point I wanted to make. There's a kind of spiritual uplift in that light, the light of the American day."

"I see," I said.

"Let me ask you something."

"Mm?"

"I want to ask you something."

"Okay."

"You sing sometimes, don't you? While you're driving? In the day-time? In that amazing light? You start singing sometimes, right?"

"We often sing," said Albertine. "One of us better than the other."

"Sure. I knew it. You see? I told you I've been there. I sang too, when I was on the road. Couldn't hardly stop some days. I was a singing fool. Driving along. Singing. A singing fool."

He picked up his beer bottle. I think he meant to take a drink before he went on, but something came over him. He paused with the bottle half raised.

"But," he said. He nodded at us, just once. "But," he said again, with added emphasis. Then he took a pull at the bottle. He wiped his mouth and said, drawing the words out as he delivered them, "At eventide, something happens. Something happens to the tone of the country. The bright American day gives way to the dark American night. Does that seem obvious to you?"

"Well—"

"There's more to it than you think. Something ominous seems to fill the sky. It's not darkness exactly. Because the American night is never really dark. There are always lights, the lights that make the dark places darker, like the bright notes in a saxophone solo that make the blue notes bluer. One of those moody saxophone solos. You can't make a moody saxophone solo out of silence. You need some notes. And you can't make the ominous American night out of darkness alone. You need some neon. You need some fluorescence."

"That—that's just the way it was when we arrived here this evening," said Albertine. "What light there was somehow made the night darker, and made this place seem threatening."

"Yeah," he said. "It's part of the package. The buzzing neon light in the sign, like it's going to burn out any minute. The way the 'No' in 'No Vacancy' flickers on and off uncertainly or randomly, as if it was tryin' to send you a message. All part of the package."

"The package?"

"Yeah," he said with a chuckle. "The owners used an 'atmosphere service,' Retro-Glo. They gave it that feeling of the kind of place you'd only stay in if you were on the lam or cheatin' on somebody. A few tricks with the lighting. Knock the furniture around some. Generally scuff the place up. Hell, I could've done all that. And for a lot less. But these guys were really talented with paint. Repainted the whole place, everything fresh, but it looks old, worn-out. You ought to see the work they put into grease spots. Real artists. I couldn't have done that. I couldn't have done any of the electric stuff, either. Like the automatic odorizers."

Albertine wrinkled her nose. "Odorizers?"

"Yeah. You get your choice. We use cheap booze and stale cigarettes. Place down the road uses the cold sweat of fear. We tried it. Kind of overpowering. Not for us."

"This process of community redefinition seems to be a growing phenomenon," I said thoughtfully. "In fact, the entire town of Babbington, New York, my home town, has been redefined based on the day when I returned from a solo flight I made to Corosso, New Mexico, aboard an aerocycle that I—"

"Holy shit!" he said. "Look at the time! I had no idea it was so late! I hate to bring this symposium to an end—"

"This will just take a minute. I—"

He rose and extended his arms, beckoning to us to get up, and then herded us toward the door.

"Sorry," he said, "but I've got to make my rounds, do some paperwork—you know how it is—too much to do and not enough time to do it."

"What I thought you'd find interesting," I said, "is that Babbington actually has a redefinition authority that—"

"Good night, Giggles," he said, swinging the door closed behind us. The lock clicked. The neon sign buzzed. The night claimed us.

Chapter 23
A Muddleheaded Dreamer

I WAS ROLLING ALONG through a small town, and as I rolled along I began to see the many ways, mostly small, in which it resembled Babbington. You can imagine how this moved me, a boy so far from home, whose thoughts, while he was rolling farther and farther from home, so often turned backward, toward that home that late he'd left, noticing the similarities.

"You see Babbington everywhere," said *Spirit*.

"You're right," I said, struck by the truth of it.

"And you see dark-haired girls everywhere, too."

"That's right, too."

"It's getting annoying."

"I think it has something to do with wishful thinking," I admitted. I was going to say something more on the subject of wishful thinking. I don't remember what it was going to be. I never got to say it.

"Watch out!" shrieked *Spirit*.

"For what?" I asked.

"That dog!"

Dog? What dog was she talking about? Oh. That dog.

I squeezed the brake levers with every ounce of strength I had. The front brake grabbed with such suddenness and force that *Spirit* pitched forward, up and over her front wheel. I was thrown from my seat and flew a couple of yards before striking the pavement. (NOTE: I have not included this brief flight in my tally of the distance I was airborne on the journey. It would have been wrong.) *Spirit* landed upside down. Like her,

I pitched as I flew, so I landed flat on my back. I lay there, unmoving. I assumed that I must be injured, too injured to move, much too seriously injured to get up. I figured that, any minute now, a crowd of the curious and concerned would rush to form a ring around me, buzzing with speculation about my condition, putting odds on my survival. In the movies, someone always rushed forward to command the quickly assembling crowd to stand back, give the victim some air, and avoid moving him. I waited for the crowd and for the person who would take command of the crowd.

Time passed. I heard no crowd, no buzz. No commanding voice.

I opened my eyes. Someone was standing over me, looking down at me.

"You okay?" he asked.

"I'm not sure," I said.

"Why don't you get up?"

"I think I should wait until I know if I've broken anything."

"Like what? Your watch?"

"I don't have a watch. I meant a bone. I might have broken some bones. One anyway. I might have fractured my skull."

"Does that happen to you a lot, fracturing your skull?"

"Um, no. It's never happened to me before."

"I don't think it's happened to you now, either. You just flipped over your handlebars, that's all. I done it lots of times."

"You have?"

"Sure. I get a little tanked up, there's no telling what I might run into. Over I go."

"You have an aerocycle?"

"Aerocycle? Is that what you call this?"

"Yes."

"What's with the wings?"

"She's—it's—supposed to be able to fly," I whispered.

"Why are you whispering?"

"Oh, I don't know—must be something in my throat—dust."

"You're whispering because you don't want your bike to hear you, aren't you?"

"Heh, heh, heh."

"You talk to your bike, don't you?"

"Me?"

"Yeah, you. You talk to your bike."

"Well—"

"So do I. We all do. Come on, get up. You're okay. Let's go see how *she* is."

He extended a hand. I took it, and he helped me up. He was wearing a black leather jacket with *Johnny* written on it, dark sunglasses, a white T-shirt, a cap like the ones that taxi drivers wore, blue jeans, and motorcycle boots. He had long sideburns and a grin that resembled a sneer.

"I shouldn't have braked so hard," I said, dusting myself off.

"Six of one, half a dozen of the other," he said with a shrug. "If you'd hit the dog, you woulda gone over just the same."

"You think so?"

"Oh, yeah. I hit that dog maybe four or five times. Went right over, just the way you did. Didn't hurt me none. Didn't hurt the dog none, neither."

Together, we righted *Spirit* and walked around her, inspecting her for damage.

"What's this?" he asked when we got to what was left of the banner advertising Porky White's clam bar. "'Kap'n Klam is coming!' Is that you?"

"No," I said. "It's my sponsor. It used to say 'Kap'n Klam is coming! The Home of Happy Diners,' but that's all that's left of it."

"Must embarrass her," he said.

"You think so?"

"Dragging a ratty old thing like that around? What do you think? Of course it embarrasses her. I'd get rid of that if I were you."

I began removing it while he continued his inspection.

"She's got a cracked chassis," he pronounced a moment later, shaking his head sadly.

"Really?" I said, crouching down to look at the part of her frame that he was running his fingers along.

"Ask her if she's in pain," he said.

"I—um—are you serious?"

"Of course I'm serious. I can't ask her. She's not my bike. She wouldn't hear me, and I wouldn't hear her."

"*Spirit,*" I said, "are you okay? Are you in pain?"

"Am I in pain?" she said. "It's one long line of pain from my nose to my tail."

"You've cracked your chassis," I said.

"Am I going to die?"

"No, no. Of course not. You're going to be—just a minute." To the biker I said, "She—she's in a lot of pain."

"Awww, the poor thing," he said, caressing her chassis with tenderness and affection.

"Can she be fixed?"

"Oh, sure. We got a guy in town can work wonders. Practically bring a bike back from the dead. I've seen him take a twisted mass of metal and make it back into a bike again."

"You're going to be fine," I said to *Spirit*. "We're going to get you to a doctor."

I PUSHED HER along the street, following Johnny, who was riding an enormous motorcycle, just chugging along at walking speed, balancing the bike now and then by putting a big boot on the pavement, allowing it to drag along. He turned down an alley, and I followed. At the end of the alley there were dozens of motorcycles, or, as I realized when we drew closer, parts of dozens of motorcycles. They were in various stages of disassembly—or reassembly.

"Oh, no," wailed *Spirit*. "You're not going to let them do that to me, are you?"

"No, no," I said. "They won't have to—just a minute." I asked Johnny, "Are they going to have to take her apart?"

"Nah," he said confidently. "She's just got a thin crack in a couple of pieces of her tubing. Big Bob'll take those out, bolt new tubing in, and she'll be good as new. Between us," he said, lowering his voice, "she'll be better than new. Whoever did the original assembly job wasn't—"

"I did it," I said.

"Nice job," he said. "Considering."

WE LEFT *SPIRIT* in the care of Big Bob, who promised that she would be ready for the road when I was ready to leave in the morning.

"Come on down the pool hall and have a beer," said Johnny. "Meet the gang."

The pool hall? A beer? The gang? Was he talking to me?

"Me?" I said.

"Yeah, you," he said. "You're shaken up. You've had a crash. You are deserving of the hospitality of the MDMC."

"What's that?"

"That is the club. Specifically, those are the initials of the name of the club."

"What do they stand for?"

"That is known only to the members of the club."

"A MOMENT'S INATTENTION," Johnny was saying. "That's all it takes for a rider to get himself in trouble."

"Or for a young aviator to come crashing to the ground," I said with the wisdom and exaggerated precision of a kid who's had a couple of beers.

"Or a young aviator," said Johnny, saluting my wisdom with a tilt of his beer bottle. "Now the thing is, if a rider—or an aviator—comes to grief through inattention, he's likely to feel ashamed of himself. He knows that there's no shame in crashing if crashing is not his fault, but—"

"And even if it is his fault," I said, "he shouldn't feel any shame if he crashed for a good reason."

"A good reason? What would be a good reason?" Johnny asked.

"Hmm?"

"What would be a good reason for crashing?"

"Well—ah—for one thing—how about—trying to fly too high, the way Icarus did."

"I don't—"

"Wait, wait, I know what you're thinking. You're thinking that the reasons for Icarus's crashing—vanity, pride, willfulness, and foolishness—are not good reasons."

"Yeah, well—"

"Well, let me tell you, Johnny, just between us, there have been times while I've been rolling westward en route to New Mexico this summer when I envied Icarus."

"That so?"

"What's the story, are they out of beer here?" I said, peering into my empty bottle.

"You want another?"

"Sure. Where's the waitress with the tight sweater?"

"Hey, Marie," he called, "how about two more?"

"Yes," I said, shaking my head to show that I, too, found what I was saying difficult to believe, "I have envied Icarus not only for his flight, but even for his fate."

"He crashed, right?"

"Yes." I sighed. I shook my head. "He crashed."

"Tough luck."

"But Icarus at least crashed from overreaching, which a young aviator may consider a noble error, even a good reason, and Icarus also had the advantage over this particular young aviator of having actually soared above the earth, while *Spirit* and I seem everlastingly anchored to it."

Marie brought the beers.

"Ah," I said, "it's the beautiful Marie. You know, Marie, back at home, in Babbington, New York, I used to read those Larry Peters adventure books—I was just a kid back then—and the Peters family had a maid named Marie, who was a real beauty, but she couldn't compare to you! What hair! What eyes! What lips! And what a sweater!"

That got me a laugh from Johnny and a swat from Marie. Could life possibly get any better?

"As I was saying," I said, "my crash came about through the less-than-noble failing of allowing my mind to wander. In my defense, I will point out that a trip like mine has its long, tedious stretches, and that such stretches dull the senses. There's really no telling what kind of thoughts a young aviator may come up with, or what trouble they may get him into."

"Hey, don't be too hard on yourself, Petey," said Johnny.

"I know," I said. "You're going to tell me that my inattention was only a minor factor in the equation."

"I was going to say, in your defense—"

"You're going to say that most of the fault belongs to the dog. The cur was crossing the main street of the town as if he owned it."

"I was going to say that inattention is a common failing. You can take it from me. I have extensive experience in inattention. Some of it beer-induced, I admit." He smiled at his bottle and took another swallow. "Your second failing is also a common one," he said, in a cautionary tone.

"Oh," I said. "Wha's da?" I laughed, amused at the way my lips had tripped me up. "I mean, what's that?" I said, as precisely as I could. I looked at my bottle. Was this the same one Marie had brought a minute ago? I looked around the room. Had it always been turning like this? Had the other members of the MDMC always been arrayed in a circle around Johnny and me, watching, listening, with their arms folded across their black leather chests?

"Overreaction," he said.

"Overreaction?" I said. "Me? Pffft."

"I seen the whole thing. You overreacted."

"I had to do smothing," I protested. "I mean mosthing."

"Overreaction is often a consequence of inattention," he said.

My head dropped to my chest for a moment.

"You've got your inattentive rider rolling along, being inattentive," he explained. "Then suddenly he's startled out of his inattention by the screams of his woman, who's riding behind him, holding on to him for dear life. He asks himself, 'What the hell is she screaming like that for?' He snaps his head up—"

I snapped my head up. I think I heard a deep rumble of hearty laughter from the guys in the gang.

"—and sees a dog in the road in front of him."

"Crossing street zif he owns it," I contributed.

"What does he do? Does he calmly slow the bike down and nimbly avoid the obstacle? He does not. He overreacts. He slams on the brakes and wrenches the wheel sharply."

"Not his fault, though," I asserted. "Dog—"

That was my final contribution to the discussion.

I WOKE UP ON A POOL TABLE, another first for me. You will probably not be surprised that I didn't know where I was when I woke. I felt the felt beneath me, and when I rolled over I occasioned a clattering of balls. I sat up, thought better of it, stretched out again, and slept some more. When I awoke fully, some time later, the pool hall was full of the light of midday, pouring through the storefront windows. I climbed down from the table, staggered to the door, and let myself out.

I had to find my way to Big Bob's on my own, but it wasn't hard. That is, it shouldn't have been hard. Everybody in town seemed to know the way. With my head full of fuzz, I kept losing my way, and I had to ask many times before I finally arrived at the end of the alley with the ranks of damaged motorcycles. *Spirit* was there, waiting for me. With some anxiety—with a lot of anxiety, to tell the truth—I asked Big Bob what I owed him.

"It's been taken care of," he said. "Paid for by the MDMC."

"Paid?"

"That's what I said."

With a mighty roar, Johnny appeared at the other end of the alley, mounted on his bike. "Petey!" he called. He thundered the length of the alley and came to a stop beside *Spirit*. "How you feeling?"

"Not so hot," I said.

"That is often the state in which a new initiate finds himself the morning after his election to the gang."

"Election? To the gang?"

"That's right. By unanimous vote, you are now a member of the MDMC."

"A member?"

"Full-fledged."

"Since I'm a member—do I get to know what the initials stand for?"

"You do," he said. "The name was originally suggested by my father." He glanced upward and said, "Thanks, Dad." To me he said, "The old man was always telling me, 'Johnny, you're nothing but a muddleheaded dreamer who never does anything but ride around on that damned motorcycle in the aimless pursuit of adventure, and that's all you're ever going to be,' so one day I said to myself, 'Johnny, he's right! That's exactly what you are, and that's exactly what you want to be. Enjoy it. Just get on your bike and *go*.' So I assembled a bunch of like-minded individuals, and we formed the Muddleheaded Dreamers' Motorcycle Club—and now you are a member. You are officially a muddleheaded dreamer."

"But your father was wrong!" I said.

"About my being a muddleheaded dreamer?"

"I don't know about that. I mean he was wrong to call the pursuit of adventure aimless because—*Spirit* and I were talking about this just yesterday—if you're pursuing adventure then just about any route you take is the right route if it leads you to adventure—so if you're having an adventure, you're always on the right track, and—"

"Petey," he said, raising a hand. "Cool your jets, man. If you're gonna stay cool, you gotta get a grip on yourself. I'll have to straighten you out. Remember what I said? Hmmm? Don't overreact."

I GUESS that "Don't overreact," was the advice that Johnny wanted me to take with me when I left, but I heard something else in addition to that. I heard what he had said when he told me about his father. I heard him saying, If you're a muddleheaded dreamer, enjoy it. Just get on your bike and *go*." I haven't done a very good job of restraining my tendency to overreact—ask the girl in the furniture store about my reaction last week when a sofa that Albertine and I had ordered wasn't delivered on time and I'll bet you hear the word *maniac*—but I have done a good job of admitting that I am a muddleheaded dreamer, a full-fledged member of the MDMC.

Chapter 24
Pre-Traumatic Stress

I WAS ON THE ALERT. I was keeping an eye out for dogs. I had the feeling that we were in the area of my crash, the crash that had been more the fault of the dog than the muddleheaded dreamer at the controls of the aerocycle, and I didn't want history to repeat itself.

"You seem on edge," said Albertine.

"I am. I'm tense."

"What's the matter?"

"I'm on the alert for dogs."

"Dogs."

"With every fiber of my being, I'm watching for any dogs that might suddenly dart in front of us and cause a crash."

"Was that one of the duties of the guy riding shotgun?"

"In the westerns, you mean?"

"Yes."

"Hmm. Let me check."

I had barely begun a random ramble through my memories of westerns that I'd seen at the Babbington Theater, looking for dogs that might have darted dangerously in front of the steaming team hauling a hurtling stagecoach over the dusty plains, when suddenly, there it was, the threat that I was on the watch for: a dog.

It was a small dog with spindly legs and large ears, the kind that you may have heard people refer to uncharitably as a long-legged rat or, for short, a rat dog. The dog was at the end of a leash held by a woman who was standing on the curb. Both the woman and the dog seemed to intend to cross the street, but neither of them was paying any attention to the traffic. The woman was pressing her cheek to her shoulder to hold a cell phone to her ear. In one hand she held the leash that ran to the collar of the rat dog and also a purse, open. She was peering into her purse in search of something, shuffling through the contents with the hand that held no leash. The dog was looking up and down the sidewalk for someone to trip.

"There's a dog now," I said.

"Where?"

"Right there, on the sidewalk. See the woman poking around in her pocketbook? She's got a rat dog."

"It's on a leash."

"Right. Probably nothing to worry about. Still, I do want to keep you informed, to alert you not only to danger but to potential danger."

"What about that other dog?"

"What other dog?"

"The one that might run in front of us in the next town."

"We'll avoid that dog when we come to it. Right now, I'd like you to concentrate on missing this dog. Uh-oh. There they go. They're stepping into the street."

Albertine slowed the Electro-Flyer. The woman and her dog took a couple of steps, oblivious to the traffic. Albertine veered a bit to the left. The woman quickened her pace. Albertine veered a bit to the right. The woman stopped in the middle of our lane. Albertine stopped. From behind us came the sound of screeching brakes.

The woman and the rat dog snapped their heads in our direction and registered surprise. Then the woman thrust her cell phone at us. It was a rude gesture. "Watch where you're going!" the woman shouted.

The dog frowned and said, "Yap!"

The woman and the dog continued walking, noses in the air.

The driver of the car behind us leaned on the horn. Then he shot forward with squealing tires, swerving out and around us, lurched up beside us on the left, then slammed his brakes when he saw the woman and the dog, now directly in his path. Voices were raised. The dog became particularly animated.

"This is getting ugly," I said to Al.

"I think I'm just going to back up," she said, throwing an arm across the seat and looking toward the rear as she reversed, "then make an illegal U-turn," she added, whipping around to the left and slipping into a gap between oncoming cars, "and try another route."

THE ALLEY WAS THERE, where I remembered it, and at the far end was Big Bob's, with a collection of broken motorcycles in front.

"Big Bob around?" I asked a beefy guy who was idling in the door-way.

"Big Bob?"

"Big Bob."

"Big Bob hasn't been around for—oh—about twenty years."

"Took that last ride, eh?"

"Huh?"

"Died?"

"Oh, yeah. Died. That's kind of a colorful way of putting it: 'took that last ride.' I like that."

"He's got a way with words," said Albertine.

"Actually, I was hoping I might find a guy named Johnny. He used to be the leader of the MDMC."

He chuckled. "You mean Dr. Wylie," he said, "the distinguished director of the prestigious Algan Institute, the world's foremost clinic for the treatment of pre-traumatic stress syndrome."

"I don't think that could be the same—"

"Oh, yeah," he said. "It is. It's the guy you're looking for. Johnny Wylie. Formerly a muddleheaded dreamer, now a prosperous quack."

"You mean h-he was c-cured?" I stammered.

"Let's say he heard the call of the open wallet."

"Just what is pre-traumatic stress syndrome?" asked Albertine.

"The unsettling complex of stress-related disorders that results from contemplating the traumas we haven't suffered yet, but might," the biker explained.

"Are you trying to be funny?" I asked.

"Certainly not," he declared. "Pre-traum is big business. Nearly thirteen percent of the general population is convinced that they're suffering from it, thanks mainly to Dr. Wylie's books and infomercials."

"Where is this Algan Institute?" Al asked.

"Right here in town. You ought to drop in. You'll get to see Johnny in action. Just tell them you think you might be suffering from pre-traum. After all, you probably are."

"I don't think so," I said.

"We did almost have a crash," said Albertine. "That's got me a bit tense, nervous, edgy."

"You say that you *nearly* had a crash?" the biker asked.

"That's right," said Albertine.

"But you didn't actually *have* a crash?"

"No," I said. "Fortunately, I was riding shotgun and—"

"Would you say that if you *had* had a crash, you might be suffering from post-traumatic stress syndrome now?" he asked me.

"Possibly," I said. "I'm not sure how traumatic—"

"As it is, you *didn't* have a crash," he said to Albertine, "and yet you're feeling tense, nervous, and edgy! That's pre-traum. Classic. Drop in at the Institute. They'll let you sit in on a group session—but take my advice: keep your hand on your wallet."

THE ALGAN INSTITUTE occupied a stately mansion on the tree-lined main street of the town, set well back and surrounded by a wrought-iron fence.

"Impressive," I said to Albertine.

"Are we going to go in?"

"I don't know," I said. "All these years, I've thought of Johnny not only as a muddleheaded dreamer but as perpetually such. I think I expected to find him and have him say to me, 'Hmmm, Petey, what do you say we get on our bikes and just *go*.'"

"Hmmm, and what about me, Petey?"

"Well, he would have been all over you, of course. I might have had to mess him up some."

She rang the bell.

"Yes?" said a woman's voice from a speaker beside the door.

"Peter Leroy and Albertine Gaudet to see Dr. Wylie," I said.

"What's troubling you?" asked the voice.

"Nothing. I just—"

"We nearly had a crash," said Albertine.

"Ah!" said the voice. "You say you *nearly* had a crash?"

"That's right," said Albertine. "A woman with a small dog—"

Something whirred, something clicked, and the door swung open.

We entered a marble hall. Some distance away there was a desk, at which a woman in a crisp suit sat. We hiked across the hall and eventually arrived at the desk.

"I wonder if it would be possible to see Dr. Wylie," I said.

"You nearly had a crash," the woman said with professional sympathy. "I'm sure that Dr. Wylie would like to help you. Who is your insurance provider?"

"Insurance?"

"Your health insurance provider."

"Oh—I—"

"A charming man at Big Bob's told us that we might sit in on a group session and see whether it was the right thing for us," Albertine said.

"Very well," the woman said. "There is a group in session now. Follow me."

She led us a few hundred yards across the entry hall to enormous double doors that she flung open without ceremony, revealing a group of people seated in a circle. I recognized Johnny immediately, even without his sideburns and black leather jacket, and I would have recognized him even if he hadn't been wearing a white lab coat with the name *Dr. Wylie* on it.

We had obviously interrupted the session. Everyone turned in our direction. The doors thudded closed behind us. We found our way to empty chairs, trying our best to disappear.

"Go on, Stan," said Johnny.

Stan, a thin, nervous young man, said, "As I was saying, I'm suffering from the stress that I feel from the trauma that generations as yet unborn are going to have to suffer as a result of the selfishness and stupidity of the generations that preceded them, including my own."

"That is just a bunch of abstract bullshit," grumbled a young woman seated next to him. She nibbled on her fingers.

"I think it's an interesting example of sympathetic pre-traum," said a young woman seated on the other side of him. "I'm starting to feel some of it myself."

"Nyeea," snarled the first young woman.

"I have a sympathetic soul," the second young woman claimed.

At that moment, the doors burst open again and we all turned toward them. The woman in the crisp suit stood there, and beside her was the woman with the rat dog. The doors closed behind the woman and her dog, and she surveyed the available chairs. She chose one that was a mere two chairs to my right. She plopped the rat dog onto the one that was immediately to my right.

"Rrr," said the dog cordially.

A small man, meek and bald, raised his hand.

"Yes, Mr. Tripp?" said Johnny.

"I just want to say—if nobody minds—that this most recent arrival has provoked in me a reaction that I would have to describe as a completely new instance of pre-traum that I hadn't been suffering before now."

"And that is?" Johnny prompted.

"I'm feeling how painful it would feel if I were bitten by that dog— and not just the bite—but the anxiety I would feel after being bitten when I would be asking myself, 'My god, what if the dog had rabies?'—and now, now I'm beginning to feel the anticipation of the feeling of the rabies needle. I'm told that they inject you with an enormous needle in the stomach—"

"Oh, I can't stand it," said the girl on Stan's right. "I hate hospitals! The smell! I'm anticipating it. It's making me sick! Get the dog out of here!"

"My dog is a certified emotional-support dog," said the rat dog's owner. "He is highly trained, and his presence is essential to my well-being." She began rummaging in her purse again, as she had when she was crossing the street, and eventually she produced a document, which she unfolded and handed to Mr. Tripp. He perused it.

"This seems to be legitimate," he said sadly.

"What do you mean 'seems to be legitimate'?" said the dog's owner. "It most certainly is legitimate."

"It's just that I never heard of an emotional-support dog before."

"Rrrr," said the dog. Its hackles began to rise.

"Sorry, fella," said Mr. Tripp. To the woman, he said, "A guide dog, yes. A service dog, yes. But an emotional-support dog, that's a new one on me."

"Rrrr," said the dog with undisguised contempt.

"Perhaps our visitors would like to let the group know what it is that has brought them here to the Algan Institute," said Dr. Wylie, turning pointedly toward Albertine, me, the dog, and the dog's owner.

"After you," I said to the dog's owner.

Everyone stared at her in anticipation. So did her dog.

"I think Dr. Wylie wants to know what sort of pre-traumatic stress you are suffering from," I said.

She gave me a long look. I think she was asking herself where she had seen me before. I disguised myself with a look of deep concern.

She looked at her dog and then put her hands over its ears. The dog looked puzzled.

"I'm suffering from pre-traumatic stress induced by the anticipation of the inevitable death of Mr. Pfister."

"Someone close to you?" asked Dr. Wylie.

The woman inclined her head in the direction of the dog.

"Your dog?" said Mr. Tripp.

The woman nodded yes.

"A triviality!" declared Tripp.

"Hardly!" said the woman.

"The death of your dog?" scoffed Tripp. "I'd call that next to nothing compared to the suffering of an entire generation of children as yet unborn."

"When Mr. Pfister dies," the woman lamented, "I don't know what I'll do. I don't see how I can possibly go on. And yet I know that he must die. The day will come. I can envision that day as if it were today. I can feel the grief that I will feel as if I were feeling it now. I'm a basket case. That is, I will be a basket case. When it happens. And it nearly happened today. I had just arrived in town, and I was crossing the main street, trying to find my way here to the Institute, when a car came upon me suddenly, silently, as if it had sprung up out of nowhere, headed straight for Mr. Pfister. I had to yank him out of the way with a sharp tug of his leash—and I nearly killed him. What if I had? Oh, my god, my god, what if I had?"

"Life is a grim farce," groaned the woman who hated hospitals.

Voices were raised around the group. A lively debate seemed about to begin. Al and I saw the opportunity for a getaway and decided to take it.

We had reached the door when Dr. Wylie called out to us, across the developing fracas, "Wouldn't you care to contribute something before you leave?"

"I think we're in the wrong place," I said as I opened the double doors. "It's my fault. I got the wrong impression—somehow—I don't know—I guess I'm just a muddleheaded dreamer." I closed the doors behind us.

Chapter 25
The Second Most Remarkable Thing in the Life of Curtis Barnstable

Travel has the serious defect of taking one away from the stimulus and criticism of contemporaries. . . . One is too much alone, too much the passing stranger.
V. S. Pritchett, *Midnight Oil*

THE TOWN was called Cornfields. The road that led to it, and through it, and away from it, was straight. At intervals, that road was crossed by other straight roads, each of them cutting across it in precise perpendicularity. It was an unremarkable place, but it got me thinking. It got me thinking about the naming of places, about paucity and plenitude, and, of course, about Babbington.

"What's with you?" asked *Spirit*.

"I was just musing, ruminating. Why do you ask?"

"I thought I heard you mutter something like 'paucity and plenitude.'"

"Well—I—I might have."

"You'd better stop for the night," she said. "You need a break."

I saw, ahead, to the right, a single farmhouse.

As I made my way up its driveway, a boy about my age came out the front door and stood on the porch, watching me approach. When I stopped and put *Spirit* on her stand, he called a greeting: "What in the world are you doing here, of all places?"

"I'm on my way to New Mexico," I explained. "I was hoping that I could spend the night here."

"Here? With us?"

"Yes, if you're willing to put me up."

"This is very unusual," he said. "Remarkable."

"Can I stay?"

He opened the front door and called into the house, "Mama, there's a boy here who arrived on an airplane and wants to know if he can stay overnight."

A great rumbling laugh rolled out the door, followed by a gleeful declaration: "Curtis Barnstable, I swear you are the most imaginative child there ever was! A boy on an airplane! Where do you get your ideas! Why, of course he can stay! We put up all the aeronautical boys that come our way! Oooh, I tell you, Curtis, you are going to wear me out with laughing. You drive away the dullness of the day!"

"You can stay," he said. "Have a seat."

"Thanks," I said.

We sat in rockers, side by side. Quite a long time passed. The day was hot. Insects buzzed in the cornfields. Nothing happened.

Then, across the buzzing silence, a bus appeared, on our right, far down the road, and lumbered toward the intersection. With a wheeze, the bus sighed and settled to a stop, and we could hear its door open though it was on the opposite side from us.

Curtis looked at me. "This is a big event," he said. "Hardly anybody ever gets off the bus there."

The bus rumbled, shook itself, and pulled away, leaving behind, in the hovering dust that it had raised, a dapper man in a well-tailored suit. He squinted in the glaring light and looked around, evidently trying to get his bearings, as if the place where he found himself was not at all where he had expected to be. He looked out over the cornfields, and he looked out over the plowed fields. He looked briefly in our direction, then looked away.

Time passed. The man began to look increasingly uneasy, and increasingly annoyed. I began to wonder if chance had played a trick on him, sending him to this place in the middle of nowhere as a joke.

Now and then a car passed. The man regarded each car as it approached, leaning slightly toward it quizzically, apparently wondering whether it might hold the reason for his having stopped there, the someone he expected to meet.

A truck roared by, and the well-dressed man recoiled slightly at its approach. As it passed, it raised a cloud of dust that settled onto the man. He began brushing at his suit. He was still brushing at it when another car approached, on the side of the road opposite him, slowed, and stopped. The man stopped brushing the dust from his suit and peered at the car querulously. A thin man, almost scrawny, with a prominent Adam's apple, got out of the car. The car drove off. The thin man was also wearing a suit, but it wasn't as well tailored. It hung on him. He was wearing a hat. The first man was not. The two men stared at each other across the intervening width of the roadway. The second man put his hands in his pockets. For a while, the two men kept looking across at each other, as if neither was willing to speak first. It almost seemed like a game, some school-yard game that the first of them to speak would lose.

They were distracted by the approach of a crop-dusting plane. It appeared in the distance, lowly humming, and came on in a lazy way, crossing the fields of corn without dusting them, then moving closer over the plowed fields, the pilot then dropping white dust as the plane came nearer. Both men watched it. The second man, the skinny one, commented on it. Calling across the road to the well-dressed man, he said, "Funny that a plane should be dustin' crops where there ain't no crops."

Another bus came along, from the left this time. It stopped where the skinny man stood. The skinny man boarded the bus. The door closed. The bus pulled off. All of us who had been left behind watched it go until it was out of sight.

The plane made a turn at the end of its dusting run and came back, veering this time closer to the road, then drifting farther still, until it was over the road rather than the fields, and headed right toward the well-dressed man.

He saw it coming at him. He stood there and watched it coming at him. He didn't seem to believe what his eyes were seeing. He leaned toward the plane for a moment, as if to get a better look at it, to see if he could decide whether it was really doing what it seemed to be doing.

Then he leaned back from it, as if he might avoid it. The plane dropped lower, until it was nearly at ground level.

Then the pilot of the plane began firing at the man. I recognized the staccato crackle of machine-gun fire from all the war movies I'd seen at the Babbington Theater.

The well-dressed man crouched, as if he might make himself invisible or dodge the bullets. He quickly realized how futile ducking was, though, and he began to look for somewhere to run, moving quickly, not frantically, but urgently, ducking and dodging. The plane passed over him. The pilot had missed him.

The plane made a lazy circle, as easy and unhurried a maneuver as if the pilot really were dusting crops and didn't care much whether the job got done or not, then came back at the man from the other direction, firing again.

A car appeared in the distance, approaching. The man dashed into the road, waving his arms, trying to signal the driver to stop. The car swerved, and it swung around the man. He seemed for a moment as if he might be about to lunge at it, grab a door handle and let himself be dragged away, but he didn't, and the car continued on, useless.

The plane completed another turn. The man looked this way and that, hesitated a moment, and then ran into the cornfield.

The plane followed.

If the man had expected a safe haven in the corn, among the stalks, he didn't find it. The plane came directly on, toward him, slowly, a biplane especially fitted out to be able to fly so slowly, and began dusting. A cloud of dust began streaming from the plane, spread in the air, and settled onto the cornfield.

Another truck appeared in the distance, barreling along purposefully. The legend on the side of the truck read Magnum Oil. The dapper man burst from the cornfield, driven by desperation now, taking a chance that must have seemed to be his only chance. Waving his arms, he ran directly into the path of the truck. He wasn't going to let this ride get away as the car had earlier. The truck driver must have thought he was crazy, but he wasn't going to hit him, so he hit the brakes, hard, and the truck began to slide to a stop, the brakes struggling against the momentum of so large a truck with so heavy a load. It looked as if the truck wouldn't stop in time.

The man would be hit. What he had hoped would be his salvation would kill him instead.

The plane came on.

The plane was coming from one direction, the truck from the other.

The man was in the middle.

At the last moment the man threw himself to the ground, flattened himself, and the truck rolled over him, harmlessly, its big wheels holding it above the prostrate man.

Still the plane came on.

The pilot had gone too far. He'd made a fatal error.

The plane struck the truck. There seemed to be a moment when time held its breath. Then there was an explosion. The plane exploded, or the truck exploded, or both. The plane was on fire. The doors of the truck swung open, and two men flew out—the driver and the guy who had been riding shotgun for him. They ran from the truck shouting.

A couple of other cars and pickup trucks came along, and their drivers stopped to rubberneck. They got out of their cars and trucks to get a better view. The well-dressed man saw his chance. He slipped into the driver's seat of one of the pickup trucks, shifted it into gear, and drove off.

Then everyone began to make a fuss. Curtis's parents came running from inside the house. His father wanted to know what the hell had happened. His mother wanted to know if we were hurt. The truck drivers came running up the long driveway to the house, pounded up the steps to the porch, and asked to use the phone. The porch grew crowded. Curtis's mother brought a pitcher of lemonade. His father offered bushels of corn at what he said was a good price.

By sundown, everyone had gone. Curtis's parents had gone to bed.

Curtis and I sat on the porch in silence for a while.

"Does that sort of thing happen often around here?" I asked.

"Never," he said. "In fact, before that, the most remarkable thing I ever saw around here was you."

SOMETHING WOKE ME in the night. I wasn't sure what it was. I lay awake for a while, listening, but I heard nothing. The night was full of the sound of nothing happening. I switched on the light beside my bed, got my books, and returned to Panmuphle and the Bonhommes. The daughter

had just told Panmuphle—that is, me—that it was Dr. Faustroll's habit to
substitute paper for water in his daily sponge bath:

"It has been a long time since he made that change," said Mr.
Bonhomme gravely. "He uses a wallpaper of the season, of the
fashion, or suiting his whim."

"Wallpaper," I muttered, suspecting now that I was the victim
of a jest.

The fetching child spoke up. "To avoid shocking or offending
the populace," she said, "he dresses himself, over this wallpaper, in
a shirt of quartz cloth; a large pair of trousers, drawn tight at the
ankles, made of matte black velours; minuscule gray half-boots,
with dust that he maintains, not without great effort or expense, I
assure you, in equal layers or coatings, for months—"

She hesitated.

"Yes, mademoiselle?" I said, coaxing her.

"There is something about ant lions," she said, knitting her darling brows.

"Ant lions?"

"Yes, sir. He employs ant lions in the maintenance of his
boots—that is, in the maintenance of the layers of dust on his
boots." She cast her eyes downward like a schoolgirl who has not
learned her lesson. "But I am not quite sure how or to what end
they are employed," she confessed.

"The ant lions are of no interest to me," I assured her. "Continue with his costume, if you will."

"Yes, sir," she said with the hint of a curtsy. "Thank you, sir.
He wears a vest of yellow gold, the exact color of his complexion, a
vest—or perhaps I should say a cardigan—with two rubies closing
two pockets, very high—"

"Quite the dandy," I observed.

"Yes, sir," she said. "And he completes the effect with a blue
fox pelisse."

"Whatever that is," I muttered, noting it nonetheless.

"On his right index finger he stacks emerald and topaz rings,"
she said, making the gesture as she spoke, "as far as the nail, the

only one of his ten that he does not bite at all, and he stops or con-
cludes or ends the stack of rings with a perfect molybdenum pin,
screwed into the bone of the little phalanx, the smallest bone at the
end of the finger, through the nail."

"That is very bizarre," I muttered as I noted it on my pad, "and
possibly criminal."

"By way of necktie," she went on, almost gaily now, "he passes
around his neck the ribbon of the order of the Grande-Gidouille."

"I do not know—" I began.

"It is an order he invented!" she exclaimed, with delightful girl-
ish giggles.

"And he has patented it," her father added with bourgeois gravity, "so that it will not be misused."

"Very well," I said, assuming that I had heard all. "Thank you
for your assistance," I said, intending to take my leave.

"There is something more, monsieur," said Mr. Bonhomme.

"Yes?"

"Before he leaves the house, he—"

"Yes?"

"He hangs himself, monsieur."

"Hangs himself?"

"By that ribbon, the ribbon of the order of Grande-Gidouille."

"Extraordinary."

"He hangs himself by that ribbon from a gallows he has arranged for that purpose," said the girl, with a mixture of awe and
scoffery, "and he waits or hesitates there, hanging, for some time."

"He must look ghastly," I ventured.

"Somewhere between the looks that suffocators call 'hung
white' and 'hung blue,'" she said thoughtfully.

"Almost certainly illegal," I announced.

WHEN I CAME DOWNSTAIRS for breakfast, everything was quiet.
There was a place set for me at the table, but it seemed as if everyone else
must already have eaten and begun the day's occupation. I didn't see any
food. I peeked around the corner into the kitchen, but no one was there,
and I didn't see any food in there, either.

I went into the front hall. All was still. I went out to the porch.

The man and woman were sitting in rocking chairs, staring out at the intersection where the bus had stopped the day before.

"Good morning," I said. "Where is—"

"Gone," said the woman.

"Left this morning," said the man.

"Right after breakfast," said the woman.

"Took the bus," said the man.

"W-what—where—why—" I sputtered.

"Said if he stayed here for the rest of his life he would never see anything like that again."

"Said he had to go."

"Oh," I said.

A long time passed. No one said anything. Nothing happened.

Then I said, "I guess I'd better be going too," and I left.

Chapter 26
Everything Olivia

WE SWUNG OFF THE INTERSTATE, following the sign directing travelers to the town of Olivia. The sign was unusual. It pointed in separate directions for tour buses, for deliveries, and for passenger cars. At the end of the off-ramp for passenger cars, we approached a toll gate.

"Two?" asked the toll collector.

"There are two of us," said Albertine, "but isn't it a little odd to charge tolls by the person?"

"It isn't a toll," the collector said with the weariness of one who has had to deliver the same explanation many times. "It's admission."

"Admission?"

"That's right. It isn't a toll, and I am not a toll collector. It's admission, and I am a sales associate in the Admissions Department." She pointed to the plastic tag pinned above her left breast. It said *Amanda,* and below that it said *Sales Associate.*

"I've never been asked to pay admission to a town before."

"Olivia isn't just a town," Amanda explained. "It's a museum."

"Ah!" I said. "One of those historical re-creations? That's very interesting. You see, my home town—"

"More of a personal museum," she said. "The Town of Olivia is the Museum of Olivia."

"A personal museum?" I said. "That's an interesting idea."

"Olivia who?" asked Albertine.

"Just Olivia," said Amanda. "Having her own museum and all, she has attained the rarefied status of single-name international celebrity. That's the way the brochure puts it."

"I've never heard of her," I said.

"Still," said Amanda, "she has her own museum, and I'd be willing to wager that you don't."

"Well, no," I said, "I don't, but there is a caricature of me on the wall of a restaurant—"

"Do people live here? In the town of Olivia? In the Museum of Olivia?" asked Al.

"Sure do," said Amanda. "I live here. I've lived here all my life."

"The caricature shows me as I was in my teens," I explained, "when I flew an aerocycle from—"

"You see," said Amanda, "before Olivia came along, this town had been shrinking for as long as I can remember. I watched my friends grow up and move away, even saw members of my family move away. It was getting to be a very lonely place. We were on the verge of just disappearing, but then one day Olivia drove into town. She was just passing through, like you, but she was enchanted by the prospect that she, a woman named Olivia, might live in a town named Olivia. That's the way she puts it in her introduction to the brochure. She says she was 'enchanted by the prospect.'"

"What a surprising and fortunate coincidence that she should happen upon a town named Olivia," said Albertine.

"Well, of course at that time the town was named Gadsleyville," said Amanda, "but nearly the whole damned place was for sale, so Olivia saw the opportunity and she seized it. She began buying up bits and pieces of us, and pretty soon she petitioned the town council to have the name changed to Olivia, so there she was and here we are."

"Her destiny has been fulfilled," Albertine offered.

"I doubt that Babbington would go so far as to rename the town for me," I speculated, "although I wouldn't be surprised if the idea had its supporters—"

"I wouldn't say it's been fulfilled just yet," said Amanda. "The mansion is still under construction, and the museum is likely to be under construction forever. So it remains a work in progress."

She leaned toward us and lowered her voice.

"Confidentially, just between us, Olivia turned out to be a bit of an eccentric."

"No," said Albertine with convincing surprise.

"'Fraid so. She didn't tell anybody until she just about owned the whole town that what she wanted to do was not to establish the Museum of Olivia *in* the town of Olivia, but that she wanted to establish the town *as* the Museum of Olivia."

"People would have resisted that?" I asked.

"Wouldn't you?"

"I probably would," I said, "but I'm just wondering whether the people back in my home town—"

"So, anyway," said Amanda, "that's what she set about doing."

"Do you mean that she has been turning the entire town into a museum?" I asked.

"Sure do. I thought I was pretty plain on that point."

"You were, you were," I said. "I just wanted to be sure, because it raises an intriguing question about the future of my home town—"

"You don't say," Amanda said. "Is that going to be two day passes then?"

"It sounds fascinating, Al," I said. "What do you say?"

"I'm not sure that *fascinating* is the first word that comes to mind," she said.

"Among the many exhibits that your pass will admit you to is the Gallery of Coins Found on the Sidewalk," said Amanda. "You see, when Olivia was just a girl she found a nickel on the sidewalk. Kids are pretty good at that, finding coins on the sidewalk. Kids are little, so they're right down there, right close to the sidewalk, making it easier for them to find coins than it is for you and me. Not that I don't find my share."

"I've always had that knack," I said, "the knack for finding coins on the sidewalk. I'll often surprise Albertine by presenting her with a penny that I've spotted. I could probably have a Gallery of Coins—"

Amanda turned a pair of icy eyes on me and went right on. "Anyway," she said, "Olivia picked up that nickel, and that night she put the nickel under her pillow, and while she was lying there in bed fingering the nickel, she asked herself how many nickels she might find in her lifetime. She didn't put it quite that way, of course, because she was just a young girl, but that was the question that formed in her mind. By morning she had a plan: she would save all the coins she found in the street for the rest of her life. Formulating a lifelong plan like that demonstrated remarkable foresight for one so young. That's what it says in the brochure: 'remarkable foresight for one so young.' Will that be two day passes, then?"

"Sounds good to me," I said. "This is giving me some interesting ideas, and I'd—"

"What else have you got besides coins found on the sidewalk?" asked Albertine.

"Well, there is the Gallery of Discards. Before you dismiss that as trash, I want to emphasize that *discards* covers a lot of territory. Most of us would think of trash when we hear the word *discards,* and you will find trash in the Gallery of Discards, but you will find much more than that. See, Olivia, once she decided that someday there would be a Museum of Olivia, instead of throwing anything away, she threw it into the collection. It's all there, her personal mountain of discards, categorized, arranged, and displayed. As you might expect, this is the largest gallery in town. Preservation is a complex issue in a collection so large and diverse, and the conservators are breaking new ground in the area of long-term stabilization. That's what it says in the brochure, 'breaking new ground in the area of long-term stabilization.' I told you that the word *discards* covers a lot of territory, and I wasn't kidding. You'll see for yourself. Let me just give you a for-instance: in the Gallery of Discards you will see wax effigies of all the boyfriends Olivia has dumped over the years. That's what it says in the brochure: 'dumped.' We take all the major credit cards. Is it going to be two day passes?"

"If only Proust had had the foresight to hang on to all of his discards," I said, bedazzled by the possibilities, "or to have wax effigies constructed—"

"I'm not sold yet," said Albertine. "What else have you got?"

"There's the Gallery of Bad Thoughts. What can I say? It's scary. That's what I'll say. You can try that one if you like. I've never made it past the first room. That was scary enough for me. I've heard tell that it gets a lot worse the farther in you go. You have to ask yourself how a woman like Olivia could come up with such nasty ideas. Like it or not, she was a child of the culture and she is a woman of the world. That's what the brochure says: 'a child of the culture and a woman of the world.' So she blames everybody else for her nasty ideas, that's the way I read it. That's what I hear her saying. Well, I never had any ideas like that. You wouldn't find a Gallery of Bad Thoughts in the Museum of Amanda. If there were a Museum of Amanda. Listen, I'm not supposed to do this, but since you're first-time visitors, I'll give you two-for-one. What do you say?"

"What a great deal!" I said. "I'd like to see how those thoughts are presented, wouldn't you, Al?"

"Well—"

"All right, look," said Amanda, "this is absolutely the last preview I'm going to give you. The Gallery of Broken Dreams. It is profoundly depressing. That's what the brochure says: 'profoundly depressing.' I'd have to agree with that. What it is, see, is a very, very realistic depiction of—what should I call it? I couldn't describe it for you. And even if I could, it wouldn't have the same effect on you. You have to see it. You have to experience it. I saw it once, and it was—let me tell you—profoundly depressing. An unforgettable experience. Many people return again and again. You want to take me up on the twofer offer?"

"Peter," said Albertine, "maybe we should just find someplace where we could get some lunch."

"Got an excellent restaurant right in town," said Amanda wearily. "Serves Olivia's favorite meals, including every meal that used to be a favorite but has fallen out of favor as well as the ones that are up-and-coming."

"Could we just go to the restaurant and not visit the museum?" Albertine asked.

"Technically speaking, no," said Amanda.

"The restaurant is part of the museum, Al," I said to Albertine.

"Oh, how silly of me not to realize that," said Al.

To Amanda, I said, "It could be called the Gallery of Favorite Meals, couldn't it, Amanda?"

"It is," she said.

"In my museum, if Babbington decides to establish one, we would have clam chowder—"

"Folks, I'm going to have to ask you to purchase passes or clear the entry portal," said Amanda. "Traffic's going to start backing up here."

I twisted around. I didn't see another car. "Nobody's coming," I said. "I'll make this short. Clam chowder would be particularly important in my museum because I've always thought of clam chowder as a metaphor for life—life in general and my life in particular—"

"There's a dust cloud on the horizon," said Amanda. "Might be a tour bus coming. Either you're going to have to buy a couple of passes and enter Olivia or you're going to have to turn this funny little vehicle of yours around and skedaddle. I can't have you blocking the entry."

"The kind of chowder I'm talking about," I said, "the kind that would be served in the Museum of Peter, is the kind made with tomatoes—"

I was thrown forward, against the restraint of my seat belt, by the sudden rearward motion of the Electro-Flyer. Albertine swung the car in a violent reverse U-turn and accelerated away from the admissions booth.

"Hey!" I protested.

"Don't even think of it," she said, still accelerating.

"What?" I asked.

"What you're thinking about."

"But—"

"Just file it away under Muddleheaded Dreams."

"But—"

"Unless you want to walk the rest of the way to Corosso."

"But—"

"And back."

So I filed the Museum of Peter there, among my other muddleheaded dreams, in that bulging folder.

Chapter 27
Advice from Afar

I ENTERED THE LAND OF ENCHANTMENT the next morning. *Spirit* and I crested a little hill, and we began accelerating as we headed downward. The rush of air beneath her wings gave us both a lift. Neither of us said anything, but both of us felt it. We were not quite touching the road. Downward we raced, faster and faster, growing lighter and less earthbound as we went. When we passed the sign that welcomed us to New Mexico we must have hit a bump. Something gave us a sudden upward leap, something more effective than wishful thinking. We were aloft. For a few thrilling feet, we soared through the air. I was not accustomed to flying. *Spirit* handled differently in the air, and I didn't have a practiced hand at the controls.

"Don't overreact," she warned me.

"I know, I know," I said.

My hand trembled, and her wings waggled, but we kept our course. In a moment she touched the ground again, but she bounced, and we regained the air. We descended the slope in a series of graceful flutters, and when we had spent our momentum and were grounded again, we were very pleased with our flight, and very, very pleased with ourselves.

"Whew," I said in a long exhalation of the breath that I'd been holding.

"That was amazing," said *Spirit*.

I pulled slowly to the side of the road, and we sat there, idling, recovering from the thrill of it all. We had stopped beside a tent, and we were surrounded by rose petals.

"What's all this on the ground?" I asked *Spirit*.

"Rose petals," she said.

"I don't see any rosebushes."

"I think the petals have been strewn here to make a path. See the way they lead into the tent?"

"Yes," I said. "I see what you mean. I wonder if that's the sort of thing Matthew and the other students at the Summer Institute in Corosso are planning for our arrival. It would be—"

A man poked his head from the entrance to the tent. When he saw me, his eyes popped.

"My god," he said with a great gasp. "You've come."

"Um, yes," I said. "I've come from—"

"Don't tell me," he said. "Tell everyone inside. They've been waiting for you, waiting for a very long time, and they are going to be thrilled to hear what you have to say from your very own lips." He paused a moment and then said, more to himself than to me, "You actually do have lips. Interesting."

"People are waiting for me?" I said. "They knew that I was coming?"

"They *hoped* that you were coming," he said. "Wait here. That is, wait here, if you don't mind waiting here. I don't mean to—I don't presume to—to give you orders."

"I don't mind," I said. "I'll wait."

"It's just that I want to prepare people for—your appearance. You see, we had no idea what you would look like, and I think that many people have pictured you as—well—different."

"Maybe if you have a place where I can wash up, comb my hair—"

"No, no, that's all right. Just give me a couple of minutes and—say—do you think you could come flying in on your—ah—conveyance?"

"Sure I could—" I said at once, but I heard an uncertainty in *Spirit*'s idle. Was she worried about embarrassing herself, not being able to get off the ground? "Maybe—maybe it would be dangerous—for the people inside," I said, "if I flew in."

"Oh."

"I could taxi in," I offered. "You know, staying on the ground, slow and steady. That would be safe."

"Fine. Fine. That would be fine. When you hear me say, 'The visitor from afar that we have so long awaited has finally arrived,' you come rolling in, down the aisle strewn with rose petals."

"Visitor from afar?"

He knit his brows and frowned. "You are a visitor from afar, aren't you?" he asked in an urgent whisper.

"I—um—yes—of course," I said.

"Good," he said. "Don't miss your cue."

He disappeared through the flaps. I maneuvered *Spirit* so that she and I would be ready to follow him when we heard our cue. I strained to hear what he was saying to the people inside the tent, but I couldn't hear him well over *Spirit*'s idling engine. I didn't want to shut her down, because I wanted her to be ready to make her entrance. I hoped that I would catch the words *visitor from afar* when he said them. When they came, they weren't quite what he had told me they would be, but the cue was impossible to mistake.

"I told you!" he suddenly screamed. "I told you that a visitor would come from afar—and here he is!"

I overreacted. In my eagerness to come through the tent flaps on cue, I gunned *Spirit*'s throttle, and she leaped forward, scattering rose petals and sending us hurtling down an aisle that led to a raised platform at the far end of the tent. Struggling to control her, I remembered not to compound one overreaction with another and applied her brakes gently. This taught me that underreacting can be as great a fault as overreacting. We were still traveling fast enough for me to call our forward progress hurtling.

To my surprise, eager hands reached out to me from either side, as the people in the crowd rushed to the aisle to get closer to *Spirit* and me and, if possible, to touch us. All those groping, grasping hands on *Spirit*'s wings, and a little more forceful application of her brakes, brought us smoothly to a stop in front of the platform, as if I had planned it that way all along.

"Let's give him the welcome we've waited so long to give!"

The audience rose and began to applaud. The man on the dais began beckoning to me, almost frantically, as if we were running out of time.

"Come on up here and tell us what we want to hear!" he cried.

Willing hands steadied *Spirit*. I mounted the few broad steps that brought me to the same level as the man. He spun me around to face the crowd and screamed at them again. "I told you! I told you that a visitor would come from afar!"

He turned to me, and he began to talk to me as if he were confiding in me, though he spoke in a voice that would easily reach the farthest corner of the tent.

"Years ago," he said, "people began reporting sightings of odd phenomena in the sky, sightings of unidentified flying objects that became known either by their initials, as UFOs, or by their most common shape, as 'flying saucers.'"

This was something I knew something about.

"That's right!" I said, adopting the same technique of speaking to him and to the crowd at the same time.

A sudden wave of nostalgia struck me, and I had to swallow hard and blink a few times to hide its symptoms.

"Are you all right?"

"Yes," I said hoarsely. "It's just that—when you mentioned unidentified flying objects—it reminded me of home."

A sympathetic *ohhhh* arose from the crowd.

The man gripped my arm and said, "Of course. You're a long way from home. You must miss home and all the people—or—all the comforts of home. We understand."

He was right. I was a long way from home, and I did miss its comforts. The mention of UFOs had sent my thoughts back there because back at home, so many miles behind me, in the bookcase in my attic bedroom, I had a small collection of books and magazines devoted to sightings of flying saucers and to speculation about their origins, their crews, and their methods of propulsion. I had built several models of flying saucers from balsa wood and tissue paper, and I had made detectors that were supposed to signal me when a saucer was in the vicinity. I had seen, or thought I had seen, five flying saucers above my neighborhood in Babbington Heights one summer night, the same summer night when I had also seen, or thought I had seen, a naked woman standing in her bedroom window in a house diagonally across the street.

With a bittersweet smile, I remembered the first model I had built. Some of the photographs of unidentified flying objects showed ships that looked like two saucers, the bottom one in the usual orientation when under a coffee cup, the top one inverted and placed so that the rims matched. A young literalist, I tried to make a model of a flying saucer in just that way. It got me into trouble.

"Among the general population," the man continued, "there was widespread curiosity about the sightings. Many people became anxious about these mysterious UFOs; they wondered about the intentions of their makers and feared that they meant us harm."

He paused and looked at me significantly. He seemed to want my reaction. I shrugged and said, "I don't know why." I meant it. I hadn't thought that the creatures aboard the UFOs meant us any harm, but then at the time I had belonged to the segment of the general population that consisted of kids who hoped they would get to ride shotgun in a flying saucer.

I was applauded heartily. I waved to the crowd.

"Another portion of the population was thrilled by UFOs," he said, "because those people wanted flying objects to be ships from another world, piloted by beings superior to us and concerned for our well-being, itinerant intergalactic mentors who would show us a better way."

He paused in that significant way again. I extended my hand, greeting him as one member of the segment of the population that wanted the beings to show us a better way to another, and he shook it.

Thunderous applause.

"Another segment of the population thought it was all a lot of hooey," he said in an exaggerated manner that made it clear that he thought that thinking it was all a lot of hooey was a lot of hooey. "As far as they were concerned, the ones who feared invasion were letting anxiety run away with them, and the ones who were looking forward to benevolent intervention wanted it badly enough to let imagination run away with them. As far as those skeptics were concerned, both groups were hallucinating!"

His audience loved that. They laughed, and I laughed with them.

"Then," he said, turning solemn, "something happened near here. Exactly what happened, we cannot say. Some people who were there, and some people who claim that they were there, say that a UFO crashed during a thunderstorm. Some people in the skeptical segment of the population immediately began howling that it couldn't possibly be true. 'Why,' they wondered aloud to anyone who would listen, 'would the conveyance of intergalactic voyagers be brought down by earthly weather?'"

He paused. It was another of those pauses that requested a response from me. I reached back, mentally, to the stack of books and magazines on the shelves in my room at home, leafed through their pages, and said, nodding, knitting my brows in thoughtful consideration of the likelihood that what I was saying might be correct, "It could have been the effect of sunspots on the magnetomic drive."

They hummed. They nodded their heads.

Gently, as if what he had to ask me next would cause me some pain, he said, "Would you rather we talked about something else?"

I would. I had been interested in flying saucers, and I still enjoyed speculating about their origins and the motives of their makers, but just then I was more interested in myself, and I would have preferred to talk about my travels. "Yes," I said, "I would. I'd like to tell you—"

"That's just what we hoped!" he said. "We hoped that when you came you would tell us what we need to hear, that you would offer us enlightenment and guidance."

"Enlightenment and guidance?"

"Pearls of wisdom, perhaps?"

"Oh, pearls of wisdom. Sure. I can do that. One that I remember from the fourth grade is, 'A journey of a thousand miles begins with a single step.'"

A collective gasp arose from the audience.

"Did I get that wrong?" I asked.

"No," said the leader, "not at all. I think we are all just surprised to find that it has traveled so far, that it is truly a universal piece of wisdom."

"A pearl," I said.

"Have you any others? Please, we are here because we want to hear what you have to tell us. Teach us how to live. Give us some advice."

"What kind of advice?"

"I am sure that any kind of advice you care to give us would be received with tremendous gratitude by everyone here assembled."

"Okay. Let's see. I have some advice about traveling."

"Please," he said, with a gesture that invited me to stand at the microphone and say whatever I wished to say.

"If you're going to make a journey," I said into the microphone, "and I'm speaking now as someone who knows what he's talking about, since I've just completed a long journey, or almost completed a long journey, you have to ask yourself whether you're going to travel with or without a map. If you travel with a map, you know where you're going, and you know where you are, and you know where you've been. If you travel without a map, you get lost a lot."

"I take it you are speaking of life's journey," he said, stepping up beside me and reclaiming a bit of the microphone, "and not merely of a journey in the literal sense, from one place to another."

"I—well—both."

"I see."

"Life's journey *is* a journey from one place to another."

"Oh?"

"Yeah. You know those trails of slime that slugs leave behind them?"

"I'm afraid I—"

"In the morning, you see them on sidewalks sometimes, and from the trail of slime you can see the wandering path that the slug has followed in the night."

"Very interesting. You have slugs—where you come from?"

"Oh, sure. We have slugs, snails, worms, probably everything you have here—but my point is that if we left trails of slime as we go through life, you would see a long thread of slime that stretches through space and time from birth, at a certain place and a certain time, to death, at another place and another time. It would be your slime time line, if you were a creature that left a trail of slime."

"Turning from slime, if we could, please go on and give us another bit of advice."

"Okay. Well—um—hmm—if you do get lost, don't try to retrace your steps. It's a waste of time. You can't change the past, so don't bother trying to go back there. Don't try to follow your slime time line—"

"Please. No slime. It's making some of the ladies queasy."

"Go forward," I said. "Go from where you are to somewhere else, somewhere you have never been. Go in any direction but backward."

"Aren't you likely to become even more lost?"

"If you're where you want to be, you're not lost," I said, "and if you want to be where you are, you're not lost. So you've got two choices: you can stay put and learn to want to be where you are, or you can move on until you come to the place where you want to be."

"Deep, very deep. Please go on."

"Lots of times, while you're on a journey, you think that where you're going is where you're going to want to be, and that where you are is just a place that's in your way and not the place where you want to be, but that's not always true. For instance, on my journey, I didn't stop in New York, because I thought that I wanted to be someplace west of New York, but now I think I should have stopped in New York, because I might have wanted to be there for a while."

"They say it's a great place to visit," he said, nudging himself over and reclaiming a bit more of the microphone.

"Yeah," I said. I was beginning to warm to my role as dispenser of advice, and as I warmed to it I began to discover that I had many more pieces of advice that I wanted to dispense. I was also beginning to resent the interruptions of the leader. "Another thing to keep in mind on a journey is this: don't try any funny business. If you do, people will ask you if you're trying to be funny. There is no good answer to that question. If you say that you were trying to be funny, they tell you that what you were doing or saying was not funny, and you wind up feeling like — well — like a jerk. On the other hand, if you say that you were not trying to be funny, you will see a certain look come into their eyes, as if they suspect that you might be wearing a mask and they're trying to see through it, and from then on they will treat you as if you were trying to be funny by making fun of them, and they'll hate you for it. So, don't try to be funny. You just can't win."

"Are you trying to be funny?" he asked. It was a pathetic bid for a laugh. He didn't get it.

"Are you?" I asked. I got the laugh. I was beginning to feel very good.

"Be yourself," I said to the crowd. "Be who you are. You may be a muddleheaded dreamer. People may laugh at you for being a muddle-headed dreamer. Stare them down. Stand tall. Start a club of muddle-headed dreamers. The world owes a lot to muddleheaded dreamers."

A sudden burst of applause came from a small segment of the audience. The few who had applauded quickly caught themselves. I saw a couple of them glance quickly from side to side to see if their neighbors had noticed that they had applauded.

I applauded those who had applauded and said, "Welcome to the club."

People laughed. Mostly, the people who laughed were people who had not applauded. I think they thought that I was just trying to be funny.

"Don't try to talk to people about the place where you're from," I said. "Nobody wants to hear about it. I don't know why. Maybe it sounds too strange to them. It's not what they're used to. It's not like the place where they're living or where they came from. To them, the place you come from seems—I don't know—"

"Alien?" he offered.

"That's it: alien. They act as if you came from outer space."

This brought me a warm, satisfying laugh, doubly satisfying because I had been following my own advice and not trying to be funny.

"When you're talking to people, try to stop yourself before you say something that makes you wish you had put your foot in your mouth. There are many things that you would like to say that would, if you said them, make you find out that they were things that the people you're talking to did not want to hear. Don't say those things. At least, don't say them to the people who wouldn't want to hear them. Watch their eyes. You can tell when you're getting close to the point when you ought to put your foot in your mouth if they get that look that I mentioned before. In general, when you see that look, shut up."

He leaned toward the microphone to make a comment. I gave him that look. The crowd roared. He didn't speak.

"When I was little," I said, "I tried to make a model of a flying saucer by gluing two saucers together—regular saucers, the kind that go underneath cups. If you think you might want to try it, let me give you a warning: holding two saucers in that way is pretty tricky. They can slip from your hands easily and break, and if they do your mother isn't going to like it. If you manage to get the rims glued together you will have a more stable construction, but—take it from me—your mother isn't going to like that either."

They gave me more laughter, fueling my fire.

"Recognize your failings. I'm not saying that you have to point them out to other people. I'm not even saying that you have to eliminate them. They may not even be failings, if you could get an objective opinion about them. I mean, one person's failings are another's strengths, depending on who's looking at them. But our tendency is to recognize our strengths and overlook our failings. I'm telling you that because I recognize the tendency in myself. In my case, my biggest failing is—well—I know what it is, but I guess I'm not going to tell you what it is. Let's just say that it's something that goes to show that, like everyone else, I'm 'only human.'"

That was received with a warmth that I find hard to describe. I could see that they found it funny, but there was more than that in their reaction, and I thought that perhaps they were, individually, reflecting on their failings, and concluding that, yes, they were, like me, only human.

"Another thing: you may know something that nobody else knows. You may have knowledge that other people do not have. You may have information that is known to no one else, or only to a small group of people who for one reason or another have come to know these things that other people do not know. You know what I mean, don't you? I'm talking about secrets. That is, I'm talking about things that ought to be secrets. Maybe you have traveled through the Land of Lace. Maybe you know what goes on in the Forest of Love. Maybe you are familiar with the secret rituals of the Great Church of Snoutfigs. Maybe you own a book or two that shouldn't fall into the wrong hands. If you have secrets, if you know secrets, keep them to yourself. Don't give them away. Don't sell them. Don't even betray them by allowing yourself to smile that superior little smile that says, 'I know something you don't know.' If people know, or even suspect, that you know something that they don't, they will hate you for it. They will. I know. I'm not going to tell you how I know, but I know."

He leaned into the microphone again. I nudged him aside.

"Here's a piece of advice I got from someone I didn't like. I guess that shows that you can sometimes get good advice almost anywhere if you keep your ears open. And I guess that means that you should keep your ears open. The advice that this person gave me was to be aware that gravy can hide a multitude of sins. Be wary of what the gravy might be hiding. I think I will probably always be wary of any cut of meat that's hiding under gravy. As I went on traveling, though, I got a taste of some other kinds of gravy: a certain kind of smile, a certain kind of promise, even a certain kind of goodness. Beware of any kind of gravy. It can hide a multitude of sins."

The leader coughed. He seemed about to make a lunge for the microphone. I grabbed it the way singers do, with both hands, swung it toward me as if I were dancing with it, and said, "Here's one for those of you who are waiting for 'someday,' for that day when life is finally going to bring you what you've been waiting for, that wonderful day when your dreams are going to come true, all of them. My advice? Take what life offers you and move on. If you're offered a sandwich, take it and make a graceful exit. Chances are good that you won't be offered anything else."

"I'm sure you must be tired," he tried. "You've had a long journey, and—"

"I have had a long journey," I said, "a very long journey—"

His eyes brightened.

"—and I'd like to give you a piece of advice that my—ah—that I gave myself—while I was on my journey. Don't be too quick to decide that you've made a wrong turn. It's not really a wrong turn unless it takes you away from what you're after. Most of us are after many things, so there are many, many paths that we can take to what we want. None of them could accurately be called a wrong turn. And here's a little secret: if you're not trying to get anywhere, then there are hardly any wrong turns at all."

"You've certainly given us a lot to think about—"

"In the evening, the light can play tricks with your eyes," I said, taking a couple of steps to one side, away from him, as he advanced. "If there is mist, the tricks can be even trickier. Somehow, the light and the mist form a kind of screen onto which your mind projects the images that it manufactures when it is engaged in wishful thinking. You may seem to see a castle on a mountain peak where there is nothing but a water tower. Don't bother climbing the mountain unless it's the water tower that you're after."

"We'll be sure to remember that," he said. He had gone into a crouch. I was sure that he meant to make a spring for the microphone.

"Be alert to the many meanings of the words *ha-ha*," I said, circling, forcing him to turn his back on the audience in order to keep his eye on me. "In themselves, those words have no real meaning at all. What they mean depends entirely on the motives of the speaker. Their meaning is beyond your control. Do not try to give them meaning. Do not impose a meaning on them. Look for the meaning that they have been given; respond to that, and only to that."

"Rrrr," he said, baring his teeth.

"If you're looking for a way to decide whether you can trust someone or not, check his pockets for wads of cash. If you find wads of cash, don't trust him."

He sprang. I leapt aside. He missed.

"I'm out of advice," I said. I looked at the leader. I smiled. He straightened up and started toward the microphone. Into it I said, "I'd like to end with a request, if I may." What could he do? He stopped and nodded. I turned to the crowd.

"If strangers should come into your midst," I said, letting my eyes roam the crowd, "strangers passing through, visitors from afar, take them in. Try to feel their loneliness, the terrible isolation of outsiders in an alien culture, and if they seem odd to you, if the things they say and do seem disturbingly different from the things that you and your neighbors say and do, please realize that in their loneliness those strangers may be clinging for consolation to familiar customs and trying desperately, awkwardly, ineptly to ingratiate themselves with you by trying to show that they have something in common with you. Don't reject them. Welcome them. The foods they eat, the ideas they hold, the emotions they feel, and everything they hold dear may seem weird or worthless to you, but they are neither weird nor worthless to them. Open your hearts. Open your homes. Let the strangers in." I paused. In the hush, I could hear sniffles. Then I asked, "Would anyone out there be willing to put me up for the night?"

Chapter 28
On the Street of Dreams

I WOULDN'T HAVE RECOGNIZED the place. The little college that had hosted the Summer Institute so many years before had grown into a university. I couldn't get my bearings, couldn't match the map of memory to the new data, the terrain of the facts.

"I'll park somewhere, and we'll walk around the campus," suggested Albertine. "You'll start seeing landmarks that you remember."

She parked, and we began walking aimlessly, just to see what might spark a memory.

After a couple of minutes of that, Albertine said, "Instead of wandering aimlessly, why don't we see if we can get a map or take a tour?"

I approached a man who seemed to have a professorial air about him.

"Excuse me," I said. "I wondered if it would be possible to take a tour of the campus. You see, I was a student here for one memorable summer when the institution was known as the New Mexico Institute of Mining, Technology, and Pharmacy. It was quite an experience for me. I flew here from Babbington, New York, on an aerocycle that I had built—"

"Admissions Department," he said abruptly.

"I'm not applying for admission; I just wanted to—"

"Take a tour."

"Right."

"Admissions Department."

"I seem to be missing something."

"The tours leave from the Admissions Department."

"Ah! Of course. I should have understood what you meant. The heat must be getting to me. It's—"

"It's a dry heat. Never bothers anybody."

"I guess it's just me. Where is the—"

"Admissions Department."

"Right."

"Down here, turn left, turn right."

"Thanks."

We began walking in the direction that he had indicated.

"Did anyone offer you a place to stay after you had given them all that advice?" asked Albertine.

"They were scrambling over one another to get at me," I said.

We turned left.

"Was there a dark-haired girl?"

"Ahh, yes," I said, teasing her with an exaggerated display of pleasurable recollection. "There was."

We turned right.

"Did you get lucky?"

"I—"

On the wall of a building, directly ahead of us, was a large, colorful poster, announcing the 21st Annual "Land of Enchantment Fly-In." I read it in a glance. It promised fun for the whole family. It promised kit-built, home-built, and experimental airplanes. It made the event sound like great fun, not only for the whole family, but for Albertine and me, the perfect ending to our journey. I was just about to point it out to her, when I saw that it promised something else. It promised a thrilling competition among "those daring superheroes of the air, our nation's top-ranked flying EMTs."

"Well?" she asked.

"I—" I snapped my head around, looking for something to distract her from the poster. "Were we supposed to go left and then right or right and then left?"

"Straight, then left, then right. Aren't you going to tell me what went on between you and the dark-haired girl?"

I took her arm and tried to turn her away from the poster, but she resisted, and in an eager, gleeful voice that made me think that all was lost, she cried, "Oh, Birdboy, look."

"Al," I said, "I thought something like this might happen. It's been on my mind ever since we left New York. I—"

She put her hand under my chin and raised my head. "Look!" she insisted. "If I hadn't seen it with my own eyes," she said, "I would never have believed it."

*Will Peter learn anything at the prestigious
Faustroll Institute?*

Will Peter have to take the wheel of the Electro-Flyer
and whisk Albertine away from the flying EMTs in a
thrilling white-knuckle chase?

*Will Peter return safely to Babbington and rendezvous
with the dark-haired girl?*

Will Peter and Albertine
decide to remain forever in the
LAND OF ENCHANTMENT?

*Don't miss
the thrilling conclusion
of
Peter and Albertine's exploits
in*

Flying
Part 3: Flying Home